Praise for the novels of
Tara Taylor Quinn

"Quinn smoothly blends women's fiction with
suspense and then adds a dash of romance to
construct an emotionally intense, compelling story."
—*Booklist* on *Where the Road Ends*

"One of the skills that has served Quinn best...
has been her ability to explore edgier subjects."
—*Publishers Weekly*

"Quinn ties you up emotionally as her wonderful
voice explodes into the mainstream."
—*Reader to Reader* on *Where the Road Ends*

"One of the most powerful [romance novels]
I have had the privilege to review."
—*Wordweaving* on *Nothing Sacred*

Street Smart is filled with "deception, corruption,
betrayal—and love, all coming together in an
explosive novel that will make you think twice."
—*New Mystery Reader Magazine*

"*Street Smart* is an exciting novel...
action-packed and fast-moving...
Tara Taylor Quinn has done a beautiful job."
—*Writers Unlimited*

"Quinn writes touching stories about real
people that transcend plot type or genre."
—*All About Romance*

Also by
TARA TAYLOR QUINN

STREET SMART
WHERE THE ROAD ENDS

Watch for a brand-new novel from
TARA TAYLOR QUINN
Coming July 2006

TARA TAYLOR QUINN

HIDDEN

MIRA®

ISBN 0-7783-2194-0

HIDDEN

Copyright © 2005 by Tara Taylor Quinn.

All rights reserved. Except for use in any review, the reproduction or utilization of this work in whole or in part in any form by any electronic, mechanical or other means, now known or hereafter invented, including xerography, photocopying and recording, or in any information storage or retrieval system, is forbidden without the written permission of the publisher, MIRA Books, 225 Duncan Mill Road, Don Mills, Ontario, Canada M3B 3K9.

All characters in this book have no existence outside the imagination of the author and have no relation whatsoever to anyone bearing the same name or names. They are not even distantly inspired by any individual known or unknown to the author, and all incidents are pure invention.

MIRA and the Star Colophon are trademarks used under license and registered in Australia, New Zealand, Philippines, United States Patent and Trademark Office and in other countries.

www.MIRABooks.com

Printed in U.S.A.

Dear Reader,

There are some stories that just insist on being told. They come to you without warning or explanation. They take up residence in that corner of your brain reserved for private thoughts, and they nag at you, sometimes incessantly, sometimes quietly, sometimes in the middle of the night when you aren't sure if you're dreaming or awake. If you don't heed them they take a seat and stay put until finally, out of desperation, you agree to listen and to write. *Hidden* is one such story. It first came to me almost three years ago in the middle of a long-distance telephone conversation. I listened to the story for a second, losing track of the real-time conversation because of the interruption—and I don't know that I'll ever regain credibility with the person who was at the other end of the phone and doesn't understand writers at all. And then I told the "voice" to shut up. It quieted but didn't leave.

I told the story to get lost. I was contracted for seven books, and it wasn't one of them. I didn't write that kind of book. But even as I thought the words, silently listed the reasons, I knew the story wasn't leaving.

It hung around for a couple of years, bugging me periodically, reminding me that it was waiting. And in a meeting with my agent, in reply to a question she'd asked, this story stood up from its seat in a corner of my mind and suddenly it was all I could see, all I could think about. I told my agent about it. Her response was completely positive. Surprised, I then talked to my editor, who also showed no signs of shock or hesitation. Only I remained, secretly, doubtful of my ability to pull this off.

And then I sat down to write. I opened myself to the story, and I can now honestly tell you that this is the best work I've done to date. *Hidden* is a story about people who, at least to my mind, are very real. I'd love to hear what you think about it! You can reach me at P.O. Box 13584, Mesa, Arizona 85216 or at www.tarataylorquinn.com.

Till then, enjoy!

Tara Taylor Quinn

ACKNOWLEDGMENTS

For Quinnby, Henry J, Maya and Abrahamburger, who are the angelic bearers of unconditional love and support. If they were my only teachers in life, it would be abundant.

Thank you to California senator Jack Scott for his generous insights into a day in the life of a California state senator, and to Phil Blake, EMS Management Analyst with the San Diego Fire Department for cheerfully and enthusiastically answering a plethora of questions. Any mistakes in representing either career are mine.

A heartfelt thanks also to Lynn Kerstan, who shared her hometown of San Diego with me and who not only chauffeured me around but took me to dinner. And thanks to Jill Limber for running down to her local San Diego fire station to find out what color uniform the firefighters were wearing. And to Lisa Kamps, former firefighter turned romance writer, for all the tidbits about the life of a firefighter.

1

San Francisco Gazette
Tuesday, April 5, 2005
Page 1

Single Socialite Disappears

Leah Montgomery, one of the country's most sought-after and elusive heiresses, was reported missing by her brother, San Francisco attorney Adam Montgomery, and sister, Carley Winchester, in San Francisco last night after she failed to attend the $200 a plate orphaned children's fundraiser she'd spent the past six months organizing. The thirty-one-year-old was last seen yesterday at 3:20 p.m. leaving Madiras where, according to the upscale salon's owner, Samantha Ramirez, Montgomery received her weekly massage and manicure and had her hair cut and styled, in preparation for that evening's event.

Again according to Ramirez, Montgomery

had been planning to wear a black satin gown with red lace trim. Late last night, when police searched Montgomery's penthouse condominium, they found a dress matching that description hanging from one of the two shower heads in the woman's shower. Montgomery's white Mercedes convertible is also missing.

There are no leads in the case, though police are rumored to be questioning California's newest state senator, attorney Thomas Whitehead, who was to have been Montgomery's escort at last night's fund-raiser. Whitehead was elected to the Senate last fall, just fourteen months after his six-months-pregnant, fashion-designer wife, Kate Whitehead, disappeared without a trace. Before her disappearance, Mrs. Whitehead was frequently seen in the company of her longtime best friend, Leah Montgomery.

"Mama! Mamama!"

Shaking, heart pounding so hard she could feel its beat, Tricia Campbell lowered the newspaper enough to peer over the top at her eighteen-month-old son. She could see him sitting there in his scarred wood high chair in their modest San Diego home, pajamas covered with crumbs from the breakfast he'd long since finished, wispy dark curls sticking to the sides of his head. Could smell the plum jam he'd smeared all over his plump chin, cheeks and fingers. And she could definitely hear him...

"Mamamama! Down!" The baby, pounding his clenched fists on the stained tray of his chair, was working up to a frustrated squall.

The paper fell to Tricia's lap. She stared at her son, seeing him as though from afar—as though he belonged to someone else. The little boy was almost the entire sum of her existence—certainly the basis of every conscious decision she'd made in the past two years—and she couldn't connect. Not even with him. Not right now.

"Maamaa?" The little voice dropped as though in question.

Wordlessly, she glanced down at her lap, staring at the small, grainy picture that accompanied the article. It must've been pulled from the vault in a hurry. The likeness was old, an image captured more than two years before. Taken at yet another of Leah's constant stream of charity events—a Monte Carlo night with proceeds to offer relief to recent hurricane victims.

Tricia recognized the dress Leah was wearing. The smile on her face. The picture. She'd been standing right beside her when that photo was snapped. Had posed for one herself. After all, they'd both been wearing gowns from the latest Kate Whitehead collection— gowns that were to have their own showing later that year.

"Ma!Ma! Down! Mama! Down!" The loud banging, a result of her son's tennis shoe kicking back against the foothold on his chair, caught her attention.

With a trembling hand, she pushed a strand of her

now-mousy brown hair toward the ponytail band that was supposed to have been holding it in place, watching as the toddler screwed up his face into the series of creases and curves that indicated a full-blown tantrum. And felt as though the expression was her own. Grief. Anger. Confusion. Leah was missing. Leah—her best friend. A piece of her heart.

Leah, whose memory afforded her a secret inner hold on sanity in a life that was nothing but secrets and insanity.

"Down!" The squeal of fear in her son's voice catapulted Tricia out of her seat, across the foot and a half of cheap linoleum to his secondhand chair. In no time, she had him unstrapped and clutched his strong little body tight, cheek to cheek, the tears streaming down her face mingling with his.

She was shaking harder than he was.

"...Engine Eleven respond, overturned traffic..."

"Let's go!" Captain Scott McCall dropped his sponge in the bucket of water he'd been using to clean the windows in the station's kitchen and ran for the door. An overturned vehicle on the freeway couldn't be good.

A flurry of heavy footsteps hitting cement rang through the station. Silent men, focused on the moments ahead, or perhaps the pizza they'd just ordered, all doing the jobs they'd been trained to do. Street boots off, Scott pulled on the heat-resistant pants with attached boots that he'd thrown over the side of the engine when they'd returned from a Dumpster fire that morning. He grabbed his jacket off the side mirror and jumped aboard, scooping up the helmet he'd left in the passenger seat.

Cliff Ralen, his engineer, already had the rig in motion. They traveled silently, as usual, having worked together so long they had no need for words. Scott was the captain, but he rarely had to give orders to any of the three men on the engine with him. They were well-trained, as firemen and as co-workers. He was damned lucky to have a group of guys who shared a sixth sense when it came to getting the job done.

The engine couldn't get to the freeway quickly enough for Scott. Was it a multiple-car accident? Someone could be trapped inside. More than one someone. It was interstate. A second engine would be called. Police would be on-site.

With a rollover accident, there was a greater possibility of explosion.

And a greater possibility of severe injury—or death.

Sweating, impatient, Scott clenched his fists, waiting. This was always the worst part for him. The waiting. Patience wasn't his strongest suit. Nor was inactivity.

Waiting could be the hardest part of his job because he knew what it was like to be on the other side, helpless, feeling time slip away while you waited for help to arrive….

He tapped a foot against the floorboard. *He* was help.

He and his men. The guys would secure the area. Check for signs of fire danger. Rip car doors from their jambs. Break through back windows.

And Scott, as the engine's paramedic, would...

Do whatever needed to be done. He always did. He wouldn't think about the people. He wouldn't feel. They didn't pay him to think too much. Or to feel.

Feeling weakened a man. Got in the way. Could make the one-second difference between saving a life and losing it.

Scott wasn't going to lose a life. Not if there was anything humanly possible he could do to save it.

He wasn't going to witness another life fading away while he stood helplessly by and watched.

Period.

With his door open even before Cliff pulled to a halt, Scott jumped out. He took in the entire scene at a glance—the circle of tragedy, with bystanders on the periphery and his men moving forward checking for fuel leaks, other signs of explosion danger, trapped victims.

Engine Eleven was the first on-site. Goddamn, it was ugly. A pickup truck, the mangled cap several yards away. Off to the other side, also several yards from the smashed vehicle was a trailer hauling a late-model Corvette. Whoever had been driving that truck had been going too fast, jackknifed the trailer, lost control. Judging by the roof flattened clear down to the door frame, the truck had rolled more than once.

Whoever had been driving that truck was nowhere in

sight. He hoped it was a man. Or an old woman who'd lived a full life. *Please, God, don't let it be a young woman.*

"She's trapped inside!" Joe Valentine called out. He'd worked with Scott for six of Scott's eleven years with the department.

If she's young, let her be okay, he demanded silently as he grabbed his black bag and approached the truck. She's just trapped. *Between the steel frame of the truck, the air bags and seat belt, the vehicle might have protected her.* Cliff took a crowbar to the upside-down driver's door. Metal on metal, screeching over raw nerves. He'd treat her for shock. Rail at her about the reason for speed limits. Make sure she understood how lucky she was to have escaped serious injury.

It was half an hour before Scott had his mind to himself again. He'd filled out his report. *Tuesday, April 5, 2005. 11:45 a.m. Responded to call at...*

Kelsey Stuart, the young woman who'd borrowed her boyfriend's truck to pull her recently deceased father's car to her apartment in San Diego, had been pronounced dead at the scene fifteen minutes before.

By the time she heard Scott's black Chevy pickup in the drive shortly after eight on Wednesday morning, Tricia had had twenty-four hours to work herself into an inner frenzy and an outer state of complete calm. Much of her life had been spent learning things she'd never use. But little had she known, growing up the daughter of a wealthy San Franciscan couple, that the ability to keep up appearances had also equipped her with the skills to lead a double life.

"Hi, babe!" Even after almost two years of living with this man, sharing his bed and his life, she still felt that little leap in her belly every time he walked into a room.

She was in the kitchen and plunged her hands into the sink of dirty dishwater to keep from flinging them around Scott. He wouldn't recognize the needy, clinging woman.

"Hi, yourself!"

He'd been gone four nights—part of the four on, four off rotation that made up most of his schedule, broken only once or twice a month with a one or two day on/off turn. She could have justified a hug. *If* she'd been able to trust herself not to fall apart the moment she felt his arms slide around her...

"Daaaddeee!" Taylor squirmed in his high chair, seemingly unaware of the toast crumbs smeared across his plump cheeks and up into his hair. His breakfast was a daily pre-bath ritual.

"Mornin', squirt!" Scott rubbed the baby's head and bent down to kiss his cheek, as though he was spotlessly clean. "Were you a good boy for your mama?"

"Good boy." Taylor nodded. And then, "Down!"

He lifted his arms up to the man he called Daddy. Someday Taylor would have to know that Scott wasn't actually his biological father, but maybe by then Scott would have adopted him and—

She abruptly yanked the plug in the bottom of the sink, watching as the grayish water and the residue of bubbles washed away. She couldn't think about the future. It was one of her non-negotiable rules.

Unless things changed drastically, there would be no future for her. Only the day-to-day life she had now. Only the moment.

Hearing her son squeal, followed by silence from the man who usually made as much or more noise than the little boy when the two were playing together, Tricia glanced over her shoulder.

"Scott?" She dried her hands, moved slowly behind the man she'd duped—yes, duped—into taking her in. She'd played the part of a destitute homeless woman, and then grown to love Scott more than she'd ever believed possible. Face buried in Taylor's neck, he was holding on to the boy.

Almost as she had the day before...

"Is something wrong?" she asked, her throat tightening with the terror that was never far from the surface. Had he had enough of them? Was this going to be goodbye?

Could she handle another loss right now?

He didn't look up right away, and Tricia focused on breathing. Life had come down to this a few times in the past couple of years—reduced to its most basic level. Getting each breath to follow the one before. Clearing her mind of all thought, all worry, her heart of all fear, so that she could breathe.

"You want us to leave?" she made herself ask when she could. Probably only seconds had passed. They seemed like minutes. Her arrangement with Scott wasn't permanent. She'd known that. Insisted on it.

The back pockets of her worn, department-store jeans were a good place for hands that were noticeably trembling.

"Can we put him in his playpen with Blue?" Scott asked.

Taylor's addiction to *Blue's Clues* could easily buy half an hour of uninterrupted time.

"I need to talk to you."

It was bad, then.

He wouldn't look her in the eye. Hadn't answered her question about leaving. And his thick brown hair was messier than usual—as though he'd been running his hand through it all morning.

Scott had a habit of doing that when he was working through things that upset him.

She wanted to speak. To tell him that amusing Taylor with Blue while they talked was fine with her. That she was happy to hear whatever was on his mind.

She just didn't have it in her. She'd hardly slept. Was having trouble staying focused. Jumping at every innocuous click, bump or whoosh of air. She'd even dropped Taylor's spoon earlier when the refrigerator had clicked on behind her.

With a jerky nod, she followed him into the living room, where one entire corner was taken up with

Taylor's playpen, toys and sundry other toddler possessions. She would've moved the changing table out of the crowded room now that he was older and it was easier to have him climb onto the couch rather than lifting his almost twenty pounds up to the table for a diaper change, but they didn't have anyplace to put it. Scott's house, as was the case with most of the homes in the older San Diego South Park neighborhood, didn't have a garage.

And the crib and dresser in Taylor's small room left no space for anything else. Which made the fact that they had little else less noticeable.

"What's up?" They were in Scott's room—their room for now—with the door open so she could hear Taylor.

He paced at the end of the king-size bed, staring down at the hardwood floor. Sitting in the old wooden rocker that had become a haven to her, Tricia hugged a throw pillow to her belly and waited.

Scott stopped. Glanced over at her. He sat on the end of the bed she'd made only an hour before. With hands clasped between his knees, he looked over at her.

"I haven't been completely honest with you."

Her breath whooshed out, but her lungs didn't immediately expand to allow any entry of air.

He opened his mouth to speak, then shook his head.

"What?" Her voice was low, partly because she was having trouble saying anything at all. Partly because of Taylor in the next room. But also because, as she saw him sitting there, she watched—*felt*—the struggle inside him.

She knew. Oh, not his secret, obviously. But she knew all about the dark pain associated with keeping secrets.

"I shouldn't have lied, and I'm sorry." The conversation was getting more and more ominous. Tricia wanted to scream at him for lying to her. She'd been lied to enough. Couldn't take any more.

But how could she be upset with him for something she was doing herself? No one was guiltier of hiding things than Tricia Campbell—name chosen from the Campbell's soup can she'd seen on his counter when, the morning after the first time they'd had sex, he'd asked her full name.

"Why..." she coughed. "Why don't you tell me what this is about?" If she had to find another place to live, she'd need as much of the day as she could get. Taylor had to be in bed by seven or he'd be too tired to sleep.

Still hugging the pillow, Tricia tried her hardest to ignore the far-too-familiar sense of impending darkness, the dread and panic that she could never seem to escape. She thought of the blue sky outside. Of the beach in Coronado, there for her to walk any time of the day or night. She thought of cuddling up to her small son for a long afternoon nap.

"I'm—I haven't always lived...this way." He gestured to the room.

"What? I'm keeping the place too clean? I don't mean to, I just…"

"No!" He grinned at her and Tricia's heart lightened. That quickly. It was why she'd been drawn to the man in the first place. There was something special about him and something deep in her recognized it. Even if, consciously, she had no idea what it was.

"I love everything you've done to the place. The curtains and pillows, the rugs. I love having meals I don't have to fix myself, and having help with the dishes. I love always being able to find what I need because it has a place, so I know where to look for it."

Good. Okay, then. She wasn't just using him. She was giving him a valuable service.

"Have you ever heard of McCall faucets?"

The question threw her. "Of course. They're top of the line. In custom homes all over the country. They do shower fixtures, too."

"And toilet hardware," he added.

"So?" She frowned, pushed against the floor with one bare foot to set the chair in motion. "You want to replace the kitchen faucet?"

He shook his head.

She hadn't really thought so.

"The shower?" Please let it just be that.

"No, Trish. I want to tell you that my family *is* Mc-Call faucets. *I* am McCall faucets."

She was going to wake up now and find out that this was a twisted dream, another way her psyche had dreamed up to torment her. She was going to wake up and find out that it was really only one in the morning and she had a whole night to get through before she could get out of bed and feel the promise of sunshine on her skin. Seven and a half hours to go before Scott got home from his shift at the station.

"Say something." He was still sitting there, dressed in his blue uniform pants and blue T-shirt with the San Diego fire insignia on it, hands clasped. She hadn't woken up.

"I'm confused." It was a relief to tell the complete truth for once.

"My grandfather is the original designer and patent holder of McCall faucets. The company now belongs to my parents. My younger brother, Jason, has an MBA in business and will probably take over the vice-presidency from my uncle when he retires in a couple of years."

Wake up. Wake up. Please wake up.

"Do you have a large family?" That seemed the smart thing to concentrate on until she could get herself out of this crazy nightmare.

Scott was one of *those* people? The kind she used to be? The kind her husband still was? People whose wealth and privilege instilled the belief that they were above the law? One of those people who made mistakes and knew that society would look the other way?

Scott was coming clean? When it was more important than ever that she continue with her lies?

He'd said something—about his family she presumed—and was now awaiting her response.

"I'm sorry, I missed that, I was listening to Taylor." The lies slid out of her mouth so easily these days.

His mouth curved in that half grin that usually made her stomach turn over. Not today. She was going to miss that grin.

"I said that I have numerous aunts, uncles and cousins, both of my maternal grandparents and both parents. But Jason is my only sibling."

"No sisters?" The ridiculous question, considering what he was telling her, proved to her that this was only a dream. Reassured her.

Scott shook his head. "Just a bevy of female cousins."

She felt a brief curiosity about them. Would probably have liked them. If she could've met Scott sooner, in college maybe, before she'd made the one critical choice that had ruined the rest of her life.

Staring at the braided rug in the middle of the floor between the rocker and bed, she didn't realize Scott had stood until she felt the warmth of his hand prying the pillow from her fingers. With gentle pressure, he pulled at her hand. Tricia didn't resist. In his arms she came alive.

She knew her attempt at escape through fantasies of nightmares for the lie it was.

Everything Scott had just told her was true. All true.

And everything about her—including her mousy-brown hair—was false.

2

The peace Tricia generally found in Scott's arms was elusive that morning. She snuggled up to his warmth, buried her face in his neck, inhaling the musky scent of his aftershave—a cheap drugstore brand she'd bought him for Christmas.

A drugstore brand when he'd probably been used to several-hundred-dollar-an-ounce varieties.

He'd shaved before he'd come home that morning. The skin on his neck was smooth, soft. She kissed him. A small caress that lingered.

God, let this all go away.

Scott held on to her, saying nothing, but there was a sense of things left unsaid. Of more things coming.

She had to get a San Francisco paper. It was going to tell her that Leah had turned up, healthy and happy, though embarrassed as hell for having fallen prey to the consequences of some inane idea she'd had. Wasn't it? She'd promised herself, sometime during the long lonely hours of the night, that it would.

"Taylor's going to want his walk," she said into Scott's shoulder, making no move away from him.

It was during those morning walks that Tricia usually picked up the *San Francisco Gazette* from a stand at the food mart a couple of blocks away. And unless Scott was on twenty-four-hour duty at the station, she read it at the Grape Street dog park, where no one would pay attention or ask questions. And where Taylor could squeal at the four-legged creatures.

In another lifetime he'd have had a dog. Or three. In another life, her son would've had anything and everything his little heart desired.

"I don't think he'll be too upset about exchanging a walk for *Blue*." Scott's lips nuzzled her neck, sending chills down her spine. Good chills. And chills of warning, too. She'd never have believed it was possible to experience such opposing thoughts—emotions—sensations—all at the same time.

She had to take that walk. Get away from Scott. She had to buy the paper.

And she had to stand up, face what was before her, move on. Taylor's life depended on her ability to take the next step. And the next.

Reaching up to release the ponytail that was giving her a headache, Tricia pulled back from Scott and shook her head, letting the long brown strands fall around her. She'd never had long hair before.

She'd gotten used to it. Maybe even liked it if she could get past how unfashionable it looked.

"The fresh air's good for him."

"You're angry."

She turned away. Dropped the ponytail elastic on the Formica dresser top.

"No, I'm not."

Turning back, Tricia met his gaze briefly, and then glanced at the blue fake-down comforter on the bed behind him, covering what she knew were sheets with such a low thread count that the only way she'd been able to make them soft was to wash them repeatedly with tons of fabric softener. The throw pillows she'd sewn herself from fabric remnants left over from her contract job as an independent alterations specialist at a Coronado dry cleaner. Behind the bed were walls so thin any insulation that might've been there had probably deteriorated years before, and windows whose frames were bent enough that if the wind blew just right during a storm, water would come in.

His body, leaning against the bed, captured her attention for a second. And then she looked him in the eye.

"I don't understand."

He shrugged, didn't ask what she meant. "It's a long story."

"I can always start *Blue* over if I have to."

He gestured to the bed. "You want to sit down?"

She didn't. Her nerves were stretched too taut. Tricia peeked out the bedroom door, down the hall to the living room where she could see her son happily playing, his little chin raised as he stared at his idol on the screen in front of him.

And she turned back. As much as she didn't want to hear whatever Scott had to tell her, she had to. She loved him.

With one hip resting on the bed just below her pillow, she kept both feet firmly on the floor, arms crossed over her chest.

She'd once been told that her C-cup breasts were the best part of her. At the time, she'd considered the words a compliment.

Scott closed his eyes, one bent leg pulled up on the mattress, his other foot still on the floor.

"I had it all once." His voice had an edge she didn't recognize. The man she'd grown to count on was peaceful and compassionate. He was a healer. Not a hurter.

Taylor's babyish lisp rang out from the other room, his rendition of Blue's theme song. Another episode was starting.

Plastic scraped against plastic. He was playing with his hollow square color blocks, trying to fit one inside another. Only problem was, her son hadn't quite grasped the concept that the smaller block went into the bigger one.

"The best of everything. Best home. Best clothes. Best education." He'd opened his eyes and was looking right at her, making her uncomfortable.

He knew nothing about her. But this wasn't about her. Silently, keeping her own counsel, she waited.

"I had my own servants."

He'd said that as though it was one of the seven deadly sins. Her skin felt hot. And she shivered with cold.

"On my seventeenth birthday, my father surprised me with a brand-new Porsche."

They were nice cars, though Tricia was more fond of Jaguars. Navy-blue ones. With beige leather interiors and seats that heated up at the touch of a button.

"Alicia loved that car."

What? "Alicia?"

He nodded. Tense enough that the cords in his neck framed his next swallow. "I met her in high school."

"Your girlfriend?" She wasn't jealous. Had no reason to be jealous. Obviously Scott hadn't stuck with this girl. Still, had she ever seen that warmth in his eyes when he'd been focused on *her?*

"She was more than just a girlfriend." His voice took on a distant quality, almost as though he was talking in his sleep. His sight had definitely focused inward, leaving Tricia sitting there alone.

And yet... He was sharing this with her. That meant something.

"How so?" she asked softly, dragging a blue-and-white throw pillow onto her lap, hugging it, pulling at the tasseled trim she'd sewn on by hand.

He tilted his head slightly, a restless hand coming to rest on the side of his boot.

"It sounds crazy," he told her. "Always has, even in my own mind, but Alicia was special. Different. From the first time I met her, it's like we connected. Suddenly everything in life made sense. I felt as if I'd been thrown from a hurricane into a rainbow."

Which described exactly how she'd felt when she met him. Emotion burned at the back of her throat. She felt that way about him. He'd felt that way about someone else.

"It doesn't sound crazy." But this love story didn't have a happy ending. Had the woman dumped him? For someone who was more…what? Couldn't be richer. Meaner, then? Politically motivated?

Or had their families been involved? Disapproved of the match?

"Did your parents like her?" Was she rich enough for them?

"Everyone liked her. Alicia was the only daughter of one of California's most influential bankers. But unlike the other girls at school, her attitude wasn't defined by her family's wealth. She was blond, small, popular. She liked nice things. But she spent her time thinking about poetry. And social problems—how she could help people."

Tricia had spent most of her teenage years dreaming about clothes. But she'd volunteered at the animal shelter every weekend and during the summer. Leah had taken her there. Among the animals Tricia had found peace. Security. Unconditional love.

"So what happened? I can't imagine she didn't like you."

His grin was slow, not fully present, but Tricia felt heat in her cheeks anyway.

"We were pretty much inseparable the last two years

of high school. We graduated. Celebrated our eighteenth birthdays that summer."

His was in July. Three months away. Last year had been the first she'd celebrated with him. He'd been embarrassed by the fuss she'd made—which had consisted of one new shirt and a homemade cake.

"The third Saturday in August, just before we were due to leave for college, we took the Porsche out for a long drive along Highway One."

The coastal road followed the Pacific Ocean all the way up the state of California and beyond. Tricia and Leah had run away for a couple of weeks one summer during college and driven the entire craggy coastline, marveling at the natural beauty that took their breath away, the mountains and drop-offs, the mammoth rocks and roaring waves, stopping wherever the spirit took them. They'd spent three days in Carmel.

Tricia had sworn she'd go back there with a lover someday.

She never had.

"Somewhere about a hundred miles north of Santa Monica I pulled into a deserted overlook and asked her to marry me."

This was where the story got sad. Those narrowed, glistening eyes said so.

"She turned you down?" She hadn't meant to sound incredulous, but she really couldn't believe it.

"No." He glanced up with a bit of a smile. She'd never seen a smile look so sad. "She said yes. And started to cry when the ring I nervously pulled out of the glove box fit her finger perfectly."

"How'd you manage that?" She was hurting and didn't even know why.

"Got one of her rings from her mom and took it to the jewelers."

His thoughtfulness didn't surprise Tricia. Except as confirmation that he'd always been like that. She'd occasionally wondered if he was so different from the other men she knew because of something that had happened to him. Apparently not. Apparently he'd been born thoughtful and kind.

"An hour later, flying high on life, I took a corner twenty miles an hour too fast, lost control of the Porsche and slammed into the side of a mountain."

San Francisco Gazette
Wednesday, April 6, 2005
Page 1

Socialite Still Missing

Forty-eight hours after thirty-one-year old charity fund-raiser Leah Montgomery was reported missing by her brother and sister, there has still been no word on her whereabouts. According to a police source, they have no clues other than the black gown hanging in her shower. The missing woman was apparently planning to wear it two evenings ago at a charity gala. There was no sign of struggle in her Pacific Heights security-system-controlled home. Montgomery's white Mercedes convertible has not been found.

Standing at the checkout counter at Gala Foods, her basket empty except for the fresh vegetables she'd suddenly decided she wanted for dinner, Tricia read the article a second time. Her hands were trembling so hard she could barely make out the words bouncing in front of her.

They weren't what she'd expected to read. No inane idea to explain her friend's sudden disappearance. No embarrassing statement of apology for the rash or naive behavior that had made her miss her own black-tie function. No Leah.

Dammit, Leah, what have you done this *time? Who's rescuing you from whatever mess you've created now that I'm not there to do it?*

And whose gown did you buy?

It was almost one in the afternoon. The paper had gone to press before six that morning. Perhaps Leah had been found by now.

Yeah, that was it. Tricia folded the paper, putting it on top of her purse in the metal child-seat in the front of the basket. Tomorrow she'd read all about it. The harebrained scheme. The embarrassment. Leah safe and sound and laughing it all off in such a way that everyone would eventually laugh along with her.

Taking a deep breath, hooking the hair that had fallen over the shoulder of her T-shirt back behind her ear, she pushed her basket closer to the moving conveyer belt, unloading a head of cauliflower, broccoli florets and peeled baby carrots.

The San Diego daily paper was there at the checkout—without any mention of Leah on the front page. Somehow that was comforting.

"Paper or plastic?" the older man who bagged groceries asked.

His question startled her. Brought her back to the present moment—the only moment she had to worry about right now.

"Plastic, please." She pushed her empty basket through to the end of the aisle.

"Where's your little one this afternoon?" asked Gabriella, the young, slightly plump and quite beautiful Hispanic cashier.

"Home napping with his dad." She'd snatched the opportunity to get out alone to grab the paper. Away from the house, she could freely study news from the town where she'd grown up and dispose of the evidence with no one but her eighteen-month-old son the wiser.

Only occasionally during Scott's four-day rotations on would she spoil herself, bringing the paper home to enjoy over a cup of coffee as she had the day before.

"You are one lucky woman!" Gabriella was saying, her fingers flying over the number keys of the computerized register, typing in prices for the fresh vegetables.

"Most of us just fantasize about being with a gorgeous fireman. You not only got one, but he's a good dad, too."

"And he cooks!" Tricia smiled at the girl she'd come to know. She and Taylor made at least three trips a week to the neighborhood grocer.

"'Course, you ain't nothing to sneeze at," Gabriella continued. "I'd give a year's worth of paydays to have your long legs."

"And I'd give the same to have your beautiful black hair." Tricia pulled cash out of the black leather bag she'd sewn from the bolt Scott had given her for Christmas the year before, after he'd seen her fingering it in a department store.

"You really should get one of them cards," Gabriella said, pointing to the debit machine by Tricia's right arm. "It's not safe, a woman like you carrying cash around. Not in this neighborhood."

Yeah, well, it was a hell of a lot safer than leaving any kind of paper trail that could be traced.

Picking up the plastic bag, she nodded. "I know. I'll get around to it."

It was the same reply she'd given the first time Gabriella had warned her about the neighborhood. That had been a couple of months before Taylor was born.

"Where were you Monday afternoon and evening?"

Senator Thomas Whitehead, impeccably dressed in a navy suit, cream shirt and red tie, his always freshly polished black Italian leather shoes shining, didn't immediately spit out an answer to the San Francisco detective's question. He'd come to the station voluntarily and without counsel.

He had nothing to hide. And everything to gain by carefully thought-out, honest responses.

"I was at my office until close to seven. I stopped on the way home for a steak at McGruber's, dropped a novel off at my mother's after she called to say she was having trouble sleeping. I visited with her until shortly before midnight and then went home."

Detectives Gregory and Stanton, the same team who'd interrogated him after Kate's disappearance, were seated across from him in the small room. Dirty white cement walls, gray tile floor, a single table with two chairs on either side. Their faces were grim. Gregory was the younger of the two, in his midthirties, tall, dark curly hair with a pockmarked face. Poor guy must've had it rough in high school with all the acne it would've taken to leave those scars.

"Is there anyone at your office who can verify that?" Gregory asked, head tilted to the left and slightly lowered at the same time. He was still assessing, Thomas surmised. Not yet convinced of Thomas's innocence, but not thinking him guilty, either. Thomas took an easier breath.

"Yes. My secretary was there, as were Senators Logenstein and Bryer. We're working on legislation to provide stiffer penalties for anyone bringing drugs within the state's current safe-school perimeter."

So much rested on the positive outcome of this voluntary and informal questioning by the police. His mother's health, certainly. His own emotional health. Particularly if—as it appeared—he'd just lost his wife's best friend only two years after Kate's disappearance.

His schedule and convenience were also factors. He was a very busy man who didn't have time to be hauled into a long drawn-out court case but he'd do what needed to be done. He always did.

And for his constituents, he needed to clear his name as quickly as possible. They trusted him. Depended on him. He'd been told by many of them that they slept better at night knowing he was there taking care of the big decisions for them.

Stanton, proverbial pen in hand, nodded. "Amanda Livingston still your secretary?" Shorter than Gregory, and thirty pounds heavier, too, the older detective was the one Thomas respected most.

"Yes." The fifty-year-old grandmother was perfect for him. Sharp. Reliable. Mature enough not to get emotional on him. And a great asset in his quest to win voters' trust. "She's been with me since I graduated from law school."

"And that was when, fifteen years ago?" Stanton asked. The man really needed to run a comb through that grey hair once in a while. And iron his cheap suit while he was at it.

"Sixteen. I earned my Juris Doctorate at twenty-four."

"When was the last time you were in contact with

Leah Montgomery?" Gregory didn't seem to think Thomas's education pertinent.

He allowed some of the sadness he'd been fighting for the last two days to show on his face. He'd been genuinely fond of Leah. Found her spontaneity engaging. "I spoke with her Monday afternoon."

"What time?"

"Around four." Four-eleven, to be precise. His cell phone logged all calls, received or made. As his father had taught him to do with everything in life, he'd come to this meeting prepared.

"You called her?"

"She called me."

Gregory leaned forward, practically drooling. His instinctive alertness reminded Thomas of a hunting dog. "Why?"

"To say that she wasn't feeling well." Thomas slowly, calmly lifted his folded hands to the table. "I'd agreed to escort her to a children's fund-raiser that evening and she was calling to cancel."

All he had to do was tell the truth. The rest would take care of itself.

"What was the nature of your relationship with Ms. Montgomery?" Gregory didn't quite sneer, but the tight set of his lips was enough to put Thomas on edge. And to make his smile that much more congenial.

"We know each other quite well. She was my wife's best friend. Leah and Kate grew up together, and even after Kate and I were married the two of them spent a lot of time together."

"And you had a problem with that."

Gregory's words were more of an assumption than a question. "No, I did not. I'm a very busy man. I was glad my wife had her for company."

"And now?"

"Leah and I grew closer after Kate's disappearance, understandably so," Thomas said, the ever-present pang of grief and anger brought on by Kate's disappearance stabbing once more. "My wife was a dynamic woman, and her absence left a real emptiness. Leah and I have spent some time together, trying to fill the gap where we could. Mostly in the social arena. Leah accompanies me to various public appearances. And I return the favor. That's all."

The older detective cleared his throat. "Where've you been for the past two days?" he asked, his tone friendlier than his partner's.

"Out on a fishing boat with a couple of my late father's friends. It's an annual event."

Thomas waited for the next question. And all the questions after that. He could handle them. And then he'd be free to get on with his life.

Even if that meant living in a house that was empty and far too quiet. Going to bed alone. But then he'd never been one to require much sleep.

3

The little guy went down without a fuss. It wasn't all that unusual. Taylor was a great kid. He played hard. Ate well. And slept when it was time. He was a tribute to the woman who'd borne him.

The woman who was pouring a diet soda before joining Scott in the living room Wednesday evening. There was only one lamp burning softly on a small table in the corner. As was the case most evenings when he and Tricia were home together, the television remained silent. He'd put a couple of new age jazz CDs in the player, turning the volume down low. And was sitting in the middle of the L-shaped sectional sofa, dressed in one of the pairs of silk lounging slacks from his old life that he'd never quite been able to abandon and a ten-year-old faded blue San Diego Fire Department T-shirt. He rested his arm along the overstuffed cushion.

"You sure you don't want anything?" Her voice, as she called from the kitchen, sounded normal enough.

"No, thanks." What he wanted was a beer. But if he

started drinking, he wasn't apt to stop, and hungover wasn't the way he wanted to begin his four-day-off rotation. Hungover—or worse, drunk—wasn't the way he wanted Taylor to see him. Ever.

Taylor. Why couldn't the baby have fussed a bit tonight? Distracted them? Cut into the time Scott generally lived for—time alone with the most fascinating woman he'd ever held in his arms.

"I brought you a beer," she said, walking around the corner. She didn't hand him the bottle, setting it on the low square table in front of him, instead. Then she curled up a couple of cushions down from him, balancing her glass of soda on one jean-clad thigh.

Most nights she changed into pajamas right after Taylor went down.

"Thanks." He picked up the bottle, taking a sip since she'd opened it for him. Couldn't have it go to waste.

"You looked like you could use a drink."

Scott nodded.

"So, are you going to tell me the rest of the story?" Her voice was almost drowned out by the soft music.

He'd known the question was coming. Had felt it in her look, her tentative touch, all day. Ever since *Blue's Clues* had ended that morning and Taylor had let out a wail protesting against being ignored any longer.

That had been right after he'd told her about driving his Porsche into the side of a mountain. Taylor's cry had been like divine intervention. Saving him.

"Nothing lasts forever, huh?" he asked now, glancing at the woman who'd found a way into his life despite the dead bolts he'd firmly attached to any doors that might be left.

She shrugged. Sipped. "Some things do."

"Yeah?" Divine intervention sure didn't. Taylor wasn't crying tonight. In fact, the rescue that morning had only bought him part of a day.

Or nothing at all. Because he'd spent the ensuing hours reliving the horrors. In one form or another.

"Sure."

"Name one."

"Love."

Maybe. Finding out wasn't a risk he was willing to take.

"Take Alicia, for instance. Whatever happened between the two of you, wherever she is now, the love you felt for her obviously still exists."

Obviously. He stared at her, glad the dim light made it impossible to read the message in her eyes. And his. This wasn't a time for expectations. Or declarations. It wasn't a time to break the rules.

To care too much.

"So what happened?"

Maybe if she hadn't spoken with such compassion he could have stood, walked away. Maybe.

He had to be able to walk away from her.

"She died." Like millions before her. And millions after. Like Kelsey Stuart the day before. Too much like Kelsey Stuart.

He heard Tricia's glass touch the table. Felt her sit back against the sofa. And then nothing. Heard nothing. Felt nothing.

"I did everything I could." His voice belonged to a stranger, someone who was sitting a distance away, speaking of things Scott refused to think about. "It wasn't much."

Quiet had never been less peaceful. Or a muted room more filled with loud and bitter truth. He watched a drop of perspiration move slowly down the bottle of beer. Thought about picking it up and pouring it into his mouth.

"My ability extended to a phone call on my still-operable car phone. And to waiting for someone to come and do whatever needed to be done."

"Could you get to her?"

Tricia's voice slid over him, inside him, chafing the nerves just beneath his skin with her compassion.

"We hit on her side of the Porsche. She was thrown into my lap. I was afraid the car might explode so I moved her just enough to get us clear of the wreck."

He'd made a mistake, doing that. The car hadn't exploded. And her neck had been broken. If she'd lived, he'd have paralyzed her by that move.

Someone, at some point, had said better to have been paralyzed than blown up. Might even be something Scott would say to a victim. But it didn't ease the guilt.

Neither did the beer he gulped.

Tricia didn't move, didn't reach out that slender hand

to touch him. He was immensely thankful for that, yet he hated being with her and feeling so separate. So alone.

"Leaning up against a rock on the other side of the road, I held her and prayed for someone with medical knowledge to come past. Two cars passed. Stopped. But couldn't help."

"Were you hurt?"

Depended on how she defined that. "A few cuts and bruises..." A broken left forearm where Alicia had landed, slamming his wrist against the door. Not that it had hurt. He'd been so numb he hadn't even known about the injury until hours later.

When everything had hurt. He'd gone crazy with the pain....

Scott got up, went for another beer. When he came back, Tricia was sitting just as he'd left her. Disappointed, relieved, he sat again.

"For forty-five minutes I waited there with her sticky blond hair spread over my arm, her sweet face going purple, and watched as she died in my arms."

"It wasn't your fault."

Slamming his beer onto the table with unusual force, Scott turned, pinning her with a stare that he knew wasn't nice, but one he couldn't avoid, either. Other than in bed, his passion was always firmly under wraps. He couldn't seem to keep it there at the moment.

"It was completely my fault," he said, gritting his teeth so hard they hurt. The pain was tangible, identifiable, welcome. "I was larger than life, speeding like the spoiled, immature punk I was, so certain that I was above it all. Above the law…and death."

"You didn't do anything any other kid hasn't done."

Other kids might speed. But most other kids didn't kill their fiancées while doing it.

His first reply was a derisive, humorless laugh. Followed by, "So many times I'd heard people—my friends even—say that I had it all. But in the end, I had nothing."

Depleted, Scott picked up his beer, slid down on the cushion until his head touched the back of the couch and stared at the ceiling. "No amount of money could help her hang on." The words were as soft as his previous ones had been harsh. Moving his head, he looked over at Tricia, hurting all over again. "You know?"

She nodded, her gaze never leaving his. What was she thinking? Wondering whether she could trust her son to his driving? Glad she hadn't been the one in his car, in his care, that Saturday so long ago?

"Money didn't give me the ability necessary to help her. Nor could it revive her when help finally did arrive."

He glanced away and then back, eyes open wide, completely focused on her as he finished. "No amount of money could ease the pain of knowing what I'd done, of having to face her family, to bury her, to live without her; and in the months and years that have followed, there hasn't been enough money in the world to take away the guilt…."

* * *

God, she hated feeling helpless. Hugging her arms around her shoulders, Tricia sat beside Scott, studying his hunched silhouette in the dim light, aware that there was nothing she could do. No words that would change the circumstances of his life. Nothing she could offer him to alleviate the self-loathing.

She was a woman who'd once been in control of everything about her life, and the realization left her floundering. Should she get up? Leave him to the mercies of his conscience? Go to bed?

It was his bed.

She could sit quietly. For as long as it took. If he wanted her there, she wanted to be there.

And she wanted to tell him the truth, as he just had with her. It would be such a relief. She valued his opinion. He'd tell her she was being ridiculous, worrying herself sick over Leah. All she had to do was open her mouth. She could do it. And then…

No. She wasn't going to revisit that ground. She'd been all over it. Too many times. Some things just had to be put to rest or she'd be incapable of going on. Taylor needed a sane parent.

"Not quite the hero anymore, huh?"

He'd turned his head, studying her.

"I don't believe in fairy tales."

The CD player changed discs, the clicking loud in the room. Intrusive. Tricia went to check on Taylor. She adjusted the covers at her son's waist and double-checked the latch on the side of the crib, ensuring that her small son was secure. Running a hand lightly over his fine dark curls, she sucked in a long, shuddering breath. Her integrity depended solely on being the best mother she could be.

Scott didn't need her, or her protection. Taylor did.

"I will keep you safe," she whispered. "Whatever it takes."

Calm as she returned to the living room, clear in her resolve, she settled on the cushion next to Scott. She didn't think he'd moved at all.

"You are, right now, the same man I've loved and cared about for almost two years." The words came softly, without conscious thought.

That statement was the only honesty she could give him.

He covered one of her hands with his. And started to talk. About the help his family tried to give him. The support from Alicia's parents. Sitting there with him, listening, Tricia could easily imagine the days he described. Four years of college, trying not to feel, and always feeling too much. She understood completely the despair he described, the sense that life would never again contain moments of pure joy. At the same time there was the undeniable urge to press on, simply because one breathed.

And she understood the social pressures, the parents who just wouldn't give up their need to make everything at least appear okay, regardless of whether or not things would ever be okay again.

He held her hand during the telling. At some point, as the minutes passed, her fingers stole up his arm, tangling lightly in the hair at the back of his neck, caressing him.

"I graduated from college with a dual degree in fire science and business, went to work for my father and hated the sight of the years stretching endlessly ahead," he said, as though narrating rehearsed lines.

"I was so tired of fighting it all—my memories, my guilt, my family."

Her fingers stilled along the back of his neck. "So what did you do?" Had he fallen into the same depths that had almost consumed her? Scott seemed far too strong....

"For one thing, I gave in. They'd been trying for a couple of years to fix me up, and when they introduced me to Diana Grove of the New England banking Groves, I went along with everyone's not-so-gentle pushing. Diana was sweet, beautiful, had a great sense of humor..."

A paragon of virtues. Tricia would bet she'd been honest in every way, too.

Nothing like herself. A jeans-wearing alterations specialist for a local dry cleaner, who was paid in cash only. There was nothing upper-crust about her. Not her plain brown unstyled hair. Not her drugstore makeup or homemade purse. Certainly not her non-existent bank account—or the made-up social security number on file at the free health clinic where she took Taylor.

And not the facts she hid from the world, either.

"And for the other thing?" He'd said giving in was *one* thing he'd done. She rubbed the too-tight cords of his neck, taking comfort from the contact, the heat of his smooth skin, even though she knew that in loving him too much lay a danger that could kill her. Or Taylor. She couldn't let herself need Scott. Couldn't let a sense of security tempt her to trade away the freedom she'd bought at such a high price.

"What?" he asked, turning his head to look at her. In their closeness she could see the reflections of light in his eyes, the warmth and compassion that was never missing for long, shining from deep inside.

"You said 'for one thing' you gave in. I just wondered what the other thing was."

He took her free hand, held it between both of his, stroking her palm with his thumb. It was so damn hard to keep her resistance up when he did that—when all she wanted to do was concentrate on that simple touch until it was her only reality.

"I made the decision to take control where I could. I was never again going to be in a position where I had to sit, helpless and incompetent, as I watched someone's life slip away. It wasn't enough that I had the degree in fire science. I was determined to get paramedic training, as well."

"What did your family—and Diana—think about that?"

"She was understanding. Encouraged me to do what I needed to do."

As any well-trained socially prominent wife would do with the man she hoped to marry.

"And your family?"

He shrugged, turning her hand as his thumb moved from her palm to her wrist. "They humored me."

"Expecting you to get over it."

"Something like that."

"You didn't."

"Nope." Sitting back, Scott put an arm around her shoulders, still holding her hand. "Diana didn't believe me at first when I told her I was going to spend my life using that training."

"And when she did?"

"She went along with it for a while."

"Until?" *Let me guess. Until he actually had to help some homeless or otherwise socially insignificant person and came home with low-class blood on his clothes.*

That reaction wasn't like her. It was probably true—but still, not the way she would've thought two years ago. She'd always been more of a glass half-full kind of person.

"She walked when I told her I didn't intend to live in the mansion my parents planned to give us for a wedding present."

So they'd gone as far as to get engaged. Something she'd never have the honor of doing with Scott.

"Why didn't you want the house?"

"Somehow, living a life of luxury didn't seem conducive to the job I had to do. It always comes down to those split-second decisions. I couldn't risk getting too comfortable, losing my edge." He threaded his fingers through hers. She loved the feel of silk against the back of her hand.

Moving her fingers against his, Tricia fell in love with the man all over again. If she'd met him a few years before, knew that men with character really did exist, she might still believe in fairy tales.

Scott leaned forward, grabbing his beer, which had to be pretty warm by then, and took a long sip. He held on to the bottle. "I'm never again going to be that soft boy sitting beside his mangled Porsche by the side of the road, waiting to be waited on."

"No, you aren't." But not just because he'd given up a luxurious house.

He took another sip of beer. The CD changed, filling the room with Enya's evocative tones. Tricia laid her head against his shoulder.

"I'm curious about something." Petrified, more like it, but pretending to herself that she wasn't.

Bottom line, she was on her own. Always would be. She could handle anything. Hadn't she already proved that to herself?

"What?"

"Why did you choose today to tell me all this? Your parents coming for a visit or something?"

His hand on her shoulder stilled. He didn't pull away, yet Tricia felt his withdrawal as completely as if he had.

"My parents have been on a cruise around the world for the past six months. They've called my cell phone a few times. They're due to return sometime next month."

"So you have contact with them?"

"When they're in town, I talk to them, and to my brother, every week. Once they realized I was serious about my life choices, they gave me their full support."

He talked with them every single week and she'd never known. That hurt.

And there wasn't one damn thing she could say or do about it.

She and Scott were a moment, not an item. There was no reason for her to know his family. She couldn't expect them to understand the terms of their relationship—that there was no future for them. It just made things too complicated.

And what if she liked them and they her? That would just make walking away even harder.

"Do they live here, in San Diego?"

He shook his head. "Mission Viejo. It's where I grew up."

"So back to my question—why come clean today?"

He sat forward, clasped his hands in front of him.

"I attended a freeway accident yesterday. A single vehicle rollover."

His distant tone scared her.

"The driver was a young girl, about Alicia's age…."

Tricia almost slammed her hands over her ears. She

knew what was coming. Didn't want him to have to say it.

"We got her out. I did what I could. And watched her die anyway."

Sliding a hand along his thigh, she reached for his hands. "Even the most world-renowned doctors lose patients sometimes," she reminded him softly. "Sometimes it's just not up to us…."

"I know." His answer, the accompanying compassionate smile, threw her. And relieved her.

"So…"

"It's not that I blame myself for her death," Scott continued. Fear gripped her anew, more tightly, until her chest ached with it.

"What then?"

He turned to look at her, his eyes serious. "I'm never going to recover from Alicia's death."

"I understand." She did. She just wasn't sure why it mattered right now if it hadn't the day before.

"I didn't." His words surprised her. "Not until I sat on the side of that road yesterday and felt the crushing weight of it all. Alicia's death. The guilt. I can't risk that again, Trish. Not even for you."

He didn't have to hit her over the head with it. She got it. All the way through to the vulnerable little girl lurking inside her, hoping against hope to somehow find unconditional love.

"Of course not for me." She had no idea where she found the strength to sound so normal. "We have an understanding, buster," she said, grabbing his hand, squeezing it. "No strings attached. No expectations. Today, but no promise of tomorrow. Remember?"

She hated it. Every word. But it was only under those circumstances that she could stay.

Face solemn, he studied her for long seconds while she held her breath. And then he nodded.

"Just so you aren't hoping for more," he said.

"I'm not." Not in any way that could ever matter. Not now. Not with Leah missing and her heart still so raw and hurting for Scott and everything he'd told her that day. Not while she was suffering her own guilt for the lies she was telling. So she did the only thing that felt right, the only thing that had the power to dispel the darkness. She pulled his head toward hers and lost herself in a kiss that stirred every nerve in her body until there was no coherent thought left other than to assuage the ache between her legs.

And the hardness between his.

4

Thursday morning brought more bad news. Senator Thomas Whitehead sat behind his mahogany glass-topped desk, hands steepled at his chin as he faced the best defense attorney on his team, Kilgore Douglas. Thomas still maintained a penthouse office at the downtown San Francisco high-rise that housed the law firm he owned—although he no longer practiced there.

"Kassar found reasonable grounds to issue search warrants." Kilgore came right to the point after announcing that he'd just heard from Detectives Stanton and Gregory.

Judge Henry Kassar. Democrat. Openly opposed to every Republican branch in Thomas's family tree.

Sharp pain stabbed at Thomas's stomach, but only for the second it took his mind to take control, issue calm. "To search what?"

"Your home. Cars. Offices. Everything."

"I have nothing to hide." But it wouldn't look good to his constituents. And once doubt was cast…

Damn Kassar. Thomas had wiped the floor with his Democrat opposition—who'd been fully endorsed by Kassar—during last year's election. The man would stoop to anything to get his own back. He'd seen Thomas's remarks to the press as a personal attack. It wasn't personal at all. Publishing a man's accomplishments or lack thereof, as the case might be, was just part of politics.

Douglas, resting against Thomas's desk, glanced down at the papers he held, nodding. Thomas recognized the blue folder. It contained the complete record of Thomas's experiences with San Francisco's law enforcement—one traffic ticket when he was sixteen, and everything relating to Kate's disappearance.

The familiar jolt that shot through him as he stared at that folder, remembering his beautiful and spirited wife, hurt worse than usual today.

"I don't like it," Douglas said. "You have an airtight alibi. They shouldn't still be poking around. I plan to appeal."

Douglas was the best on his team, but only because Thomas, once the city's highest-paid defense attorney, wasn't practicing anymore.

Thomas shook his head. "Appeal on a warrant decision is so rare, it would play right into Kassar's hands, drawing even more attention to me. Besides, if we do that, some people are going to think I have something to hide."

"You know as well as I do that your being clean won't stop them from finding potential evidence if they try hard enough."

"They won't try. They don't have a case and they know it. They don't want to come out of this with egg on their faces, either. Kassar aside, as far as the D.A. is concerned, this is merely a formality. So he can tell the mayor, and the mayor can tell his voters, that it's been done. San Francisco's second wealthy young beauty has just disappeared. They have to turn over every stone on this one."

These were all facts he was comfortable with. Still, out of curiosity...

"What were the reasonable grounds?"

"You're associated with both women."

"What wealthy young woman in San Francisco *don't* I know?" Thomas asked. In the past ten years, he'd done enough campaigning, socializing, smiling and schmoozing to get elected president of the United States if he decided to make a run for that office. "What wealthy *person* don't I know?"

"You were the husband of one and escort of the other."

Thank God that well-known fact was all they had to go on. He was innocent in both cases, but the prosecution might come to a different conclusion—the wrong conclusion—if they had all the facts.

"They're going to see if they can find something among my things—phone calls I've made, bills I've paid, food in my refrigerator, whatever—that might connect the two disappearances."

He hadn't practiced courtroom law so successfully for seventeen years without learning how to outthink the prosecution.

"Leah and Kate were best friends."

"So maybe they ran off together!"

Douglas chuckled without any real humor. "You don't really believe that."

Thomas rubbed his hand across his face, an unusual display of weakness. Revealing emotion, especially negative emotion, was something he almost never did. A Whitehead kept up appearances at all costs. In his world, that rule had been the most important condition for sustaining life. Breathing came in a close second.

"No," he said, looking up at his attorney and closest friend. "I don't believe that." His voice broke and he stopped a moment to calm himself. "Kate and I... we—"

"I understand, buddy." Douglas's hand on his shoulder kept him from making even more of an idiot of himself.

"Sorry," he said, standing. The ability to detach himself had always served him well—in the courtroom and in life. He wouldn't lose it again.

"Hey, Thomas, this is me. No need to apologize." Douglas rounded the desk, shoving the folder back in his hand-tooled leather briefcase. "Frankly, man," he continued, his voice a little muffled as he bent over the chair in front of Thomas's desk, latching his case, "I don't know how you do it. If it were me and I'd lost Kate—let alone the baby—they'd have had to pull me out of the river. And now Leah. It's...unsettling, you know?"

"I know." Arms crossed over his chest, Thomas stood beside his desk, nodding slowly.

Douglas straightened, stared at him for a long silent minute. "Yeah, I guess you do. Listen, you want to hit the club tonight? I could use a drink."

"Maybe." He'd be drinking, that was for sure. "As long as Mother's okay."

"What's it been, six months now since your father died?"

Thomas nodded.

"How's she doing?"

"Like the rest of us, I guess. She has good days and bad ones. Nights are the hardest."

Shaking his head, Douglas moved to the door. "You guys have had it rough lately, but you know what that means."

"What?"

"That your turn's coming for something really big."

Thomas was counting on that.

Scott's four days off made it difficult for Tricia to get to the paper every morning, but that didn't stop her from driving herself crazy until she had the most recent edition of the *San Francisco Gazette* in her hands. She hated lying to Scott, hated being impatient with him when he accompanied her and Taylor on their morning walks, and then suggested going to the Grape Street dog park so the little boy could run and play with the animals. For some reason, her son was smitten with dogs.

She'd never had a pet in her life and she'd certainly never considered having one that not only lived in the house but shed, drooled and didn't wipe after it went to the bathroom. But watching Scott and Taylor with the unleashed pets in the park, she couldn't help laughing.

And wishing that life was different—that she had a place where she felt secure enough to buy her son a puppy.

Still, she made excuses every day to get out of the house on her own. Thread she'd suddenly run out of. A quick trip to the grocery. A rush job that she'd forgotten had to be delivered.

He'd raised his eyebrows at that one, but had said nothing.

Which was pretty much what she got from the *San Francisco Gazette*. Nothing. Senator Thomas Whitehead had returned from an annual fishing trip. He'd stopped by the precinct the moment he'd heard about the heiress's disappearance and no arrest had been made.

He was in the clear. Again.

On Saturday, the last day of his off-rotation, Scott stood in the doorway of the smallest bedroom in his modest three-bedroom home, watching the woman he thought of far too often for his own good. She sat there, some kind of dark garment in her hand, doing nothing.

He always wondered where she went when she did that. But he didn't ask. The answer could very well take him into territory they'd agreed not to travel.

"You almost done?"

She jumped, bent her head for a second, and then turned to him, her ready smile in evidence. "Almost, why?"

Whatever had been on her mind, she wasn't sharing it with him. Not that it mattered. He had no business knowing what made her jump in the middle of the night—or in the middle of the day when her lover spoke to her from a doorway in their home.

Soon after Tricia had moved in with him—which had been right after he'd met her, six months pregnant, in a bar where he used to hang out with the guys on his shift—he'd given Tricia this room for her sewing. He didn't know anything about what she did, since he'd never seen his mother or his cousins so much as hold a needle, but even he could tell she was skilled at it.

He didn't mind giving up his office/weight room for the sewing machine the dry cleaner had lent her so she could work at home while her baby was young. In the almost two years that followed, they'd added a cabinet from the flea market to hold her growing collection of materials, threads, scissors and tape measures, buttons and fasteners.

And she'd painted the room yellow with white trim. Not his style, but around her it looked good.

"The little guy'll be up from his nap soon. How about a trip over to Coronado?"

As far as he could tell, it was her favorite place in the world—or at least in the San Diego area.

"To walk on the beach?" Her smile didn't grow, it relaxed. She was back with him.

"Sure. And maybe get a burger downtown. I promised Taylor some French fries."

"Can you give me fifteen minutes to finish these?" She held up the dark garment—a pair of women's slacks. They were creased where she'd been holding them. "They're the last of an order, and we can drop them off while we're there."

She looked so damned cute sitting there with minimal makeup on her flawless light skin, her long silky hair hanging down the white button-up shirt she was wearing over a pair of faded jeans. Compelled by something other than his own thoughts, Scott moved closer, catching and holding her gaze. Accepting the invitation he read in those deep blue eyes. He'd never seen such blue eyes on a brunette.

Or at least that was the reason he gave himself for the way they caught—and held—his attention even after nearly two years of living with her. Sleeping with her. Waking up beside her.

"Sounds good." He finally uttered the words that were waiting to be said. He couldn't quite remember the question he was answering.

His lips lowered, touching hers as, eyes slowly closing, she lifted her chin and nodded. Adrenaline shot through him, a streak of energy igniting every nerve in his body on the way through. Her lips were so soft, almost innocent, and so intent on passion he shook with it. She was moist and fresh and burning him all at once.

"Oh, God, woman, what you do to me," he mumbled against her mouth, falling down to his knees between her legs, pulling her head with him. Tricia's hands slid up his shoulders, pressing into him, her touch sending chills across his skin.

"How long did you say it would be before he woke up?" Her voice was ragged, as was the chuckle that accompanied it.

He had no idea. Couldn't remember when he'd put Taylor down. Or what time he'd interrupted her.

"Ten minutes. Twenty if we're lucky."

Hands on her waistband, Tricia raised her bottom off the chair, and slid the jeans, with panties inside, down over her bare feet. "Let's get lucky," she said, her blue eyes glowing as she grinned up at him, her unsteady fingers meeting his at the button on his jeans.

He'd never known a woman whose hunger matched his. And that made him even hungrier. They'd done this in bed a few hours ago. It should have been enough.

"Hurry," she said, the tip of her tongue gliding lightly on his neck.

He was so hard it hurt to shove the jeans down. Scooting her bottom forward on the chair, he tilted her just enough to fit him and then slid home.

Quickly. Again and again.

Thank God for home. It made life worth living.

* * *

"Mama, down!"

Laughing, Tricia leaned down to steady her son in the sand. With one hand wrapped firmly around his small fingers, she glanced up through her sunglasses to stare at her own reflection in Scott's mirrored lenses. "Seems to be his favorite phrase with me these days," she told him.

"A guy's gotta see what he can do for himself," he told her, bending to take Taylor's other hand. They were a family, the three of them, laughing and kicking up sand as they strolled barefoot, jeans rolled up their calves, along the Coronado beach line. A moment in time.

That was just about how long it lasted. Taylor tugged at their hands. Tried to run. Laughed when Scott scooped him up, throwing him into the air, and before she knew what was happening, Tricia found herself sitting on the sand, an observer, while Scott and Taylor played a baby version of football with a shell Taylor had picked up.

Mostly the game consisted of Scott letting Taylor "catch" the shell and then chasing after the toddler, whose legs tripped over themselves in the sand, ending in a tickle tackle that had him screaming with glee.

And filled his hair with sand, too, she was sure. Not that she cared. Taylor's squeals were so joyful they were contagious. She sat there grinning like an idiot when what she needed to do was get to a newspaper. She'd yet to see Saturday's issue. Turning, looking for a newspaper box, she suddenly noticed the tall man in the distance. Noticed him because his slacks and dress shoes were hardly proper attire for the beach? Or because he didn't seem to react to Taylor's joy?

He was staring at the baby, though, and all thought of newspapers, of football games and joy fled Tricia's mind. Taylor ran several yards up the beach with Scott in mock pursuit. Tricia followed their progress from the stranger's perspective. He was watching them.

And, she was fairly certain, her as well.

Heart pounding, she stood, cloaked herself with the protective numbness that kept her mind focused and moved slowly up the beach. Had he seen them together? Did he know that she and Taylor were a pair?

If not, she had to keep it that way. Anyone looking for her would be looking for a woman with an eighteen-month-old boy. Not a woman wistfully watching a man with one.

And if he'd seen them together?

Then her walking off alone would at least throw him. Taylor was safe with Scott. Would be safest with him if something happened. She had to go. Separate herself from them. Be a woman on her own, unencumbered, unknown, spending a quiet Saturday alone in Coronado.

A brunette who'd lost twenty pounds in the past fifteen months wearing store-bought clothes and big plastic sunglasses.

Up the beach a couple of yards was a road access. Tricia took it, not once looking back. She didn't know that man and child, had never seen them before in her life. Leaving them was nothing to her.

God, let me escape before Taylor sees me. Calls out to me. Let me go before Scott notices....

She didn't breathe until she made it to the street—and then almost passed out with dizziness. She walked on. Half a mile. Maybe more. Unhurried, glancing at the flowering bushes, the palm trees lining the road. The resorts in the distance. Maybe she was on vacation. Or perhaps she was there on business.

Maybe her folks had a condo on Coronado Island.

Yeah, that was it. A condo. She could play that role. *Had* to play a role in her mind if she was to give the appearance of being someone else. A woman on the run looked like a woman on the run—a woman whose body was so filled with fear it hurt her muscles to move.

Tricia was a woman visiting her parents' condo. Appearances were everything. They had to be. Without them, she and Taylor would've been dead two years ago.

A car passed. A light-blue Toyota. Going too fast. Probably because a high-school-age boy was driving. He had a young girl in the passenger seat.

No sign of the man. She couldn't be sure he wasn't behind her, though. She didn't hear footsteps. Didn't see shadows.

Pulling her bag over her shoulder while she walked,

Tricia took out a tissue, dropping the pack in the gravel. Bending to pick it up, she looked back between her legs. And saw the dress slacks. He'd stopped, too. Was leaning against a lamppost, lighting up a cigarette. His hair was blond. And too long. He needed a shave. And he should lose about thirty pounds.

Mouth dry, Tricia was sweating beneath the sun as though it were midsummer rather than a balmy April day.

Scott and Taylor would have noticed her missing by now. Scott would be worried. She'd have to come up with something damn good to explain this. An urgent need for a bathroom might do it. Guys didn't usually ask questions when a woman needed to take care of personal matters.

The man was still there, facing in her direction.

If she had to, she could always meet up with Scott at the house later. He'd return there eventually. It would be better, though, if she could get to a phone and call his cell. He always had it with him in case of an emergency at the station. The bathroom excuse would be more credible if she called him.

If she had a chance. She was away from Taylor now. It might be the perfect time to get her. After all, she was the commodity; the baby had been unnecessary baggage.

She walked on. She could feel the man following behind her. Was he merely visiting relatives on the island? Stopping for a smoke because he had the time and nothing better to do? Still, she'd spent countless hours on

Coronado Beach since arriving in San Diego and she hadn't seen many vacationers there in dress slacks and shoes.

None that she could remember.

Maybe she was overreacting. It wouldn't be the first time since this nightmare had consumed what had once been a satisfying life.

And yet, what if she *didn't* react? What if she grew complacent, quit watching, quit taking action—and was found?

Tricia turned onto the next major street, strolling slowly—and watching. The possible price if she relaxed her vigilance was too high to pay.

She was a woman on vacation at her parents' condo. She'd go to her grave with that story if she had to. If it meant Taylor lived.

5

"Hi, it's me."

"Trish? Oh, my God. Thank God." He'd picked up his cell phone on the first ring. "Where are you? What happened? Are you okay?"

It was worse than she'd thought. He was more upset than she realized he'd be. After all, it wasn't as if they had any kind of commitment to each other. Or expectations. She was just a woman he'd picked up in a bar, slept with, shacked up with, no strings attached. She'd only been gone half an hour. And he had to have known she'd come back for Taylor.

Which meant he was just plain concerned.

And that wasn't good.

"I'm fine," she said, her chest still tight with tension as she peered around her from the pay phone on the patio at the Coronado Del—one of the island's plushest resorts. Tricia's favorite, not that she had anyone in her life she could share that with.

"Where are you?" She could hear Taylor babbling

happily in the background. The baby's chatter made it easier to take the note of anger edging into Scott's voice.

"At the Hotel Del. My stomach was upset and I had to find a bathroom, fast." Not at all sexy or glorious. But, as it turned out, the truth. And better yet, a truth that would work as a perfect cover now that the danger, if there'd been any, had apparently passed.

When she'd veered into the Del, the man who'd been behind her disappeared.

"I would've driven you!"

"I know, but Taylor was having so much fun and I didn't think it was this far."

Lame. Too lame. Scott wasn't a stupid man.

"You're half a mile away!"

He was talking like a husband.

"I'm really sorry, Scott." About so many things that were out of her control. "I thought there was a public restroom at the top of the road," she lied, "but it was closed for renovation and by that time I figured it would be quicker to walk to the next place rather than turn around and go all the way back to you and then have to hike to the car. I had no idea it would take me this long to find a public restroom."

Please don't let there be a sign for one on the road, making this an obvious lie.

Things were getting too difficult.

Scott's sigh was long and clearly distinguishable. She could hear her son babbling in the background.

"Mama?" She recognized the warning tone of impending upset in Taylor's baby sounds.

"She's right here, sport." Scott's voice was kind, reassuring. "Okay." The word was louder as he spoke into his phone. "I'm just glad you're safe."

Turning her back to the pay phone, nestled into the half-booth along a wall on the edge of the courtyard, Tricia took one more glance around, just in case.

The stricture on her chest loosened a little more. "Yeah," she said, "me, too." And then added, "I'm really sorry." More than he'd ever know.

"You don't need to apologize, love. I overreacted." He sounded so sincere; he was accepting this so easily. "Is your stomach better?"

"Yeah."

"Then walk out front. We're pulling up now. We missed you and want you back."

Tricia had to blink back tears as she hung up the phone, avoiding the eyes of the guests she passed on her way through the resort. If she'd still been free to indulge in dreams, Scott would have been the star of every one of them.

Scott thought he'd had himself completely under control. He'd put the episode behind him. Was completely on board with the program. He and Tricia were ships passing in the night. So it was turning out to be a longer night than he'd figured, they were still just passing.

She owed him nothing. And he wanted nothing except the moments she was with him.

Lying in bed on Saturday night, staring at the shapes of moonlight and dark gray shadows on the ceiling, he willed himself to let it go.

God, it was hot. Kicking off the covers he lay there, nude and exposed. But it wasn't the physical exposure that had him feeling so raw.

Arms beneath his head, he closed his eyes. Told himself to rest, something eleven years on the department had taught him to do on command. He instantly saw a vision of Tricia—lying on the beach, bleeding. In the first run-through she'd been mugged. Her clothes were torn, that bag she'd sewn and been so proud of was gone, she was bruised, but otherwise all right. She heard Taylor call out to her and opened her eyes, focusing. A small smile spread over her face as she reached out a hand....

With Taylor on one hip, he bent to pull her up and suddenly it was scenario two. She was lying on the beach again, but it was hours later. Taylor was with Joe Valentine's wife—not that he'd ever been with a sitter, as Tricia was one of those moms who'd yet to trust her firstborn to anyone else's care.

Except for him.

Which said a lot.

Just as his heart started to settle, the vision was back. The guys were all out with him, looking for her, but he was the one who found her. Nude. Injured. Bleeding.

He couldn't stand the thought of someone doing that to her. Of her experiencing such degradation and pain. He started to cry.

Eyes open, Scott concentrated on the ceiling again. It was tangible. Real. And Tricia was breathing beside him.

He had to stop this. Had to care less. He just wasn't sure how to go about doing that.

Turning, he faced the closet several feet from the bed. The closet where her meager collection of clothes hung side by side with his uniform pants and dress shirts.

She was hiding something from him. He'd always known that. So why was it beginning to matter so much? Why *now?*

Returning to his back, Scott's mind wandered over the past decade and a half. He'd experienced a lot of hell in those years. And was still standing. He was a survivor. He was—

"What's wrong?"

Her soft voice was both a blast of cold air and a warm soothing breeze. He needed her comfort—and she was intruding where he couldn't let her be.

"Nothing."

"You're not sleeping."

"Just hot."

"Scott McCall, I've been in this bed with you when it was a hundred degrees outside and the air conditioner was broken and you were still asleep the minute your head hit the pillow."

He turned his head, studying the shadows of her face in the moonlit night.

"When you moved in here, we promised no questions."

She didn't look away. "I know. I'm sorry. I've just felt a distance in you all day and figured I'd make it easy on you."

He frowned. "Make what easy on me?"

"You're getting ready to tell me it's time to end things. And I understand. You're probably right. I'll start looking for a place for Taylor and me in the morning."

She could walk out on him just like that? If so, he'd made more of a mistake than he'd realized. He'd thought their enjoyment of each other, at least, was mutual. He'd thought that when they eventually parted it would be with regret on both sides.

"I'm really sorry about today," she continued, licking her lips as though they were too dry. "I never should've run off and left you with Taylor, forcing you to be responsible for him."

"You didn't force anything. As long as he's in my home, I *am* responsible for him. If nothing else, the law would hold me accountable. And that responsibility," he added, staring back at the ceiling, "is of my own choosing."

"Well…" Her voice was thick and she sounded as if she had something in her throat. "Thank you."

Silence fell. A million things ran through his mind. Words to say. Warnings to himself. They were jumbled with emotions he didn't completely understand. She'd fall asleep soon, and then he'd be free to work it all out. He didn't have to report until eight in the morning. He had hours yet.

When Tricia pulled the covers up to her shoulders and moments later, scratched her neck, Scott knew she wasn't any closer to falling asleep than he was.

"I wasn't planning to ask you to move out. I don't want you to."

A reply might have made him feel better.

"Unless you need to, of course. In which case you have my full support and the use of my truck and any muscle you need to move Taylor's things."

"I'm a free spirit, Scott."

"I know."

"If you have expectations I'm only going to disappoint you."

"I don't."

"I can't live my life always being a disappointment."

"You aren't a disappointment." Life was, maybe— the circumstances that had brought them together at this place and time, when neither of them was in a position to get involved.

"I can't stay if my being here hurts you." Though their bodies were close, they weren't touching, separated by the covers. She hadn't moved. Neither had he.

"It's not your being here that hurts me." He wasn't supposed to hurt at all anymore. His whole life was organized around that principle. It was a decision he'd made years ago. And upheld without fail.

"What does?"

The air return flipped on, blowing thinly across the bed, across his skin. Scott started to get hard. All he wanted was to pull the covers off Tricia's delicious body, roll over on top of her and just live.

He pulled the corner of the sheet over his thighs.

"I wouldn't call it hurt."

She continued to stare in his direction. Did she see him more clearly in the dark, without the distraction of light and color? *Really* see him? Or did the darkness allow her to pretend?

"What, then?" she asked.

He might as well tell her. It wasn't like he had anything to lose. She was going to leave eventually anyway.

"I'm just curious," he murmured.

"About what?"

"You."

She rolled onto her back, her head facing up. "What about me?" Her voice had grown more friendly and that in itself rang as a warning to him.

"Your inconsistencies."

"Such as?" He might have been responsible for some of the distance between them that evening. Right now, it all came from her.

"You speak as though this modest lifestyle is all you've ever known, but when you need to use the restroom, you go to the Hotel Del."

"It was the closest—"

"No." He turned his head, pinning her with his stare

although he knew she couldn't see that. "It wasn't. There was a motel five minutes down the road with a public restroom sign in the window. It's like you didn't even see it. Which would often be the case with someone who's grown up with only the best. Without even realizing it, you learn to disregard anything less as if it doesn't exist. Because in your reality, it doesn't."

"Well, I—"

"It wasn't just that." Scott cut her off as soon as he heard the prevarication in her voice. "It was the way you moved at the Del. You demanded your share of space, as though you belonged there."

She rolled over to look at him. "I walked out the door!"

"If I hadn't lived an affluent life myself, I probably wouldn't have noticed, Trish, but today wasn't the only time. You get this…air about you. An air of privilege."

She sat up until her head and shoulders were resting against the headboard. "So I'm a snob."

"It's not a snobbish air. More, it's a sense of self. A natural awareness of worth. I think it's something bred into wealthy children. Something they take with them wherever they go. Sometimes it's as simple as the way you stand or the way you move about a room."

"I had a persnickety aunt. She made me spend one summer at a camp where they taught tomboys to be ladies."

He believed her. He also believed she'd been born wealthy.

"I told you about my past," he said.

"I didn't ask you to."

She had him there. Still, it bothered him that she didn't reciprocate. Was it pride?

He'd like to think so.

And feared not.

"You don't trust me." Trust could be freely given— at least the kind of trust where you could tell someone your secret and know it would be safe.

"I don't trust anyone."

He sat up, too, leaning against the headboard, taking the sheet with him. "It's pretty obvious someone's hurt you. Badly." He was trespassing and knew it. The terror he'd felt that morning on the beach, when he'd known she was gone and had no idea where to begin searching, no idea if she was in danger or if she'd ever done anything like that before, drove him on.

"I'm guessing it had something to do with Taylor's biological father."

Her silence gave him nothing. It could indicate agreement. Or a refusal to be drawn into a conversation she'd asked not to have.

"But that doesn't have anything to do with *me*. You've been here almost two years, Trish. I responded to your overtures of friendship in a bar, in spite of the fact that you were obviously pregnant and every other guy there was ignoring you. I brought you home and offered you a place to stay, no strings attached, no sex required. And when you let me know you wanted sex, that you needed a new experience to replace the memory of the baby's conception, I was very careful. Hell, we birthed that baby together! I would think you'd know by now that you can trust me."

When she turned her head, Scott could see the sheen of moisture in her eyes, reflected by a ray from the moon shining in the opposite window.

"It's not you I don't trust," she whispered. "It's me. And because I can't trust myself, I can't trust anyone else."

He didn't understand.

"I…made…choices. Bad ones. Really bad ones."

Skin growing hot, Scott remained still. This was what he'd wanted, wasn't it? To know?

"They affected not only my life, but others as well, and I never saw it coming. I had so much confidence, so much blind trust in my ability to make good decisions, that I almost died. Worse, I could have caused someone else's death."

Tears welled up in her eyes. He could count on one hand the number of times he'd seen her cry. And two of them had been within the past couple of days.

"That would be murder, Scott. And all because I trusted my judgment where other people were concerned." She slid back down, pulling the covers up to her chin as she blinked away any hint of emotion. "I don't anymore."

She must, at least a little. Even if she wasn't ready to acknowledge it to herself. She was here, wasn't she?

And so was Taylor.

* * *

Tricia tried to sleep. She closed her eyes. Went to the safe place inside where, no matter what was happening on the surface of her life, things were exactly as she wanted them to be.

The place was always the same. A meadow. With cool grass, a light breeze blowing. The sun always shone in her meadow, no matter what time of day she went there. It kept her warm, but wasn't hot. A brook trickled nearby. Birds sang there sometimes. Other times heavenly music played. It had to be heavenly because there were no electronics in her meadow—not even beneath the white canopy that had netted sides to keep out any bugs and a down floor upon which she could lie.

Tonight the meadow was elusive. She could get there, but kept popping back out, to an inexpensive mattress in a modest home in San Diego, lying next to a man who, in her meadow, would've been a fairy tale prince. But who, in real life, presented as much danger as he did safety. The biggest danger of all was making her want things she couldn't have. Things that could endanger her life. Or Taylor's. She couldn't afford to become too soft. Or trusting. She couldn't afford to feel secure.

That was when runaways got caught.

Still, she did want things. She wanted him.

He was still lying half-propped against the headboard and she knew he was awake.

Sliding one hand from beneath the covers, Tricia entwined her fingers with his. Many nights she'd fallen asleep with their hands interlocked.

"I want to stay."

He didn't react until, several seconds later, she felt the pressure of a light squeeze against her fingers. He slid down slowly, his body touching hers all the way down.

"I want you to stay," he replied, just before his mouth covered hers.

And, really, that was it for them. Another bout of incredible lovemaking. Another moment when, injured as they were, they could each connect with another human being. Another moment of forgetting.

A brief moment of perfection in a life that wasn't perfect at all.

6

San Francisco Gazette
Sunday, April 10, 2005

Tricia quickly checked the date above the headline as she stared at the newspaper box on the corner of Redwood and 30th Streets, a short mile down the road from Scott's house in South Park. Seeing that today's issue had replaced yesterday's, she slid her quarters into the slot, pulled open the front and grabbed the double-thick Sunday edition. Scott was at work, Taylor asleep in his stroller.

The sweet scent of roses and carnations coming from the flower stand nearby reminded her of home—of fresh-cut flowers on the table. Color everywhere. Sunshine and blue skies.

Paper resting on the stroller's canopy, Tricia pushed her small son toward Fern Street and the crossover to North Park. With the paper growing heavier with every step she took, Tricia knew she had to calm herself. Her hands were shaking, her knees weak, threatening to give out on her.

Balboa Park, San Diego's pride and joy, had acres

and acres of parkland, flower gardens, museums and even the zoo. It would be a good place to go. Its elegance—and sheer size—its buildings and businesses would provide her with the company she needed to alleviate her panic while still affording the privacy that had become a necessity. And when Taylor woke up, they could play on the swings. He loved that.

The thought of her son's laughter as she held him on her lap and pushed them both as high in the air as she dared chased away some of the fear that seemed such a natural part of her these days.

Past pink hibiscus, pine trees, down streets with two-foot-high beige walls surrounding grassy front yards, Tricia slowly pushed the stroller, concentrating on the rhythm of the wheels crossing cracks in the sidewalk, on the soft April air, on the mustards and browns of Southern California homes and plants.

Whatever was in that paper would still be there in half an hour, when she was in a better state to comprehend it. Yesterday's scare with the man in dress pants watching her on the beach had taken its toll. Or maybe it had been her immediate reaction—the way she'd walked off without a word, leaving her son playing with her lover in the sand—that was unsettling her so completely. Had she really changed that much? Hardened that much? Hurt so much that something vital inside her had snapped, allowing her to shut herself off and simply go?

Or was she just stronger now? Better prepared? Able to do whatever she had to in order to protect her son?

Had there really been someone watching her? Or was she becoming paranoid?

At the park, she pushed the stroller toward the yellow metal swing set just off a cemented common area, stopping at a stone picnic table beneath the shade of a palm tree. Brushing back damp hair from Taylor's flushed cheeks, she adjusted the canopy above him, loosened the straps on his denim coverall and slid the brown sweater down over his chubby little arms. He didn't stir.

Smiling, Tricia watched her son, followed the even cadence of his breath, and knew another perfect moment—a second when everything in her world was just as it should be. As it was *meant* to be. The love she felt for Taylor, the joy he brought to her life in ordinary moments—these things were larger than any evil that might lie in wait. That joy was worth any inconvenience, any pain she had to go through.

For now and for always. To have had these moments, raising the innocent little person who was such an integral part of her, made everything else worthwhile.

Satisfied that Taylor was fine for another few minutes, Tricia slid onto one end of the bench, setting the paper in front of her. There was no one around that early on a Sunday morning, so she didn't have the peripheral protection of the crowds that would appear later, drawn by the museums, restaurants and shops. Still, she was out.

And alive.

There was nothing on the front page. Not even a teaser. Nothing in the whole first section. Which didn't necessarily mean anything other than that Thomas Whitehead—or someone equally influential—was paying to have the news hidden somewhere inside the paper. Money couldn't stop freedom of the press, but it sure had a way of making some stories less visible.

Pages shaking as she held them up, gaze moving more rapidly across each sheet as her heart rate sped up, Tricia turned a page. And then another.

Panic rose in her throat. Another day with nothing couldn't be good.

Or maybe it could be, a calming voice said inside her mind. If, like Tricia, Leah was alive and well…

Page 25. Section E

Blood Found on Car Seat

Police found blood on the front passenger seat of Senator Thomas Whitehead's Miata convertible on Saturday after obtaining a warrant to search from Judge Paul Kassar. The lab report, released late yesterday afternoon, compared the blood sample with records from missing heiress Leah Montgomery's personal physician. According to the report, the blood found in Senator Whitehead's Miata matched a DNA sample taken from Ms. Montgomery at twelve years of age as evidence in her parents' divorce case and resultant paternity suit.

The senator was brought in for questioning just before 7:00 p.m. last night. He had apparently been at his mother's home, where he was watching television with her. He told police that, while he was unaware of any blood on the custom-ordered black velour seat, Ms. Montgomery had been menstruating Monday morning when he'd picked her up for a quick breakfast before dropping her at her office on the top floor of the Madison building downtown. When asked by reporters why he hadn't mentioned in his previous interview with police that he'd seen Ms. Montgomery on Monday, the senator replied that they'd asked only when he'd heard from her last. He blamed his oversight on emotional distress caused by the heiress's disappearance less than two years after his wife's.

Whitehead said that Ms. Montgomery had been wearing a yellow pantsuit during last Monday's breakfast. When asked if he'd noticed any bloodstains as she got out of the car to go into the Madison Building, the senator answered simply, "no." Restaurant sources confirm that the couple had a table for breakfast and that Ms. Montgomery was wearing a yellow pantsuit. According to waitress Tina Bellows, the couple appeared to be engaged in an intense conversation.

Forensics physician Adam Foster reports that the blood from Senator Whitehead's car could be menstrual blood. There is no way to distinguish between a woman's cyclic bleeding and blood from other parts of the body. Foster was also unable to determine exactly how long the blood had been in Whitehead's car, but based on coagulation, suspected it had been there for several days. Ms. Montgomery has been missing since Monday.

A search of the senator's house, offices and two other vehicles earlier in the week produced no reported evidence. Detectives Kyle Gregory and Warren Stanton, who are heading the investigation, refused to comment, but one police source told the *Gazette* that the Miata's search was delayed because Whitehead had lent the expensive sports car to Ronald Atler, an attorney at his firm who'd eloped on Wednesday. County marriage records confirm that the marriage took place. Atler was unavailable for questioning.

The dirt under the swing set was clean, processed. Tricia liked the natural grass surrounding it, and the yellow flowering weeds springing up all over the ground. That something so fragile-looking could live so abundantly meant that life endured.

Or at least weeds did.

Holding her baby to her chest with both arms wrapped around his body and the swing's chains, Leah pushed off, keeping the swing in motion. Taylor squealed, his tiny fingers grasping hold of her white sweater and a few stray strands of hair. She hardly noticed the pain. Didn't care about anything so unimportant.

Leah would survive. She was strong. Resilient. Determined.

"Did Mommy ever tell you about the time she and her friend Leah were riding double on Leah's horse and the saddle broke?" She leaned her face down to Taylor's neck, soaking in his clean baby scent.

"Horsey! Horsey!" With his little legs straddling her waist, Taylor bobbed up and down. "Mommy, horsey!"

"Yes, Mommy's kind of like a horsey today, isn't she?"

God, she loved this kid.

And she'd loved Leah, too. Her entire life.

That day on Cocoa, it had been the middle of August the summer before their senior year of high school. They'd been seventeen, too sure of themselves, maybe. Feeling invincible the way teenagers do. They'd taken the horse at breakneck speed, galloping over country roads and fields outside San Francisco, intent on nothing except getting as far away as they could, to someplace unreachable by motor vehicle. Someplace hidden from anyone looking for them. Someplace private, secret, for only the two of them. A place either of them could run to, where only the other would know where to find her.

Up in the mountains, after a couple of hours' riding, while they were galloping down a hill, Cocoa's expensive English saddle broke. Sitting behind the saddle, her arms around Leah, Tricia had felt the cinch straps give, saw the seat move. And knew they were goners.

Not Leah. No, holding on to the reins, her friend had slipped her boots from the stirrups, slid behind the saddle, half on Tricia's lap, and shoved the broken equipment off the horse. They'd continued on, riding bareback on the saddle blanket, as though nothing had happened.

Leah looked danger in the face and didn't look away. She stared it down and won.

Taylor laid his head against her chest, fingers still clutching her sweater. His eyes were closed against the wind, but he was wearing a huge grin. Tricia pushed off again. And again.

She should have told Leah.

Yes, and at what risk? Taylor's life? Your own?

She pushed higher. The baby squealed and lifted his head, staring straight at Trish with eyes so dark and trusting.

Taylor, sitting here so precious and so happy, is a fair trade for your best friend's life?

God, how could she possibly choose correctly? There was no right answer.

Not then. Not now.

But if something had happened to Leah—and if Thomas was responsible—she didn't think she'd be able to live with herself.

"How was your day?" Scott held the cell phone as he stripped off his shirt, standing in the bathroom at the station. Then he wedged the phone between his shoulder and ear, reaching for soap and a towel. The guys would give him a hard time if he was in here too long.

And there was no way he was saying good-night to Tricia out there with all of them listening, razzing him, minding his business.

"Fine." It had taken too long for her to answer and Scott's neck tightened.

"What's wrong?"

"Nothing. Just…lonely."

Oh. Well…good. He was, too.

"It was kind of an intense weekend," he said.

"Yeah."

"Hold on, will you?"

"Of course."

He splashed a handful of water over his face, swiped it with a soapy washcloth and towel and quickly brushed his teeth.

"So what'd you and Taylor do today?"

"Swung in the park. Had lunch at KFC. Watched old *Lassie* videos."

"With Timmy?" Taylor had a real things for dogs. Blue ones. Smart collie ones. And mutts in the park.

"Yeah."

Pants unbuckled, ready to slip off at his bunk, Scott faced the door. He had to be getting back out there. "What'd you have for dinner?"

"Macaroni and cheese."

She hated it about as much as Taylor loved it, which

meant she'd probably eaten very little. He rubbed at the ache in his solar plexus, left the bathroom and walked outside. The guys would rile him about his obvious need for private conversation with the woman he'd picked up in a bar and been stuck with ever since, but at the moment he didn't give a flying damn.

"You haven't been thinking too much, have you?" he asked quietly as soon as he was outside. "About last night, I mean? Having second thoughts about staying?"

Not that he didn't have second thoughts about her being there. At least once a day, it seemed. Especially at times like now, when he felt so helpless and out of control. Her past was a void and he sensed danger there and it frightened him.

But she didn't need him to worry about her. She could take care of herself.

"No."

Okay, well, fine.

"I…" She stopped, sighed, sounding almost frustrated. "I want to tell you something that has no relevance to anything, but I don't want you to ask any questions. Is that fair?"

"It is in my book." He'd accept anything as fair if it meant she was going to talk to him. Not that he wanted to hear so much that he'd have to get further involved. He just wanted to know enough so he wouldn't have to worry.

"I—when I was growing up, I had this best friend.

Leah was her name." Tricia's voice took on the soft note that melted him. So loving, compassionate. Honest.

"We met when we were three—our mothers knew each other. Neither of us ever had another close friend after that."

If he hadn't known Alicia, he probably wouldn't have understood that. "Didn't you get sick of each other?"

"Not really. We just fit, you know?"

He hadn't, before Alicia. "Yeah."

"Anyway, I was thinking about her today. Remembering the summer before we graduated from high school."

Leaning against the back wall of the station, surrounded by yard and a privacy fence, Scott slid down to the cement, intrigued as hell. If this was what his questions last night had brought him, glimpses of a younger Tricia, he hadn't made such a bad mistake in forcing the issue.

"We found this clearing. It was a cliff, really, high above the tracks for an old mining train."

Which could've put her in a million places in California and Arizona alone.

"We christened it our sacred place and whenever either of us had a problem or needed some time alone, that's where we'd go. Inevitably, if one of us went up, the other one found her there. It was kind of weird."

"Some psychic communication going on there, huh?"

"I don't know. I'm not sure I believe in any of that stuff. I just know that's what usually happened."

"So what made you think about it today?"

Had she heard from her friend? Or had she needed some time alone, an escape to work out problems?

"Nothing in particular." Her voice changed, became more cheerful. She was putting up those damned social walls again.

"When's the last time you were there?"

"I don't know. A while ago." She paused and then, to his surprise, continued in a softer tone. "We could only get there on horseback, but a few years ago we discovered this old cart trail that wound up one side of the mountain. An old hermit lives up there, about half a mile down from our cliff."

There was something significant here. Scott had no idea what. Or why. But his instincts were loud and clear. As they'd been the day before, when she'd disappeared and gone all the way to the Hotel Del to use the bathroom.

Ignore them, man.

"A hermit," he said, mind racing in spite of his directive. "Did he ever talk to you?"

"Sometimes. Whenever we stopped. He was a nice guy. Stooped, skinny, with this long gray beard. Grandfatherly, sort of like a gnome. I think he kind of adopted me and my friend. You know, growing up in the west you hear about these guys who live their whole lives alone in the mountains or the desert, but I'd never met one before."

She was talking. Telling him more about her life in five minutes than he'd heard in almost two years of living with her.

He'd never met one of those old hermits. But, like her, he'd always heard about them. "So, he lives up there all alone?"

"Yeah. He's a pretty amazing old guy. He was actually born up there." Scott couldn't help grinning at the quiet animation in Tricia's voice. This was one of the most captivating sides of the woman who was turning his world on a different axis. A side he saw far too seldom.

"He says, and I believe him," she went on, "that his great-grandfather was a merchant in San Francisco—a competitor of Sam Brannan's. You ever hear of him?"

The cement was getting hard under his butt. "Wasn't he the guy from San Francisco who made a mint during the Gold Rush?"

"Yeah, by selling shovels!"

"I remember reading about him in high school. When he heard about the discovery of gold, he bought up every axe, pick and shovel to be had, then ran through town telling everyone about the discovery of gold...."

"Something the two men who'd found it wanted to keep secret, of course," she said.

"Yeah, old Sam Brannan never dug for gold but it made him richer than most. A true entrepreneur." Scott's voice didn't drip with admiration.

"Remind you of someone you know?"

"More than one." The cool night air, the full moon and the sky filled with stars, were perfect for a man who was searching for peace.

"Money can do funny things to people, huh?"

"You speaking from personal experience?" he asked.

"You see me spending lots of money?" The edge was back in her voice.

"You were telling me about your hermit friend. Something about his great-grandfather and Sam Brannon?" he asked quickly before she could shut down on him.

"When Sam got so rich in town, virtually running the hermit's great-grandfather out of business, the destitute man settled on one of the northernmost mining trails off what's now Highway 49 to run a depot with his wife."

Tricia never used names. Not her friend's. And not the hermit's. Scott figured that was intentional. He rubbed the back of his neck, telling himself he didn't care. Her secrets—or reasons for keeping them—were nothing to do with him.

As the old saying had it, ignorance was bliss. And if she was involved in something illegal, his ignorance was also his innocence.

"His grandfather and father were born up there." Tricia was continuing with her story. "So was he and so were his six older brothers and sisters. After the Gold Rush, when all the trails closed down, his grandparents and parents stayed up there, raising their kids off the land, growing their food, home-schooling them. At one time they had quite a ranch. But eventually as the trails disappeared and the area grew more and more remote, all his siblings moved away. He never did."

"Did he ever marry?"

"Not that I know of. He didn't say. And I didn't ever ask questions."

Because that was her nature? Or did she not ask questions because she hadn't wanted any questions asked of her? And even if that was so, how could he find fault with it? In the beginning, Tricia's lack of inquisitiveness was one of the qualities that had drawn him to her.

Scott glanced over as the big metal door squeaked open. They really needed to oil that thing. Cliff looked out at him, revealed by the fluorescent bulb inside.

Scott raised his eyebrows. An answering shake of the head from his engineer, assured him that all was well. With a quick nod, he let Cliff know he was fine. The older man went back inside, leaving Scott in darkness.

"How does he get his food?" he asked Tricia now.

"Grows most of it." She paused and he heard water running in the tub. He'd never met a woman who liked bubble baths as much as Tricia did.

Not that he was complaining. As soon as he could afford it on his paycheck, he was going to knock out the front wall of the master suite and install a jetted tub big enough to fit them both—with McCall faucets.

"Otherwise I'm not sure. Maybe he has someone who brings stuff up from Reno."

Scott straightened, stood, his palms sweating. Was Reno the closest major city to this mountain retreat, then? Did that mean *she* was from Reno?

Had she just given him the first real piece of information about herself? Was she starting to trust him?

It shouldn't matter. Didn't matter. Couldn't matter.

But it did.

Scott spent another five minutes telling her goodnight, all the while admonishing himself to forget it. Let go of things that weren't his business.

And by three in the morning, when he lay in his bunk in the station still wide-awake, listening to Joe snore above him, he knew he wasn't going to disregard a damn thing. He already felt responsible for the death of one woman; he wasn't going to stand by helpless a second time.

7

Thomas had known Leah was having her period. What did that say about their relationship?

That they were intimate.

Tricia sat at her sewing machine early Monday morning. She'd slept little the night before. Mostly by her own choice. The couple of times she'd fallen asleep she'd woken up from nightmares soaked with sweat. There'd been no Scott to comfort her.

The nightmares were getting worse.

Thankfully she had a lot of sewing to get done for a drop-off on Coronado Tuesday afternoon. Her only client—a Coronado dry cleaner—was keeping Taylor fed and clothed. Not that Scott wouldn't help if she'd let him.

Where was her gold metallic thread? She'd seen it recently. Glancing up at the peg board of threads in front of her, Tricia's gaze moved down the rows. And, as all the colors blended together, forgot what she was looking for.

Instead, visions of Leah and Thomas Whitehead together flashed through her mind—making her sick. It couldn't be.

But Leah had been in his car. That much was irrefutable. They'd had breakfast together and been involved in an intense conversation.

Dropping the one-of-a-kind evening gown she was redesigning from off-the-shoulder to something a bit more becoming to the wealthy—and rather plump—Mrs. Gainhurst, Tricia stumbled down the dark hall to an equally dark kitchen. The sun wouldn't be up for another hour.

But she needed some coffee. Laced with brandy. Not that she had any in the house. She hadn't drunk alcohol since she'd found out she was pregnant with Taylor.

Before that, however...

No, she couldn't go back to that time. Those memories would take her so far off course she risked being unable to return to the present...

Holding her head, Tricia leaned against the cupboard, waiting for the coffee to drip. She'd made it strong. Just because she hadn't had any sleep didn't mean her son would be lacking energy.

Leah and Thomas? Eyes closed, she lifted her head to the ceiling. There had to be some logical explanation. A legal battle, maybe. Or some favor Leah was begging for her kid's charity. Thomas, in his newly elected position and with his obsessive need for voter appreciation, would be a good bet for big bucks.

It couldn't be any more than that. As she reached for

a coffee mug, a moment of peace settled her stomach, if not the nerves that felt ready to jump out of her skin.

And the blood on the car seat?

Sloshing coffee over the side of the cup, Tricia set the pot down, slid down to the cold linoleum floor and buried her head in her hands.

Either Thomas and Leah were intimate enough for him to know that she was having her period. Or Leah had been in his car hurt—and he was covering that up by lying about his knowledge of Leah's private bodily functions.

For the life of her, she couldn't figure out which scenario was worse.

Both made her wish she was dead.

When the next call came in from the team of San Francisco detectives, Thomas was out speaking to a group of impressionable young men at California's most elite all-boys' boarding school, Kingsley Prep. His high school alma mater. Sitting on the dais at ten-thirty Tuesday morning wearing a black silk suit, white shirt and his red Kingsley tie, he started when the cell phone vibrating against his hip indicated an incoming call.

Recognizing the number showing on the phone's display, he felt his smile slipping, but just for the split second it took to steady himself.

The only reason Kilgore Douglas would be calling him here was if there'd been more trouble over the Montgomery woman's disappearance. He'd hoped to be done with all of that. Had counted on it.

The talk didn't go particularly well, the boys much less impressed than he'd expected. They hadn't laughed at many of the little asides he'd delivered to charm and engage them. Which was further cause for internal unrest. He generally came away from these talks buoyed, remembering his own busy days within the walls of Kingsley, recalling his early popularity. And usually that was accompanied by the adulation and respect the current group of boys heaped upon him. After the past week, his worry over Leah, he'd really been looking forward to this morning.

Thomas didn't like being disappointed.

Nor did he like being summoned.

"What's this about?" he asked his attorney as they met in front of the police station.

"Forensics went through Montgomery's condo with a fine-tooth comb. They found something."

Holding the door for his attorney, Thomas followed the other man inside. "I have not seen that woman since Monday morning. I certainly didn't kill her."

Would he never be free from the pangs of regret? The loneliness? Didn't anyone understand how hard this was on him?

"I know."

Good. That felt better.

"I'm assuming there's still no word on her whereabouts?"

Douglas's form-fitting navy suit jacket moved as if one with his shoulder as he shrugged. "Not unless that's what we're here to find out." He switched his brown leather briefcase to his left hand, reaching with his right to push the elevator button. In this particular precinct the interrogation rooms were all on the second floor.

When he'd met this team less than two years ago, they'd been on the first floor. In another precinct. Closer to downtown.

Just thinking about those first days after Kate's disappearance, reliving, even from this distance, those nights of coming home to a house devoid of his wife's energy was enough to make him stumble a step or two.

That was why he tried not to think about Kate, beyond acknowledging the constant emptiness in his house, his life. When he thought of all the money he'd spent on private detectives only to turn up nothing…

"Let me do the talking," Kilgore Douglas said as the elevator doors slid open on the second floor.

"I prefer to speak for myself."

"And anything you say can and will be used—"

"I know the drill, Counselor," Thomas said, forcing himself to smile at his employee and friend. "I appreciate that you're just doing your job and looking out for my best interests as a friend, but I'm not guilty of anything. And until I'm accused, I simply want a second set of eyes and ears, not a defense attorney."

"Fine." Douglas's smile was somewhat distant. "Agreed."

Kilgore Douglas might be the highest paid attorney

in Thomas's firm, but Thomas, even semiretired, was still the rainmaker.

San Francisco Gazette
Wednesday, April 13, 2005
Page 24. Section E

Heiress's Condo Searched

New evidence turned up on Monday at the condominium of missing heiress Leah Montgomery. The search by the city's top forensic team was instigated, due, in part, to the persistence of Montgomery's family, particularly her sister, Carley Winchester, wife of San Francisco councilman Benny Winchester. This latest search turned up something significant enough to have Senator Thomas Whitehead called back in for questioning. Police are releasing no further information at this time.

Whitehead left an appearance at Kingsley Prep, his high school alma mater, yesterday morning to appear at police headquarters. After an hour in an interrogation room with detectives, Whitehead, accompanied by defense attorney Kilgore Douglas, emerged minus his customary smile. He refused to comment to the press. No charges have been filed. Leah Montgomery, recently voted San Francisco's most eligible "bachelorette," has been missing since she failed to

appear at a children's charity function she was
due to host last Monday.

"What's with you today?" Patsy Benton, owner of Island Dry Cleaners in Coronado, watched as Tricia hung
up the garments she'd brought in.

Startled at the pointed look from the woman who was
the closest thing she had to a friend these days, Tricia
bent down to her bag. She drew out a long brown dress,
reached for the cheap metal hanger that gave clothes
points where they should be rounded, and shrugged.
Taylor was in front playing with Doris, the older woman
who handled the counter for Patsy.

"Just tired," she said when she was fairly sure she could
pull off a nonchalant air. Truth was, she needed something
from Patsy but hadn't quite decided whether to ask for it.

The risk was so great. Either way.

"Scott's at the end of another four-day shift. I haven't
been sleeping well."

"Yeah, well, if I had that man in bed beside me, I'd
be awake when he was home!" Patsy, a self-made
woman, was a little rough around the edges, but completely genuine. Tricia trusted her more than she trusted
most people—other than Scott, of course.

And for someone who didn't even trust herself, that
said a lot.

"You got your hair cut," she said now, glancing over.
Patsy had just turned thirty-five and, having recently
taken a course that had convinced her she could create

any reality she wanted, was bound and determined to be beautiful and married by thirty-six.

"Yeah." The muscular, five-foot, three-inch woman brushed her hand against the short, dishwater-blond bob. "I'm scheduled for a makeover next week."

The back room, smelling like freshly laundered shirts, felt safe, evoking a sense of security. "You don't need a makeover," Tricia told her, not for the first time. "You just need the right clothes to enhance your attributes, and a bit of confidence will take care of the rest."

This morning Patsy was wearing a tight black short-sleeved shirt that emphasized her oversize biceps. And a pair of army pants. On a more petite girl, the outfit would be cute. On Patsy, the getup looked masculine.

"I've got clothes out the wazoo."

"Mmm-hmm. I know. But not the right ones."

"And next you're going to be telling me that you're the person to provide me with them. And charge me an arm and a leg for sewing up some rags from the remnants you've got stacked in that sewing room of yours." The words were laced with Patsy's signature sarcasm.

"I'll do it for nothing."

Patsy's generous mouth literally dropped open. "I know you're a whiz at fixing things," she said, motioning toward the silver lamé cocktail dress Tricia was hanging. "But fixing things isn't like starting from scratch."

Judging by Tricia's cheap jeans and T-shirt, she couldn't blame Patsy for doubting her abilities. She certainly wasn't putting any supposed designer talent to use on herself.

"I know." Tricia's breath was coming in short, tight spurts. What was she doing? Testing the waters? If she could take one small step, maybe she could follow it with a leap?

Was she completely insane?

"I play around with ideas," she said now, choosing her words carefully. "You know, drawings and stuff. I've been thinking lately that it'd be fun to actually try to do more with them."

"You really think you can?"

I know I can. "I'm not sure, which is why I wouldn't charge you. But I'd like to try."

For Patsy. No one else. Just this once. Because the other woman had been so good to her, paying her in cash, no questions asked, right from the first.

And because she needed something to focus on, something challenging, if she was going to keep the demons at bay and retain her sanity. She needed a diversion if she hoped to have the capacity to deal with whatever lay ahead.

Patsy, head tilted, half grinned. "If you're serious, I'm going to take you up on that," she said. "I'll pay for whatever supplies you need, material, everything."

"Okay, but only because I spent my last fifty-eight dollars on a bus pass this morning and I want to get started right away." Picking up her empty garment bag, Tricia folded it, shoving it down inside her purse.

Leaning against the desk in the back room where she spent most of her days, Patsy frowned. "You know, woman, with the money you've spent on those passes, you could've bought a clunker car that'd be a whole lot more convenient for your city-to-island runs."

Uh-huh, and then she'd have to get a driver's license....

"But when it broke down, I'd have neither the car nor the money for a bus pass."

"I'm surprised McCall doesn't let you take his truck. It's not like he needs it sitting there for days at the station."

What was it with the people in her life lately? Pushing for answers to questions they'd never asked before. Had she been here too long? Was it time to move on?

Or was it some subtle change in her that had prompted the change in them?

"Scott and I keep all our possessions separate. Things stay neat and clean that way."

"You're nuts, girl." Patsy rolled her eyes. "I'd have had that man to the altar a year ago."

"There's a lot to be said for doing things my way," Tricia said over her shoulder as she headed for the front of the shop. She could hear Taylor laughing, hear his little tennis shoes on the outdoor carpet by the door. Maybe it was a bad idea to ask Patsy for help. "With fewer expectations, there are fewer reasons for disappointment, which means fewer arguments."

"Yeah." Patsy was right behind her. "But think of all the making up you're missing out on…"

A gold lamé gown with black Lycra strips across the bust and below the waist hung at one end of the room-length revolving rack that held orders waiting for pickup. A three-year-old designer gown.

A Kate Whitehead original.

Tricia stopped so abruptly Patsy bumped into her.

"What?" the dry cleaner asked, looking around them in concern.

Tricia shook her head, focused on the floor for the second it took to get her breath back. "Nothing." She glanced up at Patsy, eyeing the confused woman for a long moment.

In the end, she didn't have a chance to make any decisions. Tricia just opened her mouth and the words that came out were nothing like the little speech she'd rehearsed on the bus. It was after reading the paper on the way over this morning that she'd begun thinking about it.

"I need some help."

"You got it."

Still meeting Patsy's gaze head-on, Tricia said, "No questions asked."

"Okay."

"I mean it." The stern voice was one she hadn't used in many, many months.

"Oka-a-ay." Patsy's gaze didn't waver. She stood her ground two inches away from Tricia.

"You know everyone on this island."

"Pretty much."

"So you can find me a private detective who's competent enough to get me one little piece of information—without being so competent that he follows up on it or surmises anything I don't want surmised?"

Patsy's brown eyes narrowed. She didn't respond.

"Not that there's anything *to* surmise. I just don't want the complication of any false assumptions."

Nodding, Patsy appeared to be thinking.

"Somebody who'll forget he ever knew me."

She hadn't made a mistake. She'd given Patsy nothing she could do anything with.

"Arnold Miller."

Heart beating faster, Tricia stood there, thinking it through, ensuring that she made no errors. It wasn't too late to stop this. All she had to do was walk away.

And let the guilt eat her alive. If Leah needed her, if she could help and she did nothing...

"Mamamama!!" Taylor's voice rang out from the front of the store.

If she did this, if she was found out, her son's life could be in danger. That was something other people might not believe, but Tricia knew the truth beyond doubt.

"Do you want me to call him?"

Could she do it? Leah's life against Taylor's? The baby squealed as though Doris had tickled him.

Taylor wasn't currently in danger. Leah very well could be.

"He's not some hotshot out to prove himself?" she asked.

"Used to be," Patsy said, leaning back against the rack holding the gold-and-Lycra Whitehead gown. "He pushed things a little too far and there was retaliation. A little girl died. His little girl. He's still, hands down, the best investigator around. He's also a drunk. Can't keep it together long enough to solve a case. But I know that one of the most sought-after divorce P.I.s on the island uses him pretty regularly for fact-finding."

"Okay, let's call him."

8

There were no Tricia Campbells listed in Reno. Scott wasn't surprised. He hadn't expected the answers to come easy. Turning off the computer in his bedroom Thursday night, he grabbed a book he'd been reading about the history of Ireland, traded jeans for a pair of light-cotton pajama pants then propped himself up in bed and tried to read, waiting for Tricia to finish her shower.

With her hair being so long, she liked to wash it at night so it had time to dry naturally. Scott generally liked to help her. Tonight he was tired.

And determined not to lose the distance they'd set up between them at the very beginning. It had occurred to him during the past couple of long, slow days at the station, with no one but bored guys for company, that perhaps he was beginning to care about her too much.

"I've never seen those before," she said. She was standing, naked, in the doorway between the bedroom and attached bath, a towel wrapped around her head.

She'd missed a drop of water on the top curve of her left breast. And another just below the groin.

Scott's blood ran down to his dick.

"My mother bought them for Christmas a couple of years ago." But that didn't explain why he was wearing them to bed. He'd been sleeping nude since he'd graduated from college.

Her blue eyes narrowed slightly as she stared at him for a few seconds and then, nodding, she turned away, reaching for the short violet cotton gown she had hanging on the back of the bathroom door. Still holding the book, not quite ready to give up on the idea of reading it, he watched as she brushed her teeth, combed her hair, put lotion on her legs.

She always did that, or let him do it, after she shaved. Which meant those long, slim, softly muscled feminine legs would be smooth as silk tonight. His first night home in four days.

Then, switching off the bathroom light, she padded barefoot to her side of the bed. Though she didn't normally wear any more than the brief gown to bed, he'd half expected her to stop at her dresser for a pair of panties. She didn't.

And that sure didn't help his surging blood. Still, the tension he'd felt in his back and neck all day dissipated just a bit.

Maybe sex was all he needed.

"You've seemed kind of remote today." He was careful to keep his tone neutral. There was no room between them for accusations.

"I'm sorry." She slid under the covers, her leg brushing up against his through the sheet and comforter separating them. "I'm just caught up in ideas for Patsy. I really want to get this right for her."

She'd talked of little else that day, though he could have sworn she'd used the project as a shield. Maybe she was feeling nervous about their closeness as well.

Could be he'd made a colossal mistake telling her about his past—his other identity. He'd let her know him a little too well for his own comfort, and apparently for hers. As nearly as he could figure—and he'd spent far too much time figuring—that morning the previous week when he'd confessed all seemed to be when things had started to change between them.

Only the small lamp on his side of the bed was still lit. He should turn it off, slip underneath the covers with her. Reach for her. A little forgetfulness...

Her toes moved up and down his calf, touching him through the covers still between them.

"Who's Taylor's father?" His stomach dropped when he heard his own question fall starkly into the silence. He should take the words back. He sat there with that knowledge, waiting to see what would happen next, feeling an almost morbid curiosity, as though detached from the whole thing.

Her feet pulled away from his leg. And that was all.

After a couple of long minutes, Scott picked up his

book. Read about the Vikings coming into an Ireland made up of separate warring clans that left them vulnerable to takeover.

"Where is he?" The book fell closed in his lap.

She turned over, showing him her back.

"Is he here? In San Diego? Over on Coronado?" *Had he taken leave of his senses?*

There was no movement on the bed at all. He took a deep breath. And another. Considered going out to the kitchen for a beer. Might have done so but he didn't feel like drinking.

"Listen, Trish, I'm not trying to give you a hard time here. But the other day, when you went missing like that, it scared the hell out of me."

There. He'd admitted it. To himself. To her.

She still said nothing, but rolled over onto her back, her head turned slightly toward him.

"I was scared for you, thinking you'd been abducted or badly hurt. And I was scared for me and Taylor, too."

"I'm sorry."

He sighed, ran a hand through his hair. He really needed to get it cut again, much as he hated the bother. "You don't have to be sorry. I understand and accept your explanation. I don't care about that. But what if something had happened?" He turned to look at her but she didn't quite meet his gaze.

"I have no legal rights to Taylor, no way to enroll him in school. If some stranger comes knocking at the door claiming rights to him, I have no way of knowing if they're valid or not."

"We agreed not to—"

"For that matter," he interrupted, realizing he had no patience for reminders at the moment, "I have no idea whether there's even anyone out there to contact about him. Anyone who'd need to know if something happened to you."

"There isn't."

There was no logical reason for him to take satisfaction from that response. So what did it say about him that he did?

"What about his father?"

"There's no one named on his birth certificate. You know that. And without that, no one has a claim."

"There's always DNA testing. If someone suspects he might be the boy's father and cares enough to pursue the issue."

Shadows danced across the room, making ghostly shapes on the wall.

"If someone cared enough, don't you think he'd already have done that?"

So the guy knocked her up and took off. The thought shouldn't surprise him so much. It was an age-old story. Happened all the time.

It just didn't seem to fit with his vision of Tricia. She wasn't the type of woman a guy ran from.

And then something else occurred to him, cooling his blood. "Do you know who he is?"

She glanced over at him, her brows raised.

It was a fair question. Considering.

"What do you think?" she asked.

"You do."

"Of course I do."

"Is he alive?" His gut told him to shut up. He didn't often ignore that message.

"Last I knew."

"When was the last you knew?"

"Listen, Scott, this isn't going to work." She sat up, shoved aside the covers, her legs over the side of the bed as though ready to take off. She twisted around to face him. "I can't do this. I understand that you've reached a point where you need answers. I do. Really."

He doubted it. How could she understand something he didn't get himself?

"You're absolutely right, too," she continued. Being right had never sounded so much like a death sentence. "With Taylor here, in your care, you deserve to know his pertinent information. But I'm not giving it. No amount of…anything…is going to change that."

He didn't doubt the sincerity of her statement. The truth was in her eyes, her posture, the tone of her voice. He was looking at a woman who'd been pushed to her limit.

And since, until half an hour ago, he'd done very little pressing, he had to assume that there was someone else—something else—putting on the pressure. Either now or in her past. To such an extent that she wasn't healed yet.

Would she ever be?

"I hate to wake Taylor," she said, standing. "You know how fussy he gets. So if you don't mind, I'll sleep on the couch tonight and then make other arrangements tomorrow."

He had no idea what to say. Except *no*. To everything. To her leaving. Her refusal to tell him anything. To trust him. To his feelings for her. For Taylor.

"Where will you go?"

"I don't know. I'll find someplace."

With what, her non-government issue photo ID? It was all the plastic he'd ever seen in her purse.

Plastic she could've picked up from a booth at the beach or any number of other places, depending on her connections.

Particularly if she was somehow mixed up with the California drug scene. Or, more importantly, trying to escape it. Depending on whom she'd been involved with, escaping the illegal underground could be as difficult, as seemingly impossible, as getting away from the Mafia of the 1940s. A drug connection could explain her apparent familiarity with moneyed ways.

"Where?" he asked again. She was pulling on some jeans.

He needed sleep. Had to be overreacting. She was probably the daughter of some rich guy who'd kept his pampered offspring pinned too tightly beneath his thumb.

When she'd gotten pregnant, she'd been afraid of daddy's ire and run. He'd heard that story more than once, too.

"I don't know yet."

"Back to the shelter you were staying at when I met you?"

"No."

"Why not?"

"It was for pregnant women."

A privately run, no-questions-asked place for pregnant runaways and battered women, mostly. He'd checked it out.

"You have no credit cards, no proof of income."

"Where there's a will there's a way."

There was no doubt she believed that cliché. He'd wager a bet she'd already proved it true.

It was then, between one second and the next, that he panicked. Right or wrong, healthy or not, he wasn't ready for her to leave. He would be someday. But not now.

And while he might lack the power to persuade confidences from her, he knew how to make her stay.

"It would be much better for Taylor if you stayed here."

She stopped, head bent, wearing jeans and the short cotton gown. "I can't."

"Yes, you can." For the first time that night, his words carried the feelings he held for her in his heart. He hadn't wanted that to happen; he was just too tired to resist. Or even to understand completely why he should try.

When she turned to look at him, there was a glimmer of moisture in her eyes. She wasn't crying. Tricia wouldn't. Not at a time like this. But she was struggling to maintain control.

And his heart settled. She wanted to be there. He wanted her to be there. They were both consenting adults. Case closed.

"No more questions, I promise." He held out his arms to her.

And without another word she quietly slipped into them.

San Francisco Gazette
Friday, April 15, 2005
Page 1

Senator Indicted!
Grand Jury Charges Him With Murder
Of Missing Lover

Senator Thomas Whitehead was charged late yesterday afternoon with a class-one felony for the kidnapping and murder of well-known San Francisco philanthropist Leah Montgomery after police discovered the missing woman's car.

The white Mercedes convertible was discovered yesterday morning by police divers at the bottom of the Pacific Ocean, just off the coast of San Francisco. Police are searching the ocean and miles of beach for Montgomery's body.

Whitehead, 40, showed no emotion when he heard the charges read. First degree murder brings a maximum sentence of life in prison. In order to ask for the death sentence under California state law, prosecutors would have to prove "special circumstances," such as multiple murders, murder for financial gain, murder with torture, murder of a peace officer, murder of a witness, or murder by a previously convicted murderer.

San Francisco detectives Kyle Gregory and Warren Stanton called Whitehead in for questioning earlier this week, after having conducted a thorough search of the heiress's condominium, a search requested by Montgomery's family.

Police have not released any information regarding either the search or further evidence being presented by the prosecution. But Carley Winchester, sister to Montgomery and spokesperson for the family, said in a press conference early this morning that Whitehead was "a murderer and a liar." Contrary to Whitehead's continuous claims to the contrary, Winchester asserts that her older sister, by two years, has been having an affair with the senator for months.

While leaving the courthouse, Whitehead denied the charge but refused any further comment. Winchester accused the man of denying her sister's love, and called him a murderer. Whitehead, surrounded by attorneys and security officers, moved on to his waiting car. Winchester was led away by her mother and younger brother, both of whom concurred that Winchester's claims were true.

Less than two years ago, Whitehead was questioned but never charged in the disappearance of his then-pregnant wife, Kate Whitehead.

Montgomery, who has been missing for eleven days, is survived by her mother, Marion, brother, Adam, sister Carley Winchester, several cousins and many friends.

Whitehead was released on a $100,000 bond and ordered not to leave the state.

Trembling, Tricia walked the beach on Coronado, willing it to hold her up, to take her burdens, to calm her with the even cadence of its waves, its salty smell, its promise of life ever after. Newspaper pages blew across the sand, someone's morning leftovers. The San Diego daily. With the same headline carried by the *San Francisco Gazette.*

Leah dead?

Tricia felt dead, too. Or worse. Buried alive.

Short of its being Taylor's name in the papers, this was her worst nightmare.

And it was her fault.

It had never dawned on her, during all these months of living every possible scenario in her mind, that Leah would sleep with Thomas Whitehead. She'd worried her friend would hate her for what she'd done. Worried how Leah was getting along alone. Worried about what Thomas Whitehead might do to someone else...

But the great Senator Whitehead and Leah? Those hands on her body?

Running for a rock, Tricia grabbed her ponytail, bent over and vomited. Again and again. Until there was nothing left in her stomach. No energy—or feeling—left in her body. There was only her mind. The tortured visions playing themselves out.

And then, dropping her hair, she stumbled slowly down to the ocean to wash her face. An older couple asked if she was okay. She barely heard them, nodding without fully looking at them and began to walk.

She had to get home. Taylor would be waking from his nap. She and Scott had promised him a trip to Balboa Park that afternoon, which was why she'd made the quick run to the island to drop off Friday's order while the baby was asleep. She didn't want to be late. Scott already had too many questions.

Leah couldn't be dead. They hadn't found her body with the car. She'd run. Was safe someplace, finding a Scott to love her, to support her. She had to be. Anything else was unacceptable.

Calm, depleted, Tricia walked back up the beach, oblivious to the sand in her tennis shoes or the sun beating down on her.

Leah dead?

She passed an alcove, a little cave created by weather

and waves against some boulders on the beach. A haven. A hideaway.

Leah hadn't been nearly as emotionally strong as Tricia. Hadn't lived through the fights and beatings that had been such a large part of Tricia's childhood. She was strong, but she wasn't tough enough to run, could never leave the security of the elite society that loved and adored her, could never leave her sister or brother, her mother. Her security was the source of her strength.

Leah might be dead. With a hand to her mouth, barely catching the cry that escaped, Tricia fell inside the boulders and sobbed.

How many times in her life had the papers misquoted people? Twisted facts? Regardless of what she'd just read, her best friend *couldn't* be dead.

Please God, don't let her be dead.

9

"Engine Eleven respond. Building on fire, Juniper and 30th Street…"

Riding silently beside Cliff in full turnout gear Saturday afternoon, Scott eyed the dark black smoke already filling the sky a few blocks away. They were heading toward a two-story commercial building—a deli with an apartment above it. Everyone was safely out of the deli. So far, there'd been no report that anyone was home upstairs. No one trapped. Within spitting distance was an appliance place. And less than spitting distance behind it, a residential neighborhood with houses practically stacked on top of each other.

Ralen took the corner at forty. Scott barely noticed.

As far as he could determine, the biggest danger facing them was the exposures—the nearby buildings that could be in danger. He'd tend to that first, and let Joe and Cliff take care of ventilating the burning building. He hoped there'd be enough high windows to do the job. Cutting a hole in the roof was always a last resort. He'd checked their ventilation fan himself that morning. He'd been bored. Too many thoughts.

"Engine Eleven, child trapped in second-floor bedroom…"

He didn't *feel* as the radio crackled with the bad news. But as his eyes briefly met Cliff's he communicated that he'd be the one to go in. There was no question.

"Child trapped!" he hollered to the two men in the back of the truck and then gave his mind over to the work at hand—and the part of him that would do the job without fail, without the kind of deliberation that would slow him down.

He was going to save a life.

"Damn, man, that was gutsy out there today." Sliding his chipped mug of coffee along the scarred wooden table at one end of the station's kitchen, Cliff pulled out a chair and sat across from Scott. His wrinkled and stained blue uniform pants and T-shirt looked about as bad as Scott's.

He shrugged. It wasn't as if he'd made any conscious decisions. He'd just acted.

"You come down yet?" Cliff asked.

The adrenaline rush. It was, for some of the guys, the sole reason for doing the job. "I've come so far down, I'm at the feeling-beat-to-a-pulp stage." It would pass soon enough, too.

Cliff nodded toward the nearly empty mug between Scott's hands. "You want me to refill that?"

"Nah." Scott would've shaken his head if he'd had the energy. "I'm going to crash."

Joe and Steven, his fourth, had already hit the bunks in the other room. They'd had three more calls since the fire that afternoon.

"For an hour, maybe," Cliff scoffed. "It's Saturday night."

Which meant drinking and driving. Smoking illegal substances. Numerous acts of supreme stupidity in the name of fun. And calls to 911.

"At least it's only a one on," Scott said more to himself than his colleague. They usually had a couple of them a month. One twenty-four-hour shift on followed immediately by one off.

"The doc says Vera's ready for another go." Cliff's low voice was soft.

Peering at his engineer's lowered head as Cliff stared at his coffee cup, Scott didn't know whether to congratulate the man or commiserate—give advice or shut up. He'd played it both ways in the past. And wasn't sure either one had helped.

"When?"

"Next Friday—our first day off rotation."

"And this is what she wants?" he asked, meeting Cliff's eyes before the other man looked away again. "What *you* want?"

"Yeah." Cliff nodded, turned his mug a full three-sixty on the table. He'd yet to take his first sip of coffee. "We want a kid, you know?"

A year and a half ago, he wouldn't have understood how that desire could drive people to do whatever it took. It still wasn't for him.

"You could always adopt."

"That's what I keep telling her." Cliff pushed his cup aside, slouched back in the hard wooden chair, his arms crossed over his chest. "She says she wants *my* baby and as long as they tell her there's a chance, she has to try."

He frowned. A kid was a kid. Taylor wasn't his, but he still—

No, Taylor wasn't his. Period.

"She almost died losing the last one." Scott wasn't sure how involved he should get, but felt he had to tell his friend what he was thinking.

Cliff's blond hair, usually brushed back, hung down over his brow. "I know."

"Couldn't that happen again?" He'd assisted with a fair number of births during his career. Seemed reasonable to expect that Vera, who was fibrocystic, was more at risk than normal.

"It could," Cliff said, his eyes narrowed as he finally looked at Scott head-on. "I'm telling you, man, I'm half tempted to call and have the lab destroy my goods. Having a kid isn't worth losing Vera."

"She'd just talk you into donating more."

"I know."

"So tell her what you just told me. That you can't risk losing her."

Cliff watched him silently for a moment. Then, nodding, he sat up, grabbed his mug and took a couple of healthy swallows.

Scott had a feeling his engineer was going to be spending a lot of hours on the phone that next week. Not that he hadn't done a fair amount of standing out back himself lately…

"So what gives with you?"

"Nothing." Scott considered heading in to bed but couldn't manage the effort. He slid down in his chair, resting his head against the top rail. A bit harder than a pillow, but for someone who'd learned to sleep almost anywhere, it would suffice.

"Yeah, tell that to the ants out by the trash. You've been so distracted lately even Steve noticed."

Steve was a great firefighter, one of the best, but about as lacking in personality as anyone Scott had ever met.

"I'm giving top performance on each and every call," Scott said, not quite as relaxed as he lay there with the chair digging into his head. "If any of you have complaints, take them up with—"

"I wasn't talking about the job, man," Cliff interrupted. "You single-handedly performed another miracle today, going into that wall of fire, running out with a burning kid, rolling with her until the flames were out—and all without so much as bruising her," he reiterated, as though Scott hadn't been present at the scene.

Cliff's account was so exaggerated, he felt he *hadn't* been there.

"She wasn't burning," he corrected. "Just her clothes were."

"Yeah, that's why she has first- and second-degree burns on three quarters of her body," Cliff responded dryly.

"Not her face, though," Scott said. Thank God.

"Because you'd buried it in your chest."

He'd done his job. As he'd been trained to do. Nothing else. And was relieved when Cliff finally let it drop. He concentrated on drifting off.

"So, you having problems with Tricia?" Cliff's deep voice, as soft as it had been when he'd first mentioned Vera, interrupted his counting of sheep.

Why the hell had he thought this chair would be comfortable enough to let him doze off? He kept his eyes closed anyway. "What makes you ask that?" he asked as though half asleep. Willing himself to be half asleep. On his way to fully zonked. Maybe it was the sheep. He'd been working with ordinary white ones but maybe the color was too bright. Maybe if he used a dark breed, something in black…

"The length of time you were on the phone with her the other night," Cliff was saying. "The expression on your face before you noticed I'd come outside."

Shit. He thought he'd seen Cliff right away. Had the guy gone back inside and come out a second time, more loudly, to get his attention?

"Joe and Steve were wondering about her, too."

And Cliff, being the one Scott confided in the most, had been elected to find out?

He opened his eyes to glare at his friend. "You guys think because you were with me the night I met her, that somehow gives you squatter's rights on the relationship?"

"I can't speak for them, but my throat still hurts I was cheering so loud when you left with her," Cliff said gruffly. "Even if she *was* pregnant. Hell, man, we been together, what ten years or more and she's the first woman I'd even seen you speak to twice."

"Your point is?"

"I encouraged you to get friendly with her. I feel responsible."

"Well, don't." Scott thought of black sheep. And then just had black thoughts. "You absolved yourself of all responsibility when I let her move in with me right after I met her. At the time, you shared your opinion, just as loudly. And you were sober that time around," he mumbled when Cliff didn't get the hint and leave. His eyes drifted shut.

Scott couldn't even remember all the derogatory things his men had called him—and when that didn't work, Tricia—once they found out she'd not only left with him, but, seven months pregnant with another man's child, moved herself in.

"So what's the problem?"

Scott opened one eye, then the other. Eventually,

reading the concerned and determined expression on his colleague's face, he gave up on immediate sleep.

"I'm not sure." He sighed, sitting up to rest his elbows on the table and give the back of his head a rest. "She's hiding something—big—and I don't know what."

"Big as in how? Like Christmas or a birthday? A drug deal? Another man?"

The words twisted his stomach a little tighter. "I don't know. Just big."

"Bad big?"

"Not good."

"You think she's got someone on the side?" It wasn't an illogical question. In their profession, they were gone from home for days on end, and affairs happened pretty often.

"No. At least, not as in being in love with someone else."

"But you think there's someone."

"I think she's involved in something." He was saying more than he wanted to. And wouldn't have said anything at all if he hadn't been so damned tired. Or trusted Cliff with his life.

"Like what?"

Getting up to pour himself fresh coffee, he brought the pot to top up Cliff's mug. "Anybody's guess," he said. He'd spent far too much time concocting possible scenarios with no results to show for his effort. "But whatever it is, it's not making her happy."

"Maybe it's financial."

"Maybe." He'd considered that more than a few times. She could be in big to someone who was suddenly putting on the heat. "I don't think so, though. She's making decent money and while I don't pry, I know she's got a little nest egg saved." Only because it was rolled up in a gravy tureen at the back of his kitchen cupboard. He'd happened upon it one day when he was looking for something to put the flowers in that he'd bought her on the way home from work shortly after Taylor was born. He'd been surprised when he'd found the nearly four hundred dollars tucked away.

That was when he'd known for sure that she had no bank account. She'd been saving for another trip to the used baby-furniture store. He'd offered to open a bank account for her, but she'd declined—politely, sweetly and without explanation.

He'd noticed the tureen several times since then, and it had never been empty.

"What about drugs?"

Scott shook his head. "There's not enough money to suspect she's into anything like that and no sign at all that she's a user. No pupil variations, erratic behaviors, appetite fluctuations, mood swings, excessive energy, lethargy or needle marks. Hell, she hardly drinks."

"Okay, I can see you've thought that one through." Cliff's grin didn't make light of the situation, but lightened the moment.

"So it's not drugs, money or a man. What's left?"

Scott shook his head, taking a slow sip of coffee. If they got another call tonight, which the odds said was about one-hundred percent likely, he was going to need the caffeine. "I have no idea," he admitted. "Take yesterday, for instance. She comes home with red eyes like she's been crying, you know? Claims it was allergies— that the wind was blowing on Coronado."

"Could be true. It's allergy season."

"Yeah, and in the two years I've known her, she's never been allergic to anything."

The station reverberated with the eerie silence that fell in the absence of normal sounds and activity. A silence made that much more noticeable by the awareness that bells and sirens could erupt at any moment.

"She could be pregnant."

Cliff's words knocked the wind out of Scott as tangibly as if he'd punched him.

"She's on the pill."

"Women forget."

Especially women who spent a lot of nights in bed alone.

"Could be she's afraid to tell you. Afraid you'll think she did it on purpose, to trap you."

Scott *felt* trapped. And constricted and tied up. Handcuffed. In jail, behind bars, unable to escape. She couldn't be pregnant. He couldn't be a husband and father. He wouldn't be able to empty his mind of all worldly concerns to walk into burning buildings, to rescue burning little girls. He couldn't do that if he had anything in the world he cared about more than the person inside the fire.

And if he had a wife…a child of his own…

Still, a hidden pregnancy would certainly explain Tricia's inexplicable behavior on Coronado the Sunday before. The sudden onset of a stomach ailment. It might not explain walking all the way to the Hotel Del, but pregnant women were known to have odd cravings. Why not odd requirements regarding toilet standards?

It could also explain the unusual evidence of tears the day before. Even women who didn't cry much or easily were prone to unexpected tears while pregnant. Especially during the first few months of hormonal adjustments.

Oh, my God. She could be pregnant. He should be angry. There was no room for even a hint of anticipation.

How far along was she? Did she know if it was a boy or a girl? Was she planning to have it?

He had to know.

And couldn't ask her. He'd promised no more questions.

She could very well leave if he pushed. And especially now, with a baby possibly on the way, he couldn't take that chance.

Still, he had to know.

It took Arnold Miller five days to get back to her.

You get what you pay for, Tricia mumbled to herself

as she waited outside Island Dry Cleaners for the half-bum half-detective to show up.

Of course, the fact that he could only reach her through Patsy's and she hadn't been on Coronado over the weekend made things a little tougher on him. Except that Patsy had told her he'd only called back that morning.

Still, if he had something…

Sweating in her jeans and button-up white blouse, Tricia turned in the hot sun outside the dry cleaner's to see Taylor through the window, inside playing with Doris. His presence calmed her. Always. He was larger than life—larger than her life. As long as Taylor was okay, she was, too.

No matter what.

She saw him halfway down the street—or rather, noticed how the crowd parted around him, the good people of Coronado keeping their distance from the unkempt and smelly man walking amidst them with his unsteady gait. Gray-haired and unshaven, wearing dirty beige pants and a faded dark-blue T-shirt with a hole just below the chest, he could easily have passed for a man twenty years older than the forty-something she knew him to be. Even bent over, folded in on himself, he was a tall man. Had probably been quite imposing once upon a time.

His watery blue eyes trained on her as he approached, but there was no sign of recognition.

"Mr. Miller?" she called as he approached the dry

cleaners. A couple of older women wearing tennis shoes, T-shirts and fanny packs, carrying at least three shopping bags apiece, looked over at her but their conversation never missed a beat.

The detective shuffled past.

Tricia took a couple of quick steps toward him. "Mr. Miller!"

He stopped. Turned. "Yes?" He blinked, glanced around and then nodded as though he'd just remembered why he was there.

He gripped her arm, apparently stumbling. "Ms. Campbell, good to see you again."

The hand was as dirty as the rest of him. Tricia took hold of it anyway, steadied him. She'd always heard that beggars couldn't be choosers, and only now had some practical understanding of what it meant.

At least he didn't reek of liquor as he had the other day.

"Shall we walk?" he asked, his voice at that moment firm and competent. Patsy had told her he had his moments; she was obviously right. Their first meeting had been the previous Wednesday. At her request, Patsy had called her friend who called the divorce attorney who'd agreed to send Arnold Miller over if he could get him to answer his phone. That day she'd given him the hundred-dollar bill Patsy had paid her for the work she'd just delivered.

A quick glimpse through the window assured her that Taylor was happy with Doris. Tricia took a slow step forward. And then another. She glanced over her shoulder, not that she'd be able to tell if someone was watching her. Following her. She'd seen no sign of anyone since that day on Coronado. But that didn't make her complacent.

"Did you find out what evidence the cops found in Ms. Montgomery's apartment?"

He nodded. Stubbed his toe against a crack in the sidewalk and stumbled again.

"You going to tell me what it was?"

"Eventually." Hands in his pants pockets—one of which was ripped half off—the man actually grinned at her, giving her a brief glimpse of what he'd once been, before tragedy struck his life.

She stopped in the midst of pedestrians who had to circle around her. "Listen, Mr. Miller, I paid you good money for that information and—"

The man was a couple of feet in front of her, still shuffling along. Tricia ran to catch up with him.

"No one calls me 'Mr. Miller,'" he mocked her. "I'm not fit to be Mr. Anything. And I'll tell you what you want to know as soon as I'm sure that the woman who's been standing across the street watching you isn't following us—at least not closely enough to overhear what I have to say. That is, unless you don't care if we're overheard. I assumed that since you hired me, you don't want anyone to know about the questions you're asking."

10

Tricia almost tripped. And was grateful for his hand on her elbow. "There was a woman watching me?"

"She sure as hell wasn't watching them clean clothes inside the dry cleaners."

"Maybe she was waiting for someone."

"Maybe."

She glanced at him, confused by the contradictions between the drunken derelict and the experienced detective. The man was intelligent. Observant. Talented.

"You don't think she was, do you?"

"I know not. An observer has a focused way of looking while appearing not to look at all. It's recognizable every time."

Perhaps to someone like him who was trained to see such things.

She wasn't. She'd thought herself so accomplished and capable, picking out that man on the beach, taking action. But how many of them had there been that she'd never seen? For how long? Did they know everything about her? That she was living with Scott? And where? Did they know about Taylor?

The possibility made her sick.

She turned abruptly. She had to get back to the dry cleaner, to Taylor. From that moment on, she was not letting her son out of her sight.

"He's okay," Arnold Miller rasped softly.

"Who's okay?" God, was she so naive? So incapable of pulling this off? She'd thought only she knew her secrets.

"The little boy I watched you leave with the other day. He's still inside. And the woman's on the other side of the street, right where we left her."

"You watched me leave?"

"I may be a drunken bum, but I'm not stupid," the man uttered with a sarcastic chuckle. "I like to know who I'm risking my ass for, lacking in value though it may be."

"The woman's not following us?"

"We haven't gone far enough for her to have to."

Swallowing, shaking, Tricia nodded. "So what do we do now?"

"We're going up to that hot dog stand over there. You're going to buy me a cola and a hot dog, which I'll refuse to take at first. You'll show signs of insistence, I'll shrug, take them, cram half the hot dog into my mouth and you'll turn and hurry away."

She'd appear to be merely feeding the homeless. Something she would never in a million years have thought to do on her own, not out on the street, one on one. There was an old woman who often sat on a bench near the Grape Street dog park. Tomorrow, or the next time she took Taylor for a walk, she was going to bring her a bag of fruit.

"Okay." She had to get back to Taylor.

"They found a test strip from a home pregnancy test sitting on the edge of the tub, hidden by a hand towel. Interestingly enough, there was no other sign of the kit—not a box, a cup, nothing. As though someone tried to make certain there was no evidence." They'd almost reached the hot dog stand. "Not likely that someone was Ms. Montgomery. Why would she have taken such care to remove all signs of the test, yet leave the strip lying there?"

A home pregnancy test. Tricia wasn't going to be able to step up to that hot dog stand. She was going to puke.

"Did they…" Another step. The stench of ground animal parts being simmered on rollers overwhelmed her. "Did they say what the strip showed?"

He looked pointedly toward the cart. Tricia stepped forward. Anything to throw the woman off—to get back to Taylor. Not that she was going to leave the dry cleaner with her son in tow.

But then, if they'd been following her for months, they already knew about Taylor—knew everything about her.

Reaching into the pocket of her jeans for the five-dollar bill she'd tucked there, she spiraled toward the stand.

"The stick showed positive."

Only the overweight old guy behind the hot dog stand was privy to the horrified look on Tricia's face. She knew she'd slipped up, could see him looking at her strangely, as though wondering whether or not to call the cops, run or offer to help.

"One hot dog, please, with everything. And a diet cola."

She had no idea if Arnold liked diet cola. She should have asked. And what if he didn't like mustard? Or relish? With a shaking hand she held the five dollar bill suspended while the old man behind the chin-high glass squeezed various containers over the bun in his hand. What was she doing? Arnold might be allergic to catsup. She had no business ordering for someone else, taking responsibility for the life of another.

She couldn't do it.

"That'll be a buck fifty."

She heard the voice, felt the tug as he pulled the bill from her hand. She took the hot dog and can of dripping wet cola he'd removed from an ice chest at his feet. She walked away with lead in her heart. If Leah had been pregnant, there were no more questions. Everything fell sickeningly into place.

"Hey, lady, don't you want your change?"

"Keep it." She wasn't sure she said the words loudly enough for the old guy to hear. He'd get the idea, anyway, when she didn't turn around.

Leah had been notorious for forgetting to take her birth control pills.

"Here," she said to Miller, shoving the food in front of him.

When he backed up, shook his head, Tricia wanted to cry. She couldn't stand the smell. Couldn't take many more steps. Couldn't keep up appearances.

"Here," she said again, more loudly.

"She'd made an appointment with her OB/GYN," Miller said without ever moving his lips. He was still backing away from her.

As if in a trance, Tricia followed, the food held in her outstretched hands. She'd almost forgotten why they were playing this little charade. Almost, but not quite.

If Leah was pregnant, it hadn't been menstrual blood in Thomas's car. What had the bastard done to her that morning? Something that hadn't shown up later that day at the salon. Kissed her so hard he made her mouth bleed? "Bump" into her just hard enough to cause a nosebleed?

"Would you consider another job?" Tricia faced the detective. She wasn't thinking, merely reacting. But reaction was all she had.

"Depends."

"Find out who's watching me." She didn't care that she was whining, begging.

He stopped and she accidentally smeared mustard and relish on his shirt. He hardly gave it a look, clearly more interested in the hot dog than his attire.

"It'll cost you," he said, around a mouthful of half-chewed food.

Bile rose in her throat. "I don't care."

"I didn't think you did."

"Hey, you fellas feel like some chicken cordon bleu and baked potatoes?" With her son on her left hip and a big wicker basket over her right arm, Tricia walked into the station garage late Tuesday afternoon, interrupting what looked to be a rousing game of table tennis. Cliff and Joe against Steven and Scott.

It was the first time she'd ever seen Steven join in with the other guys. Something Scott had maneuvered, she was sure.

"Tricia!" The way his eyes lit up when he saw her made the day's cooking worthwhile. Hell, it made most of life's daily struggles worthwhile.

"Daddee! Daddee!" Taylor bounced on her hip, moving the handle of the wicker basket back and forth across her forearm. Tricia, taking in the welcoming looks from the three other men, maintained her smile.

Setting down his paddle on the green-painted table, Scott hurried over to relieve her of her biggest burden. "You should've called," he said, balancing the toddler on his hip. "It's not good for you, carrying all this heavy stuff."

"Daddee."

Scott glanced at Tricia. "I'd have picked you up."

"I know, but it's not all that heavy and I wanted to surprise you. "

Cliff took the basket off her arm and set it on the old

wooden table that took up half the living space inside the station. Joe and Steven gathered plates.

"Hi, sport!" Scott raised Taylor above his head, making the baby laugh out loud.

"Daddee!"

"Are you staying to eat with us?" he asked Tricia, still smiling.

She shook her head. "I have sewing to get back to," she said softly, aware of the other firefighters a short distance away. "I just wanted you to know I'm thinking about you."

Telling the other guys to go ahead and start without him, Scott walked Tricia outside. "I can't believe you walked all the way over here carrying all of that."

"It wasn't too bad. It's only a few blocks." And if anyone had been watching they'd have seen exactly what she'd needed them to see—a woman in love putting forth a lot of effort to take dinner to the father of her child. "Besides, this little guy walked most of the way."

"Daddee eat!" Taylor's sweet baby face, framed by dark curls, grinned up at Scott. And if life had been kinder, Tricia's world would have been complete at that moment.

"Are you sure you're okay?" Scott asked.

His concern was touching, if a little unusual, giving strength to the insidious guilt inside her. Scott was a good man. The best. He didn't deserve to be messed up by her. "I'm fine." She hoped her accompanying smile didn't look as weak as it felt.

"At least let me take you back."

"No way!" Tricia poked him in the stomach. "I didn't do all that cooking so those Neanderthals in there could finish everything off. Go have your dinner. Taylor and I are going to stop for an ice cream on the way home."

She'd made three stops as they walked over, just to see if anyone else stopped, too. No one had. But then, she hadn't noticed the woman on Coronado the day before, either.

Scott nodded and, with Taylor still on one hip, bent to kiss her. He lingered, his tongue running lightly along first her top lip and then her bottom one. When he pulled back, his eyes were half closed, sleepy-looking.

"You seem...better...today," he said, holding her gaze steadily.

"I am." And worse, too. While Thomas's indictment for Leah's death relieved her of having to go back— there was nothing she could do to help Leah now—it had left her with an inconsolable grief that she had no idea how to deal with. In one sense she'd lost Leah two years before, but she'd always known where to find her.

Now she wasn't even sure her friend and soul mate was alive. Suspected she wasn't.

Still, there was Scott. And the peace and warmth she felt whenever he was near.

Except when he frowned, as he was doing now. "I wish you'd tell me what was wrong."

"There's nothing to tell," she said, half believing her own words. The past was gone. Dead. Nothing. "I've decided to give up figuring out the future. I'm going to focus on us, you, me and Taylor, and let the rest take care of itself."

God, that sounded like a dream. Nirvana. The perfect life. And so unattainable. But she was going to try. At least until she heard from Miller and knew whether or not she had to move on.

Scott smiled again—a deep smile that softened his face, his eyes. "Sounds like a plan to me," he murmured, his gaze on her lips.

"I love you, Scott McCall." The blood drained from Tricia's face. She felt it go.

They didn't speak of love ever.

They weren't in love, couldn't be.

She wasn't free to love. At least not until Taylor's eighteenth birthday. And probably not then.

"I love you, too."

She'd never expected to hear that declaration. And certainly not in a fire station parking lot.

The expressionless set of Sergeant Mike Midori's face was not good news. And Thomas had counted on good news. Taking a long swig of the third bourbon he'd had in as many hours, he stood as the San Francisco police officer approached his back corner table in one of the city's lesser-known gay bars Wednesday afternoon.

"Tough day?" he asked his old college roommate, careful not to let his distaste of the establishment, or Mike's affinity with it, show. His choice of meeting place was no mistake.

Mike shrugged in answer as he sat, his back to the semidark, mostly deserted room. He motioned over his shoulder to the bartender he obviously knew well and in less than a minute had emptied half of the cold beer he'd ordered. That was when he finally glanced at Thomas.

"I've put pressure on certain people to ignore evidence, but there's nothing else I can do on this one."

Counting to ten, breathing deeply, Thomas forced himself to relax. Nothing would be gained by losing his temper. Emotion wouldn't serve him well in this type of situation.

"Tell me what to do," he finally said when he was sure he could put the proper amount of pleading in his voice. If his father had taught Thomas nothing else during those brutal years of his youth, he'd taught him how to behave in any situation.

Truth be known, he was close to begging but he made an effort not to show it.

"Look, Thomas, I did what I could. I warned the powers that be that they were wasting money prosecuting you. I discredited what evidence I could and showed concern about the real killer still being at large...."

Thomas believed him. As one of the handful of people in the world who knew of Mike's sexuality, Thomas had always been confident that he could trust the married cop and father of three beautiful little girls. Still, he knew how to apply pressure.

Scrutinizing his college buddy, he waited for Mike to start to worrying about the things Thomas knew. He had no intention of ratting on Mike. Ever. He cared about the other man a great deal. Cared about a loyalty that went back twenty years.

But things were out of control and something had to be done. Mike was the only person he knew he could trust. The only person with the power to help. Everyone knew that Mike was, hands down, the best detective in San Francisco. Practically on his own, he'd busted a huge meth operation the year before.

"I'm sorry, man." Mike shook his head. His mouth was twisted as though he'd sucked down a lemon with his beer. It didn't do much for the other guy's usually handsome face. "My hands are tied. It's two in a row— looks too suspicious."

Yeah, that was what the press was implying, too. He finished off his bourbon. Motioned for another. "I didn't kill my wife."

Mike, picking up his bottle from the slick black granite table, leaned back in his chair, looking every bit the macho cop most people—including his wife of ten years—believed him to be. "I know, man, I was with you the afternoon she disappeared," he said, running his free hand through the longish dark hair that had always appealed to women. "I *know* you didn't kill Kate. It's why I risked my job, my reputation, to stand by you, but there isn't much I can do here."

"Get them to drop the charges."

The shake of Mike's head irritated him. Or scared him, and he preferred the former. "Too late for that."

"I didn't kill Leah Montgomery. I didn't even see her. I talked to her on the phone and that is all." He wasn't quite gritting his teeth, but damn, he was close to it. He couldn't believe any of this was happening. He was a man of power. Always had been. Why were people suddenly forgetting that?

How could a loyal public, a people he'd spent his life serving, turn on him like this?

"I'm not doubting you, Thomas, but as far as the state's concerned, circumstantial evidence says otherwise and that's all it takes to convict you if the prosecutor can convince a jury."

"What kind of society sends an innocent man to jail because he slept with a consenting woman?" *Jail.* He had to fight the urge to wipe sweaty palms along his pants. This interview was too important to risk appearing weak. Or worried.

"The consenting woman was your missing wife's best friend, who, incidentally, is now missing as well. There's another coincidence. Both women were pregnant—"

"Not with my kid. Neither one of them."

Mike's gaze sharpened as he sat up. "Kate's baby wasn't yours?"

Making an instant decision, something he rarely did, Thomas reined in the rage that surfaced whenever he allowed himself to think of his wife spreading her legs for another man. He shook his head. "I can't father children."

"Can you verify that?"

With a cocked head, he perused his college roommate. "I had a vasectomy right after college," he admitted. "Mostly to piss off the old man. I wasn't going to be his pawn in the progeny game. Nor was I about to give him the chance to do to any kid of mine what he did to me."

He'd never told Kate about having the procedure, but she'd never told him she wanted children, either. Not before they were married, anyway. And afterward, she'd seemed content with his assertions that he didn't want to share her.

"That just might be your ticket to freedom, man," Mike said, his expression softening as much as a macho cop's could. "Who performed the surgery? I'll subpoena the records."

Keep calm. Breathe. You're almost home. "It's not going to be quite that easy. I found a guy who'd been struck from the medical register for performing illegal abortions. I offered him an ungodly sum of money to do the job and destroy all the evidence."

"Were you crazy?"

"I couldn't risk having the old man find out. That would've been the end of my inheritance and after taking shit from the guy for twenty-one years, I certainly wasn't walking out on what was due me." Thomas was being far more honest than was usual, but Mike knew him. He'd seen Thomas's father in action more than once. He'd understand.

Mike hesitated, drank his beer, then settled back in his chair, his body as muscled and firm as it had been in college. The punk from the ghetto looked better in a suit than Thomas did.

"You'll probably have to submit to an examination."

He'd do whatever it took. Two women trying to saddle him with bastard children were not going to ruin his entire life's work. "What about a lie detector test?"

"Maybe, but I doubt the prosecutor will accept that. It's not infallible, and we've got two women missing. Absolutely no bank account activity on either one of them. Montgomery's blood was found in your car. It probably wasn't menstrual if she's pregnant, which makes it look like you lied. Nothing in her apartment was disturbed, nothing missing. There's been no word from her, no history of anything like this, no history of mental illness. She had a charity function to host that everyone in this town knows was vitally important to her. And you lied about your sexual relationship…."

"Okay!" Thomas held up a hand. "So what happens next?"

Sitting forward, Mike took on an air of confidence. "Obviously you don't want me involved," he said. "I lose all influence and credibility if anyone knows we've been in touch—which would also cast more suspicion on how easily things were put away after Kate disappeared."

"Agreed."

"My suggestion is you lay this on Douglas. Let him take it from here."

It was the last goddamn thing he wanted to do. Admit to one of his employees—albeit a friend—that he was shooting blanks.

But if the world had to know that his wife had been unfaithful to him, so be it. He'd just have to make sure his people spun it so the public would admire him for having stood by Kate as he had, for having been willing to take on responsibility for her child. It would only strengthen his love for Kate in their eyes—and perhaps raise a little more sympathy for his pain at her disappearance. Sympathy often translated into loyalty.

His old man died six months ago—a victim of his own brutality, falling prey to a stroke during a fight with Thomas's mother. So there was no practical reason, other than pride, to keep his secret.

And when you were faced with jail, pride seemed like a small thing.

_11_

San Francisco Gazette
Thursday, April 21, 2005
Page 1

Vasectomy Might Free Senator

Key evidence used to indict Senator Thomas Whitehead in the kidnapping and murder of heiress Leah Montgomery might be just what frees him. According to an unidentified source, Whitehead's indictment came shortly after the discovery that Ms. Montgomery had been pregnant at the time of her disappearance. Whitehead's attorney, Kilgore Douglas, told reporters last evening that Whitehead couldn't possibly have been the father of Montgomery's baby, as he'd had a vasectomy just after graduating from college. The information has yet to be verified with the attending physician, but it would appear that, with this new evidence, prosecutors could be forced to drop charges against the senator.

The district attorney's office was unavailable for comment.

Kate Whitehead, the senator's wife who disappeared without a trace almost two years ago, was also pregnant.

"Leah, where are you?" On Thursday afternoon, while her son slept, Trisha paced the small house she shared with Scott and Taylor, and spoke to her friend as though she were there in the room and could hear. As children they'd believed they really did hear each other on some psychic level, even when separated.

She needed to believe that now. Standing in the front window she squeezed her eyes shut, trying to *feel* Leah, to get some sense that she was alive. But she was so consumed by the myriad emotions roiling around inside of her, she couldn't distinguish one from another.

The front yard, a mass of color since the flower garden was in bloom, failed to offer the solace she normally found there. When Scott had first brought her here, exhausted, desperate, scared to death, that flower-filled front yard had seemed like an omen to her, telling her this was the place she would be safe.

"What do I do?"

Weed the flower bed. That's what.

The bed was the entire front yard. And she wouldn't be able to hear when Taylor woke up.

And what if someone was out there, watching? She moved away from the window. Pulled the curtains.

"He's lying," she said aloud, unequivocally, without a doubt. "Thomas is lying. And I can prove that."

She waited in the too-silent room, the sun shining in, leaving a pool of bright light in the middle of the worn beige carpet. There was no response.

"Yes, I can prove it, but at what cost? Is it going to help you if I go back? If I come forward and testify?"

Nothing.

"Is it the right thing to do?"

Still nothing.

"In a sense I'm obstructing justice," she told Leah while she fluffed cushions on the couch. "And being disloyal to my very best friend if I don't come forward on your behalf, if I don't avenge whatever has happened to you."

There was a particle of dust on the coffee table. She brushed it off.

"But if you're hiding somewhere, you don't need to be avenged. You just need this all to go away. To leave you alone."

Hadn't she wanted nothing more than that these many, many months?

"Leah?" Standing in the middle of the room, Tricia raised her voice. "Answer me, dammit!"

She sighed, shook her head.

"How can I risk Taylor's life, my life, by giving that bastard a chance to reassert his control, when I don't know if going back is what's best? When I don't even know if it'll help you? But if you're alive in hiding, I *have* to go back. You won't be able to handle everything alone—you'll call for help, get caught and he'll kill you for sure if he's free."

Regardless of what's gone before, it will help others if Thomas is put away. The thought came softly in the great silence engulfing the house. The bottom line was that Thomas, a respected state senator with more clout than God and enough money to buy medical records, was a dangerous, untrustworthy man capable of murder. Even if she couldn't help Leah, her testimony would help whatever woman might be next.

It would help the state of California.

Oh, God. Tricia slid down to the floor, her back to one arm of the couch, facing a blank television screen. Could the universe ask a mother to risk her baby's life for the good of some unknown woman in Thomas's future? For the sake of some nebulous entity called society? Because if she went back and Thomas managed to pull off one of his miraculous escapes, she and Taylor would be in danger.

But could Tricia live with herself if another life was lost because of her?

Could she live with herself if she didn't do everything possible to avenge her best friend?

Head in her hands, Tricia started to shake. With trembling fingers she massaged the back of her neck. She was in pain. So much pain. Her head was going to split soon, and then she wouldn't have to think anymore.

An hour later, no closer to answers or sanity, Tricia went to get her son from his crib. Taylor was awake—full of energy and ready to be entertained.

Changing his diaper, getting lost in the grin and babble with which he conversed while he watched her face, Tricia didn't know how she could possibly walk back into the nightmare that had been her life in San Francisco. How she could possibly walk back with Taylor in her arms.

So did she go and leave him here? Without a mother? Without an identity?

Snapping the overalls, she picked him up, hugged him until he squirmed, then gently lowered him to the floor.

Did she go? Did she stay? Did she have what it took to do either?

Tricia turned on the television.

"And now boys and girls—"

"No! I'm telling you, I didn—"

"…with bleach and—"

"…find out what—"

"…up next on—"

Channel after channel sped by. Taylor had the remote. Was standing two feet in front of the set, barefoot and diapered, pushing the up arrow button. He wasn't allowed to do that.

A cartoon voice, immediately followed by country singing and then the frenetic jumble of a car commercial, calmed the panic barely held at bay as she lay back on the couch, watching the baby. He was safe. Happy. She'd teach him that the remote control was not a toy some other day.

Today she could keep him safe. She'd feed him dinner when it was time. And then they'd go to bed. He was sleeping with her tonight. She didn't really expect to sleep, not without the aid of the sleeping pills she'd left back in San Francisco, but was going to keep him close in any case.

He emitted strange little tones and squeals as he paused in his surfing to watch a toy commercial. With his diapered bottom swinging back and forth, he was attempting to sing and dance like the huge animal on the screen.

How could she possibly consider doing anything to put that little body at risk?

"…Carley Winchester will be joining us—"

"…on the fourth tee with his three wood—"

"Taylor, wait!"

The baby jumped, dropped the remote and started to cry.

"Sweetie, Mama's sorry," she said quickly, grabbing for the abandoned remote, frantically pushing backward. "I didn't mean to yell at you."

She'd made her baby cry.

What channel had he been on? Commercials, all she could find were commercials. And Taylor was wailing so loudly, having worked himself up to full-blown hysteria, that she couldn't hear.

"Taylor! Please, honey!" The baby's cries stopped for a split second as he stared at her, and then burst forth even louder. She hadn't meant to yell those last words. But she had to find that channel. It might already be too late.

Oh, God, Carley. What are you doing on television? Where are you? Please, someone...

Her fingers were trembling so hard she missed the channel button, hitting the one next to it. The television grew noticeably louder, almost competing with Taylor's screams. The baby was at her feet, clawing at her legs. She had to pick him up.

"...Carley Winchester, right after this break," the television yelled out.

A break. She had the channel. And a break.

Breathing quickly, Tricia set the remote on the carpet, scooping up the baby and hugging him to her chest, crooning words that probably didn't even make sense but comforted her because they seemed to comfort him.

"Mama's here, baby," she said over and over, her tears mingling with his, wetting both of their necks. "Mama's right here."

And she's sorry, she added silently. *Sorrier than you'll ever know.*

"Welcome back to *Good Afternoon, San Francisco*...."

Blaine Cavanaugh, local well-known bachelor and host of his own cable talk show—which she'd heard of but never seen before in her life—appeared on the screen. He was sitting in a beige tweed armchair turned at a slight angle from the matching couch next to him. A low table with fresh flowers sat in front of the couch. He placed a coffee cup on the small table.

Pulling over a stuffed Blue, Tricia sat on the floor, Taylor cradled in her lap with Blue, hiccuping and sucking his thumb.

"Blah, blah, blah, get on with.it," she mumbled when the trendily dressed good-looking blond man rattled on about the day's guests, the local lottery and a romance fiction author who was due to appear on the next program.

"Those of you following our latest scandal here in San Francisco will recognize our next guest as the woman many are calling crazy and out of her head with grief, the younger sister of missing heiress, Leah Montgomery, now presumed dead. Please welcome Ms. Carley Winchester."

And then, right there in her living room, sat Carley.

Fresh tears spurted in her eyes at the sight of the woman she loved like a sister. Her first contact with home in nearly two years. She missed belonging.

After the applause and Carley's thank-you, Blaine Cavanaugh briefed those in his audience about the unfolding drama, emphasizing the scene between Carley and Thomas Whitehead outside court the day of Whitehead's indictment, and ending with that morning's newspaper shocker.

"We at *Good Afternoon, San Francisco* had previously asked Mrs. Winchester to be a guest on our show, an invitation she regretfully declined. However, after reading this morning's headline, she felt she had no choice but to call us. She offered to appear on the show, and we knew you, our viewers, would want us to make that happen."

Carley, slim as ever and dressed in a black suit with red silk trim, her coal-black hair shoulder-length with loose curls, nodded, her face tight.

"So let her talk," Tricia grumbled. *Come on, Carley, tell me what's going on.*

"Mrs. Winchester, how do you feel about defense claims that you're out of your mind?"

"It's not only the defense." Her voice sounded exactly the same, sending a warm thread of emotion through Tricia. "It's also the police. Two years ago they disregarded the things my sister told them—mostly by saying they didn't have enough evidence to make a case. This time there's more evidence so they have to work harder to bury things. I'm not going to let them."

"So you don't think you're crazy?" Blaine asked, as though he wasn't sure which side of the story he was on.

"I know I'm not," Carley said, her voice even, convincing—just as Tricia would have predicted. "I'm an intense woman, Mr. Cavanaugh, an *intelligent* intense woman. I get passionate in my delivery, but I deliver rational thoughts."

The camera shot to Blaine, who nodded. "What made you change your mind about doing the show?"

Carley looked straight at the camera, her dark eyes open, lucid and glinting with something that dared anyone to dismiss what she was about to say.

"I will not see that man walk free a second time," she said. "Not without a trial by an unpaid jury of this town's citizens."

"Whoa!" Cavanaugh sat back. If she hadn't been so completely focused on Carley Tricia would've hated the man's "cat got the cream" expression.

"Are you saying Whitehead has someone from the police department on his payroll?"

Carley shook her head. "I doubt he'd do anything that overt," she said. "But he's a man of great power, with a family that goes back to Gold Rush days. They have holdings all over the state and fingers in so many pies, there probably aren't many people who couldn't be controlled by him."

Cavanaugh nodded again. Was he wondering about the funding for his show, or maybe the cable station on which his show appeared? He'd be a stupid man if he didn't wonder about that. He shifted, his entertaining persona slowly segueing into something more serious.

More worthy of Carley.

"And you know for sure that things have been covered up?"

"Yes."

"Such as?"

"I'd told the police Leah and Whitehead were lovers.

No one listened until I accused the senator outside the courtroom."

"Investigators seldom disclose evidence. How do you know they didn't listen?"

"They warned me very clearly to be careful about what I said, since Whitehead could sue me for defamation of character. And they said the information was hearsay only, my word against his, and therefore not worth much to them."

One hand on his chin, Cavanaugh leaned back. "But you had more to say?"

"That was just the beginning," Carley confirmed. "I knew Leah was pregnant. She'd done the test on Sunday and called me immediately afterward. I told the detectives on Monday night when I reported her missing, but she hadn't seen a doctor yet and with no proof…"

"That's why you were so insistent that forensics do a thorough search of her apartment."

Carley nodded. "I knew she'd taken the home pregnancy test but I had no idea we'd be so lucky." She took a deep breath. Blinked. The first sign of the emotion she was reining in. Tricia wanted to reach out and grab the other woman in her arms as she'd done when she was eight and Carley five and had been spit on by a boy in her kindergarten class who had a crush on her. "After they found the test strip they called her gynecologist and learned that she'd scheduled an appointment for early next month."

A pan of the audience showed rapt attention. Taylor

sat silently in her lap, one thumb in his mouth, his other hand rubbing Blue's silk-lined ear.

"At least the police are finally listening," Cavanaugh said, seemingly engrossed now in the Pandora's box he'd opened. Tricia respected him for continuing with a show that could as easily finish him as catapult him from local cable to prime time.

"Listening, maybe, but still approaching the probable deaths of two women with a disturbing lack of commitment."

"How so?"

"They charged him with murder in the first degree, one count. With a baby involved, in the state of California, that should've been two counts. And, in the state of California, two counts of first-degree murder allows them to ask for the death sentence, which, of course, they did not do."

Did a woman go to hell for feeling a surge of joy at the thought that a man might be put to death? Had Tricia foreclosed any possibility of personal happiness by wishing bad fortune on someone else?

Cavanaugh took a sip of something from the cup on the coffee table beside him. "Let's go back to the pregnancy for a moment." He glanced from the audience back to Carley. "You think Senator Whitehead knew about it, and that this somehow had a connection to your sister's disappearance?"

"I'm certain of it." Carley sat up straight, facing the camera, not the studio audience. She was talking to a much bigger audience. Or just to Tricia. "That last phone call between Whitehead and Leah, the Monday afternoon she disappeared, didn't go at all the way he said. That's the one where he claimed she was calling to say she didn't feel well, to cancel their date for that evening. But someone got in touch with me, someone who's afraid to come forward, who overheard the senator on the phone. He broke things off with her. She'd told him that morning at breakfast that she was pregnant. And knowing Leah, if he'd told her it was over, she would've refused to accept that. She'd more likely have made some impetuous threat, such as going to the press and claiming he was the father of her child. Not that she'd have *wanted* him as a father to her baby at that point, but to show the world that the man really wasn't the supporter of children he appeared to be."

"And this person really overheard Senator Whitehead say he was breaking it off?" Cavanaugh sounded incredulous. The man was definitely off his game plan.

Carley nodded.

"Wow. Hard to believe. Senator Whitehead seems like such a kind, ethical man. And everyone knows about all his efforts for the kids of California."

"Yeah, kind." There was no misinterpreting the scorn in Carley's voice. "So kind, he beat his wife."

Tricia gasped. Crouched down over Taylor as though to protect him, her gaze still glued to the television.

"What?!" Cavanaugh sat forward. "That's some pretty serious allegation!"

Carley shrugged. "So I've been told. And that's probably why no one else is willing to say it out loud. But I knew Kate from the time I was born. I could tell— probably even better than my sister, whose head was often lost in the clouds—when Kate was lying."

"And she told you he didn't hit her?"

"No." Carley shook her head. Her gaze seemed to be focused inward, and Tricia held her breath, her heart beating far to fast. *Please, no. It's not important. Or pertinent. We need to hear about Leah. Only Leah.* "On two occasions in particular, when we had plans that would've been impossible to cancel, Kate showed up with bruises on her face. The first time they weren't so bad. She said she'd slipped getting into her jetted tub and hit her face on the spigot."

Tricia moaned.

"And the second time?"

"The bruises were much worse. Covered both of her eyes, her nose was swollen…" Carley paused and another shot of the audience showed a room full of shocked-looking people. "She said she'd had her eyes done to remove the laugh lines."

Rocking back and forth, arms wrapped around the baby in her lap, Tricia barely heard when the show's host announced a commercial break.

They'd be right back with more from Carley Winchester.

She couldn't believe this was happening, that she was sitting in Scott's house, on his carpet, in his living room, surrounded by his furniture, Taylor's toys and the couple of knickknacks she'd bought since moving in, watching his television and hearing parts of *her* life story. A story she could *feel*. And yet, a story that seemed to belong to someone else...

She wanted it to stop. But it didn't. And it didn't help. The more she watched Carley's lips move, the more confused she got until she wasn't even sure who she was anymore. She wasn't sure of anything.

Except that she loved her son.

"Before we get back to the incredible story you're telling us, Mrs. Winchester, I wanted to ask you a quick question regarding your husband, Benny Winchester. He's a sitting member of San Francisco's City Council and, one would surmise, professionally acquainted with Senator Whitehead."

"They know each other, yes."

"So what does he have to say about you speaking out so harshly against a man who is, quite frankly, his political superior?"

Carley's face softened into a mischievous look Tricia recognized. "Whitehead's a Republican, Blaine. Benny's a Democrat."

The audience laughed. Even Cavanaugh, his face usually so filled with drama, chuckled.

"Still..." he began.

Carley looked straight at the camera. "My husband loved my sister. And he loves me," she said in no uncertain terms. "He's a member of the San Francisco City

Council because he'd like to make a difference, but it isn't the driving force in his life, nor is the position going to dictate his decisions." Carley looked back at Cavanaugh. "He fully supports what I'm doing."

Cavanaugh had opened his mouth, as though just waiting for Carley to finish so he could say more. He shut it again. Glanced at his notes.

"Okay," he said a couple of long seconds later, "you were telling us what you know about Kate Whitehead." His gaze rested on Carley. "Is there more?"

She sat forward, hands together in front of her, and nodded. Tricia's stomach tightened. Ached. But she couldn't turn away.

"The day Kate disappeared, my sister told Detectives Gregory and Stanton that she'd had a phone call from her. Kate had sounded odd, in a hurry, out of breath. She'd asked Leah to meet her in their usual spot, but wouldn't say any more over the phone. Leah ran out of gas on the way there. By the time she arrived, Kate was gone."

"Do you know the spot Kate referred to?"

Mesmerized, Tricia watched as Carley nodded. The cliff. She was going to tell them about the cliff. Leah had run out of gas. Who would've believed something that ordinary could have such a drastic effect on so many lives?

"...the detectives sent someone to check out the cliff, but there was nothing. Leah had already told them that. They said the phone call in no way tied Kate's disappearance to Thomas Whitehead, nor did it give them any other clues, since it wasn't unusual for Kate to ask Leah to meet her there, or vice versa. So the whole thing was dropped."

"I wonder if anyone's checked up at that cliff this time," Cavanaugh said.

"I've wondered the same thing," Carley responded dryly, appearing more and more exhausted under the hot lights. "As a matter of fact, I've wondered it out loud, more than once, while speaking with the detectives."

"We're running out of time, but tell me, Mrs. Winchester—and I'm probably getting myself into trouble here—do you think Whitehead is paying someone at police headquarters to make this go away?"

Cavanaugh smelled bigger game than a missing woman or two. Tricia's stomach hurt even more.

She wasn't surprised when Carley shook her head. "I really don't." She laughed, a sound completely lacking in humor. "That's just it, he doesn't *need* to. They're doing their jobs. They're just treading too lightly on Whitehead ground for fear of being wrong and having it affect—or destroy—their careers."

"But they did indict him."

"Yes."

"Don't you think you might be compromising the case, the upcoming trial, by releasing information they evidently thought might hurt their investigation if they disclosed it?" Before she could answer, he continued. "If nothing else, aren't you taking a chance on swaying a future jury? Making it impossible to find an impartial one?"

Carley sat forward and Tricia could tell by the twitch on the right side of her lips that it wouldn't be long before her friend lost all patience and told Cavanaugh exactly what she did think. "I'm trying to make sure there *is* a trial," she said more loudly than she'd been speaking thus far. "We'll worry about the jury when we get there."

"You think this morning's article might actually make a difference?"

"I can see history repeating itself," she said. "If there's any way the D.A.'s office can justify dropping the charges, they'll do so."

"And you don't think that the fact that Senator Whitehead had a vasectomy—surgery that makes it physically impossible for him to father children—is justification enough for believing there's more to this than anyone knows?"

"I don't care what stories Whitehead tells about his balls and who's done what to them," Carley snapped. "Someone like him could produce medical records in his sleep. I know that man fathered my sister's baby. Not only has she slept with no one else in more than a year, she said one of the redeeming factors about the whole mess was that in being pregnant with his child, she felt closer to Kate somehow...."

Tricia didn't hear the rest of the show. Didn't hear much of anything the rest of that night. *Please, Leah, please be safe. Loved. Protected.*

And please, please, please find some way to forgive me for all the things I've done.

12

She wanted sex. Her naked body curled around his like an octopus, a smooth slender leg flung over one of his, her toes hooked under his calf. Her belly pressed against his hip, one arm under his shoulder, the other wrapped around his chest, fingers tucked beneath his ribs. All of which was fine with him. The soft kisses she was placing along his neck were distracting, a pleasure and an irritation at the same time, because he didn't *want* to be distracted.

Scott shifted, sliding an arm around her back, holding her close—and moving down a few inches so that her mouth was away from his neck. She said nothing, just settled in again. He could almost be fooled into thinking she was falling asleep.

It wouldn't be the first time.

He'd heard from his parents, who'd called him at work, on his cell. They were due home in a couple of weeks and wanted him to come to Mission Viejo for the weekend. He missed them, but had avoided giving them an answer. He wasn't going to introduce them to Tricia—not the way things were. Where he saw no future, they'd see wedding rings. And he didn't want to leave for a weekend without her, either.

Thank God, in all the years Scott had been living in South Park, his family had never visited him there. They met for dinner occasionally. Before Tricia's advent into his life, he'd driven out for an occasional weekend with them. But not often. He felt out of place there—as they would in South Park. They supported his decisions; they just didn't want to see the evidence of them. And that, especially now, was probably for the best.

Scott lay there, wide awake, staring at the shadows on the ceiling.

His body wanted sex, too.

His first night home with Tricia after rotation almost always included great sex. He'd been back for two nights, and he still hadn't taken her up on her offer. In her usual way, she asked no questions.

It bothered him. Perhaps because she didn't need to be with him badly enough to insist. And because he had no idea what she was making of his reticence. Was she expecting him, once again, to ask her to leave?

How could she live like that? Always wondering if, at any given moment, she'd be homeless with an eighteen-month-old son to care for.

He wasn't quite ready. If they had sex, would he be reaching up inside her toward a baby? His baby? He felt strange about not knowing.

And yet he didn't really understand that. It wasn't as

if pregnant women couldn't have sex. Hell, he'd had sex with her two days before Taylor was born. So why should it matter?

Deciding it didn't, Scott went to sleep.

San Francisco Gazette
Monday, April 25, 2005
Page 8. Section C

Sister Takes On Senator

Carley Winchester, the younger sister of heiress Leah Montgomery, who disappeared three weeks ago today, is getting some results. She made a recent appearance on *Good Afternoon, San Francisco,* when she alleged before thousands of California viewers that the police investigation was flawed. Soon afterward, police searched an undisclosed mountainous area for signs of the missing woman's body. There was no evidence of anyone having been on the mountain recently, no tire tracks or footprints. The police questioned an elderly man who's lived on the mountain his entire life but refused to comment on the interview.

On another note, nineteen-year-old medical records show that Senator Thomas Whitehead had a vasectomy by an unnamed physician, who had lost his license to practice medicine for performing illegal abortions. The senator's personal physician confirmed the existence of barely dis-

cernible knots and a small incision scar that result
from such a procedure.

"Where were you?"

Scott was sitting at the kitchen table, a half-empty
mug of coffee in his hand.

Just once, couldn't something happen the easy way?
She'd risen at the crack of dawn, certain that she'd be
back before anyone knew she'd been gone.

She said the first thing that came to her mind. "Out
getting a paper."

"Then where is it?"

Reaching for a coffee cup and saucer, Tricia bumped
her hand on the cupboard shelf. "I read it already and
threw it away."

He had no right to subject her to this inquisition.

And he had every right.

Coffee sloshed over the side of her cup. Emptying the
saucer into the cup, she stood with her back to the
counter, took a sip, and then put the cup and saucer
down. She didn't dare hold them. Their rattling would
give her away.

Finally, she looked at her suspiciously silent lover. His
dark hair was rumpled from sleep, his face bearing the
shadow of a day's growth of whiskers. His flannel shirt
was unbuttoned, as were the jeans he'd pulled on from the
day before. His feet were bare. And he was staring at her.

Six months ago, Tricia would have crawled into his
lap, made love with him there on the chair and then

again in the shower. She braced herself with her hands on the counter behind her. "What?"

"You didn't think I'd be interested in the news?"

Shrugging, Tricia tried her best to hold his gaze. To think of him and not herself. Because she loved him and he deserved her loyalty. And because she'd never be able to remain standing if she let her mind take her into another place and time. "You don't get the paper."

"Because I'm gone so many days in the month it didn't seem financially feasible."

She nodded at his repetition of a conversation they'd had two years before when he'd offered, after she'd moved in, to have the local paper delivered now that someone was going to be at the house everyday.

Not wanting him to spend a dime on her that wasn't necessary, she'd declined. It wasn't San Diego news she was interested in, anyway.

Scott sighed, forearms on the table, and just sat. Guilt, thick and heavy, spread through her, mingling with the fear, the confusion and despair. Her son was asleep in his crib in the other room. Two walls away.

She stood in the kitchen and tried to concentrate on visions of Taylor. His chubby baby cheeks, pert rosy lips, his father's nose…

Thomas Whitehead influenced the press, falsified medical documents, and even owned one of the most esteemed physicians in San Francisco. The Whitehead family physician, who had to be lying about that small scar. Not that anyone except his physician would probably have detected it.

Thomas Whitehead had said she was a whore. That her unborn son wasn't his. Only a man who was sick beyond words would take the farce this far.

There was no stopping him. Unless…

One simple DNA test was all it would take. A few minutes of time.

And a lifetime of fear.

He'd buy his way out. He'd find a way to control her. Without warning, Tricia could feel that peculiar beating of her heart that meant she was trapped and in very real danger. She was back in that other place, that other time. She could taste the blood in her mouth as she saw her attacker approach, knowing what was coming, the slaps and punches that connected, the ringing in her ears, and while she struggled to maintain consciousness, he'd be demanding that she tell him who she'd been sleeping with….

"Tell me—"

Tricia screamed, jerked, banging her back against the counter. And then blinked. Scott was sitting at the table, eyes wide, face twisted in disbelief as he watched her.

"What?" She tried for normalcy.

"I asked you to tell me where you really were."

Glancing down, Tricia studied the scuffed toes of her tennis shoes. Dusty white tennis shoes with no bloodstains.

"Out getting a paper."

He stood. "Don't lie to me, Tricia," he said, crossing

the kitchen. "If you aren't going to tell me the truth, then say so. Just don't lie. We're worth more than that."

All the money I'm worth, and you dare to stand there and lie to me.

I'm telling you the truth, Thomas. I swear...

And the truth was never heard.

Tricia watched him approach. Knew what was coming. Tried to be ready.

"Okay!" she said when he was two steps away. "I...I didn't feel well and went for a walk, thinking the cool air would do me good and it did and now I feel better."

He cocked his head, narrowed his eyes. He didn't hit her.

"Why didn't you wake me?"

"I didn't want you to worry."

"Is there some reason I should be worried? Something going on—physically—that I should know about?"

Peering up at him, Tricia knew she didn't need to be afraid of this man. The knowledge would pass, it always did, to be replaced by the irrational fear instilled by hard experience. But for now...

"No, Scott," she said softly, removing all holds on the love she felt for him. "I promise you, there's nothing." Not physically. Not yet.

He studied her for a long time. And when he reached out, it wasn't to inflict searing pain, but to pull her into his arms, against his chest, where she could rest her face against the beat of his heart and feel safe. If only until Taylor cried.

* * *

On Tuesday afternoon, Tricia stepped into the back room of Patsy's dry cleaners and almost dropped the heavy bag of clothes she was carrying.

"What's going on?" she asked sharply, arm muscles weakened from the surge of fear that had come and gone when she'd seen the man sitting in the corner.

"I thought it was best to meet here where no one can see us," Arnold Miller answered slowly. His words were slurred, but his eyes pinned her to the wall she'd leaned against.

"Sorry, I wanted to call you, but he told me not to," Patsy said, shrugging. The sturdy blonde was sitting on her desk, frowning. She appeared more irritated with the smelly man in her store than anything else.

"You found out something," she said, nervous with Patsy there—with anyone knowing anything about her business at all—but not knowing how to ask her to leave her own establishment.

"You got clothes for me?" the woman asked, nodding toward Tricia's laden garment bag.

"Two pairs of pants, one of them drawstring, one dressier, a couple of lacy tanks, and a short jacket with funky sleeves," she rattled off, watching the drunken investigator. Did he know something important, or was he just using her as an excuse to hang out here and sleep for a while? Could she believe anything he told her when he was like this?

Getting to her feet, Patsy took the garment bag. "I'll

just go try these on," she said. "Be back in about fifteen minutes. She went up the back stairs to her apartment on the second floor.

"Siddown." Miller's order was compelling even with slurred syllables.

She told herself she was strong now. Didn't have to take orders. Unless she wanted to do as she'd been ordered. Tricia sat.

He leaned forward slowly, elbows extended as though to rest them on his knees, but missed, almost hitting his chin before he righted himself with forearms leaning heavily on his thighs. "Ish someone local," he said, each movement of his mouth exaggerated as he spoke.

Tricia backed away from the stench of stale alcohol and cigarette smoke that sailed toward her on his breath.

"Someone local is following me?"

"S'right." He gave her an almost piercing look. "Hired."

"Someone hired someone local to follow me."

Miller nodded; then froze, as though allowing himself to recover from the movement.

"Do you know who hired her?"

"Not jush her," Miller, head hanging, grew still, and Tricia had to stop herself from crying out in frustration and fear. If he fell asleep now…

"Who else?" she asked quietly.

Pushing off from his knees, he fell back against the cushioned plastic chair. "At lease two—women." He said the last word with the emphasis on the last syllable. "I got a…friend…to fo'ow zhem. Sheprate. Talk."

Mind reeling with questions, possible scenarios, various actions to be considered, Tricia clasped her hands in her lap, holding on for dear life. Taylor's occasional squeals from the front room were all that kept her focused. Miller had asked a friend to strike up a conversation. "Do they work together?"

"Don' know."

"You don't know who they're working for?"

"Nah yet." His emphasis on the *T* spewed spittle that landed on his stained and wrinkled brown tweed pants.

"But you can find out?"

"'Coursh."

"When?"

"Schoon as I'm sober."

"When will that be?"

"Don' know."

That was all. She couldn't take any more. She was going to lose her mind. Tricia rose with some half-formed thought of grabbing her purse, walking out and just walking until she was too tired to walk anymore.

And then Taylor giggled.

Falling to her knees in front of the broken man, hands on her thighs, she leaned close enough to see how dilated his pupils were. "Please Mr. Miller, I'll pay you whatever it takes, but I need you to get sober *now*. I have to know. Soon."

"I don' care 'bout…"

She put one hand on his knee and held his gaze, although it was one of the hardest things she'd ever done.

She fought back nausea. "Please. My son's life might depend on it."

He peered at her for a long time. And then heaved a sigh that almost made her lose her lunch.

"Okay. Bah only for da boy."

She nodded, satisfied. Taylor was, after all, the only reason she did anything, including getting up in the morning.

Without another word, she picked up her purse, needing to get to her son, to hold him, to remind herself that life held innocence and beauty, trust and pure, unconditional love.

What did any of it mean? If Thomas Whitehead knew where she was and wanted her dead, she would be. If he wanted Taylor, he'd have him.

Wouldn't he?

Could it be someone else watching her, then? Watching out for her? Had her mother hired someone? Or did they all believe she was dead?

Her guess was that Thomas's hired gun had not yet confirmed that she wasn't who she said she was. A seamstress who did alterations on rich people's clothes and lived with a fireman while they raised their son. And if he worked for Thomas, he wasn't going to take any chances on being wrong.

Thomas was not a forgiving man.

Really, she could understand not being recognized. Kate Whitehead hadn't stepped outside her bedroom without full makeup, including enhanced eyebrows and

a mouth artistically painted to make it fuller, more suc-
culent than the one she'd been born with, since she was
fourteen years old. Kate Whitehead had been well-
taught.

Tricia Campbell was named after a soup can.

"The old man says you had Kate followed."

Unafraid, Thomas Whitehead met this latest inquisition head-on. Before coming down to the station, he'd
agreed to let Douglas speak for him, but once he knew
that the line of questioning included the hermit, Walter
Mavis, he indicated with a brief shake of his head that
he'd handle the interview.

He'd expected the questions to be about the fact that,
at one point, his wife had had a lover—not this that was
so uncommon in California. He hadn't seen recent sta-
tistics, but he'd bet more than half the married popula-
tion had affairs.

"I did have her followed."

Prosecutors Holm and Black exchanged a glance
and he didn't have to be a scholar in human relations to
know he'd surprised them, just as he'd planned.

"Why?"

"Kate's pregnancy was hard on her." Thomas's answers came easily; they were the truth. "She was…
upset…a lot of the time." There was only so much a
man in the public eye could reveal about a family
member, particularly his wife, so he chose his words
carefully.

But he chose them. He wasn't going to jail out of loyalty to a missing wife.

"You're saying she suffered from depression?" Amy Black asked, eyes narrowed.

He'd have put it more delicately. "Yes."

"Was she treated for it? On medication?"

Hands clasped loosely on the table, Thomas shook his head. "She was one of those women who become obsessed with everything they put in their bodies from the moment they find out they're expecting. She wouldn't accept any kind of medication."

"Did you notice erratic behavior?"

"Not erratic, really, but melancholy, which can be even worse. I worried constantly that she'd take her own life. Not at home, of course—the servants were around—but she had that damn mountain she always ran to. There was no telling what she might do there. Or somewhere else, for that matter."

"So you had her followed."

"Naturally."

David Holm stepped forward. "I'm wondering then, Senator, why she wasn't followed the day she disappeared."

He'd thought all of this would come out two years ago. He'd been prepared ever since.

"We'd had a talk the night before," he said. "A disagreement, really, that turned into a compromise. My man got careless, and Kate figured out that I was having her followed. She insisted I call him off. I refused at first, but she became so upset I was afraid that knowing she was being watched might send her over the edge. I told her I'd fire the private detective if she promised not to go anywhere alone."

"So you'd just called off the detective that day that she went missing?"

"Yes."

"And you can provide us with the name of that detective?"

"Yes. Alan Klein." It occurred to Thomas that he had his college buddy Mike to thank for the fact that this hadn't come up before.

Amy Black, an older woman with graying hair, drab-colored suits and glasses that were too big for her face, sat on one corner of the table in the otherwise empty room. "Why, Senator, since you'd hired a professional, did you also ask Walter Mavis to watch out for your wife?"

"Have you been up on Miner's Mountain?" he asked.

"No."

"It's off an old mining trail barely wide enough for a single vehicle. The last quarter mile up is reachable only by foot. Not an easy place to follow someone undetected."

"I guess not," Holm said with a smile. Thomas resisted the urge to sit back, to get too complacent, regardless of the fact that he knew he'd already done his job that day.

"I loved my wife to distraction, ma'am." He pulled

from deep within to address Holm's partner. "And she spent a lot of time up on that mountain top. She used to say she got her inspiration there. She'd take her drawing pad and pencils and be gone for hours. It was a natural conclusion for me, when I discovered that the old hermit lived up there and often heard Kate's car on the old mining trail, to ask for any added protection he might be willing to give her."

"Did you pay him for his services?"

"I did not." Thank God no cash had ever exchanged hands. It could have, so easily. The angels of heaven were still smiling on him. Compensation for his miserable youth.

"Mavis says he heard Kate's car go by the day she disappeared, but that she didn't stop," Black said, her mouth a thin line. She needed some good hard sex. If she could find anyone who could get it up for her uptight ass.

"Not at all unusual. She stopped to say hello only about half the time."

Holm nodded, putting his pen in his pocket, closing his leather notepad. Douglas closed his as well.

"Since you obviously know about your wife's last trip up the mountain, why didn't you tell investigators about it—or about the existence of Walter Mavis—when she disappeared?"

Kilgore Douglas stood. "You are out of line, Ms. Black." His voice was firm, confident; it hinted at power without arrogance, an effective ploy, successful enough to earn him the generous salary Thomas paid him. "My client is not on trial for his wife's disappearance."

Kilgore held the door and Thomas walked through with his head high. He was going to stop for a drink on the way home, after all. One stiff bourbon should take care of the unease left inside him by the unsightly face of Prosecutor Amy Black.

13

She talked to Scott twice a day, stopped in to see him a couple of times, had Taylor constantly in her sight. She kept her back to the wall and looked over her shoulder whenever it wasn't. And always, every waking moment—and the sleeping ones, too, huddled in bed with her son snuggled against her, listening to the house while she tried to rest—she lived in a bubble of darkness.

Should she run? But where? And wouldn't she just be followed again? If they'd found her this time, they'd find her again.

At least here she had a full life, a disguise. And she had Scott's protection. He was someone she trusted to watch out for her son, to raise him if anything happened to her.

Here she had moments of love.

Here she was swimming in a sea of guilt.

Scott had started a four-day-off rotation that morning. He'd called to say he was bringing home a surprise and asked her to have Taylor up, dressed and fed. Just like a real dad. In a real family.

Except that Taylor Campbell had a real dad. One who believed himself powerful enough to get away with murder.

Her heart sank when she saw Scott's surprise.

"Dog! Dog! Daddee, dog!" The baby, dressed in denim overalls and a blue-and-white collared shirt with navy-and-white tennis shoes, jumped up and down, his soft dark curls bouncing with his delight.

One knee on the grass in the backyard, Scott kept an arm poised, as though ready to catch the toddler if he lost his balance. Both of them were intent on the squirming little ball of fur at Taylor's feet. "He's yours, sport. What should we call him?"

"Dog, Daddee!"

The puppy, a six-pound Dalmatian mix, darted off after a butterfly, tripping over his own feet. Taylor ran after him, giggling and squealing. "Dog, Daddee!"

"The dog's running, Taylor." Scott's grin made the moment bearable, but nothing could assuage the guilt knotting in her stomach. The puppy was one more thing for Taylor to get attached to. One more thing a little boy should be allowed to get attached to. Like a dad. One more thing Taylor might very well have to leave.

"Wun!" Taylor yelled.

Scott and Tricia exchanged a startled look. "He said run!" Her smile wasn't as painful, suddenly, as she watched her son gallop along as drunkenly as his new puppy, screaming "Wun, Dog, wun!"

For three months, no matter how she'd coaxed, encouraged, worried, Taylor had adamantly held to his repertoire of five words. He'd just added a sixth.

Thanks to Scott. And Dog.

"You shouldn't have done this." Half lying on an old maroon-and-white quilt on the kitchen floor Saturday evening, propped up against the counter, Tricia held out both hands, ready to catch the puppy cavorting on her chest should he slip and fall.

Scott, on his side next to her, leaning on one elbow, reached over to scratch the little guy behind one comically pointed ear. "He was free."

"He's going to pee in the house." There was only a momentary twinge at the vulgarity she would never have uttered in her other life.

"We'll wipe it up."

Dog pounced on Scott's finger, digging in sharp puppy teeth. "Ouch! You little rat." Scott laughed, playing keep-away with the puppy just beneath Tricia's unbound breasts. Hoping to go to bed, she'd undressed an hour ago, and pulled on the violet nightshirt and panties when it became obvious that Dog had other ideas than sleeping in a cardboard box by himself in the kitchen.

Or the bedroom.

Or any room.

The box was now outside, next to the trash can. And Scott and Tricia were facing a possible night on the kitchen floor—with a light on over the sink because Dog whined as soon as they turned it off.

"He's going to chew on stuff."

"Only for a while."

Dog rolled off her, settling between them while Scott continued to pet him gently. "And what happens when we call it quits?" She asked the question that had been torturing her all day. "How do we tell Taylor that Dog isn't his?"

She and Scott shared a bed, shared their bodies and their grocery bills. They did not share possessions.

His hand on the puppy's back, Scott, still in the jeans he'd worn that day, rubbed one bare foot against the other. He didn't look at her. His chest provided distraction for her restless gaze. But only for the second it took her to want to be there, her fingers buried in the dark wiry hair.

"You planning to go soon?"

Oh, God, I don't know. "I have no plans." Just a bunch of secrets and lies piling so high on top of me that I'm burying myself with no hope of rescue.

"Well, then…"

"Scott." She spoke firmly. And waited for him to look at her before she went on. "Things aren't great here." One of them had to acknowledge the truth—and as it was the only truth she *could* acknowledge, she figured she was the one. "We haven't made love in more than a week."

"Couples go through times of adjustment."

"Couple implies two people who have made a commitment to each other. That's not us. We're two people who are together for the moment. Period." The words hurt so much.

His green eyes were completely serious as he peered up at her. "Do you want to be a couple?"

Tricia swallowed, her mind skittering around his question. "It's not an option."

"Why?"

Dog was asleep. "We have an understanding."

"Made by us, so it can be changed by us."

It just didn't stop—the knife twisting inside her, the guilt growing heavier and heavier.

Her hands on the floor on either side of her, holding up the weight of her life, she stared at her bare feet. "The reasons we made them still exist."

She didn't even realize, or at least admit to herself, that she'd half hoped he'd argue with her until he didn't.

"Do you want to leave?"

Her gaze darted to him. "No!" It wasn't something she could lie about. That truth was just too strong to be denied.

His dark hair hanging over his forehead, he studied her silently, until all Tricia wanted to do was press herself against him. Lose herself in the only thing that made sense anymore…

"Do *you* want me to leave?"

"I brought Taylor a puppy, didn't I?"

They both looked at Dog, sleeping soundly now that he wasn't in a box by himself.

"Yeah."

"Hardly the sign of a man itching for his freedom."

"I guess not."

"On the contrary…"

Tricia met his eyes as he paused.

"It's more the sign of a man desperate enough to use bribery to get you to stay."

His love was clear to see, as he stared openly, breaking her heart, and filling it up at the same time, giving her strength when she had none left to give herself.

"Then why haven't you made love to me?" Her words were whispered, not because she feared waking either of the babies in their household, but because that was all she could manage.

"Too many walls between us."

Here it comes. He was going to push again. And take away her choices. Until she decided to blow her cover, she couldn't be anyone but Tricia Campbell. For her son's safety and her own. But for Scott's, too. If he knew nothing, he'd be innocent later.

If he knew something, he wouldn't be able to let her go on this way, a fugitive, hiding, looking over her shoulder. He'd charge forth to fix the whole mess. To make it right. Because that was the kind of man he was. He couldn't live with himself if he did any less.

It was one of the traits she loved most about him.

It was also the one that frightened her.

"So what do we do about that?" she asked, her vision starting to blur in the dim kitchen light.

"We could try talking."

She couldn't stay. This wasn't going to work. He had to have answers. He *deserved* answers. He was a good man and she was using him and—

"If I could ask you just one question, completely unrelated to the past or any future you might have that does not involve me, I'd be doing a hell of a lot better."

On the verge of standing, darting out of his life, Tricia settled back onto the floor. He'd confused her. "What?"

"Are you pregnant?"

"Of course not! I'm on the pill. You know that." She got them for a nominal fee every month from a clinic associated with the women's shelter.

"You aren't?"

"No!" And then, studying him as best she could in the dim light, said, "You sound disappointed."

Scott sat up slowly, one hand still close enough for the puppy to feel his warmth. "No! I'm not! At all!" His eyes traveled over her face, down her body, and then back up. "Well, maybe I am, just a little."

"Scott, we can't…" She was going to leave this time. She had to.

"Wait." One hand on her shoulder, he shook his head. "I know we can't. And the largest part of me doesn't want to. At all. I always take the biggest risks on the job so the other guys don't have to. I couldn't do that if I knew I had—"

"I know…." Tricia put a finger to his lips. She couldn't bear to hear him spell it out any further. "I understand."

He believed his life was dispensable, owed to make up for the life he'd inadvertently taken in a few seconds of teenage abandon. Guilt had a way of exacting its toll. And the price was eternal.

Scott lifted a hand to her face, running his fingers lightly down her cheek to her collarbone. Her skin absorbed his touch with a thirst that left her gasping. Moving carefully around the sleeping puppy he settled on her other side, sliding off his jeans and underwear before pulling her on top of him.

"That's it then?" she half teased, pushing away all the worry that haunted her. "No baby so we're back to normal?"

Scott sighed, raising his hips against hers, stroking her back lightly. "I have no idea what we are," he said. "I just know that whatever it is, I want it."

"Me, too."

"Then we'll leave the rest to take care of itself, okay? For now?"

Tricia nodded, allowing the passion she felt for him to consume her. *For now* might only last this hour, this night, and in spite of that, or maybe because of it, she gave herself completely to that moment. Sliding her panties down to her ankles she slipped one foot out and then, with the silky material hanging off her other ankle, mounted Scott, riding him slowly, watching the expression on his face change as he gave himself up to the fire burning inside him.

Long into that night she loved Scott, in ways she'd

never before loved a man, giving him everything he asked for, things she hadn't even known she had.

And all the while Dog slept beside them, seemingly unaware that the earth was shaking.

San Francisco Gazette
Tuesday, May 3, 2005
Page 1

Missing Heiress's Body Found
"Crazy" Sister Not So Crazy After All

Searchers on Miner's Mountain discovered the body of a woman lying sprawled in the middle of a broad-leafed maple tree Monday afternoon. Police believe she fell nearly a hundred feet from the cliff where Leah Montgomery is reported to have spent many hours with her best friend, Kate Whitehead, missing wife of Senator Thomas Whitehead. The body was later positively identified as that of Montgomery, who has been missing since the fourth of last month.

Searchers have been all over Miner's Mountain and the hundreds of acres of old mines and undeveloped mountainous terrain since the late Leah Montgomery's sister, Carley Winchester, appeared on *Good Afternoon, San Francisco*. In that interview, she alerted the city to a possible cover-up in the investigation of her sister's unexplained disappearance. Early yesterday morning, after dogs continued to seek out one particular spot on the cliff, a team of climbers went over the side of the mountain for the third time in a week. They would have missed the body again if not for a sudden gust of wind that blew a torn piece of Montgomery's blouse down from the tree where she had apparently fallen to her death.

No Baby Found

While earlier reports indicated a suspicion that Montgomery was pregnant, a preliminary autopsy late last night showed no signs of a fetus. Judging by the decomposition of the body, Ms. Montgomery is believed to have been dead since the time of her disappearance. A more thorough autopsy of Montgomery's remains, which investigators hope will help shed more light on the tragedy, will be performed today.

A spokesman for Senator Thomas Whitehead said this morning that the senator was greatly disturbed by this confirmation of his friend's death, stating that Whitehead fears Montgomery committed suicide. He cited the claim of a pregnancy that didn't exist (a claim she supposedly made to her sister the day before her disappearance) as indication of mental or emotional instability. Mrs. Winchester was unavailable for comment.

An idyllic night of lovemaking led to a three-day reprieve while Tricia played house with her lover, baby son and new puppy. She didn't let herself think beyond the moment, tending to practical concern only as needed—like grabbing Taylor's blue, hooded sweatshirt the evening they went to the zoo or thawing one pound of hamburger or two the day they invited Cliff and his wife for a cookout. Vera and Cliff were in high spirits, as they waited hopefully to find out if the most recent session of artificial insemination had succeeded.

She didn't read a paper. Didn't ask herself what she was going to do about anything. Didn't think of the future. Or the past. It was almost as if her spirit, knowing that she was depleted past the point of carrying on, took the reins of her life out of her hands long enough to let her rest.

Which was why it was Wednesday morning, Scott's first day back at the station, when she finally saw Tuesday's *San Francisco Gazette* headline, alongside a similar San Diego headline.

Three days of healing disappeared almost as if they'd never been.

She sat at the edge of the dog park, where she was in plain view of traffic and could make a run for it if she had to, and where she could also be seen doing exactly what she'd been doing for the past eighteen months— taking her middle-class baby for a morning stroll in the park while his father worked putting out the city's fires. Sitting there, in the warmth of that first Wednesday in May, Tricia slowly froze inside. Her son slept in his stroller and the puppy they should never have given him had worn himself out tugging at the leash to which he was tied and now lay at her feet chewing on a twig.

He'd be up and darting off again. Just as soon as someone walked by, or a bug buzzed or a bird flew. He didn't know that Leah was dead. Didn't understand what it meant.

Throat dry, Tricia read the headline again. She'd been dreading the news for so long, it hardly seemed real. Leah's body had been found. Without Leah in it. Tricia, who'd counted on their friendship to see her through every single crisis in her life, was alone now— just one woman, not part of two. All these months, the awareness of Leah's presence had kept her strong, kept her pushing ahead.

Through her whole life Leah's unconditional support had kept her sane, believing in herself.

She didn't even know that tears were dripping silently down her cheeks until she felt their splash as they hit the paper. Leah was gone.

The rest of it—the fact that her friend's body had been trapped in a tree for twenty-one days, the fact that their cliff had been the site of her death—were things she'd have to think about later. Tricia couldn't take them in right now.

Not if she was going to get her son and his puppy safely home. A car pulled up several yards away. A woman got out with a Papillon in her arms.

Leah had fallen a hundred feet and hit a tree. An impact like that could easily cause a miscarriage....

The Papillon saw Dog and barked, a high-pitched in-sistent call. Jumping up, Dog moved closer to Tricia, pushing against her ankle beneath the table, oddly silent. Scott had given her son a coward.

Taylor flinched, but his eyes didn't open. He'd be awake soon, though. The stroller almost always put him to sleep, but his morning naps were usually no more than an hour.

…and if the fetus hadn't been caught by the tree, as Leah had, marauding animals could easily have dealt with it, leaving no evidence. She and Leah used to talk about all the mountain lions, foxes, bobcats, black bears and sundry smaller creatures that shared their secret place with them. They'd had a healthy re-spect for the land's inhabitants, but, still, had valued their presence.

The Papillon barked again—much farther away now. His owner had stopped beside a masculine-looking woman who'd been in the park all morning, working with a German Shepherd.

Tricia knew she'd have to move. When Taylor awoke, he wasn't going to lie there quietly and wait for her to find the strength to get up.

You know what to do. She had almost two years' worth of practice. That woman she'd been in San Francisco, the life she'd known there—all off-limits. She couldn't think about them. She wasn't that woman anymore. Her heart had been irrevocably marked. If it was going to survive, if *she* was, she had to focus only on the present.

And what if the lack of a fetus let Thomas Whitehead off the hook? What if Leah's pregnancy had been the probable cause the prosecutor had been planning to use for motive in his case? Would they drop the charges? Cut a deal? Let him out to hurt someone else? Because he would. There was no doubt of that now.

Taylor moved. Just an arm thrown over his face. Tricia stared at him as hard as she could, willing herself to focus only on him, only on this second's reality. The park. Dog. Taylor and her. She could make it off the bench, out of the park, if there was nothing but Taylor and Dog and her.

And she would. But even as she stood, crooned shakily to the puppy, threw the newspaper she'd purchased in the trash, Tricia knew that her time was running out. Things were getting too complicated. Someone was having her watched—and he or they were doing that for a reason.

Taylor stretched. In about ten seconds his eyes were going to pop open and he'd be raring to go. Wrapping Dog's leash around her hand, she set the stroller in motion so her son would be content to remain seated for a few minutes longer.

She couldn't let Thomas Whitehead get away with her best friend's murder.

And Scott…he'd come to mean so much. Too much.

She might shut her mind off to places inside herself, but that didn't stop them from hurting. And the pain was becoming too intense to hide.

How her life had ever become so crazy she didn't know. She'd done her best, made choices dictated by conscience, not merely desire, thought of others, did for others, worked hard, shared what she had. And she'd ended up here, in a web of confusion so tight, so thick, she didn't think she'd ever find a way out.

14

Tricia was almost home, past the Big Kitchen, a quaint old restaurant that still did a decent business. She'd thought Scott was kidding when he'd first told her Whoopi Goldberg used to live there. He hadn't been. Taylor chatted away, his conversation obviously interesting to himself, although unintelligible to his mother. Occasionally he'd lean over the side of his stroller, inform her that Dog was there, and then sit back again. Maybe the balmy, seventy-degree breeze was having a calming effect on him, too.

He was a happy boy. And that was all that mattered.

Next to the bingo building on the corner was the Alano club—a place for recovering alcoholics. Tricia turned down Ivy Street. Everywhere she looked was vivid green, trees, grass—even the weeds were intensely green—interspersed with beds of boldly colored flowers. And behind it all were rows of houses, a lot of them stucco, relatively small, some with aluminum siding, mostly old, and yet each was original with a style, a personality, unlike its neighbors. Some had trash in the yards instead of flowers, but always there was green.

And the street names—they were all plants and trees—as though someone was determined to have nature remembered in the midst of urban chaos. She stopped to glance over her shoulder. A woman who was almost a block behind her looked exactly like the woman in the park with the Papillon—minus the dog.

"Let's sing," Tricia said loudly to her son as she bent once again to untangle Dog's leash. In spite of the hours Scott had spent working with the little guy during his four days off, Dog still had problems containing his curiosity long enough to pay attention to his lead. But at least he wasn't at a dead standstill anymore.

The woman in the distance had a black baseball cap on that the woman in the park hadn't been wearing. She was minus the white windbreaker, replaced by a black sweater tied around her waist, and had exchanged sandals for tennis shoes. She stopped to drop something in a mailbox on the corner.

"The itsy-bitsy spider," Tricia blurted out, reminding her son how to climb with his fingers before she gave the stroller a heavy push. As the spider climbed up the spout, Tricia told herself to calm down.

It wasn't the same woman. She was overreacting. Losing her ability to differentiate between fact and fiction.

In the song, the rains came down, and she turned the

corner. Sped up for a block. Turned again and then again. When the sun was coming out to dry up all the rain for the third time, she was back at Ivy.

And when the itsy-bitsy spider climbed up the spout again, with Taylor's heart-felt if inarticulate help, Tricia got another glimpse of the woman. Only she was even closer now. And if the bulge on her side beneath the sweater was a handgun, as Tricia suspected it might be, the woman wasn't out for a casual stroll, either.

Grabbing Dog under one arm with a quick sweep, Tricia held tight to the stroller and ran. The woman could shoot her dead, take Taylor and be gone forever. When you had enough money, anything was possible.

Thump. The stroller went over a crack in the sidewalk. *Thump. Thump. Thump.* The world became little else. The beating of her heart in her ears, unmasked by anything except the rhythm of the stroller's rubber wheels crossing crack after crack. Taylor's sudden silence, the stillness with which he sat, watching the world whiz by, scared her more than anything else. Even her eighteen-month-old baby knew something was wrong.

She ran down Ivy, stopping only long enough to go behind a car waiting at the corner as she crossed, not sure in her panic where she was headed. The houses were taller, wider, the yards larger, and still she pushed. Until she ran out of sidewalk. There was nothing ahead of her but a canyon.

San Diego was riddled with canyons. They were big. Cavernous. Covered with trees and brush, blanketing much of their acreage. There was no time to think. No time for rational decisions or hesitation. Tricia plowed through the brush, thankful that most of it was just high grass but still worried about scraping Taylor's face, scratching his eye. She prayed the stroller's canopy would protect her son from injury.

Still, a scratch or two was preferable to hanging dead from a tree, or being carried off by a fox or a mountain lion.

"Hold on, baby," she whispered. She'd get him to that cluster of trees, undo the strap around his waist with the hand holding on to Dog, and swing him up with her right. If she was quick enough, grabbed him under the arms, she could do it all while barely missing a step.

And if she had to, she'd drop Dog.

Breathing heavily, Tricia shoved ahead. A branch cracked behind her and she bit her lip. She couldn't cry out. Couldn't scare Taylor.

"It's a game, baby!" she said suddenly. "Do you like Mama's game?"

And then it was time. Her throat raw, legs rubbery, and yet energized Tricia had the baby free, against her side, and was gone.

It had taken her two months to save for the stroller she'd left behind.

"Hi, it's me."

"And?" The voice was tense.

"She took the baby to the park, walked home the long way, detoured down Ivy to the canyon and disappeared. She showed up at home an hour later and never left the house again."

"What's in the canyon?"

"The baby stroller. She left it there."

"What? Why?"

"No idea. Still had a little sweatshirt, a book, a bottle half filled with juice and a plastic bag with some crackers in the pocket on the back. I saved them for you."

"Good. Thanks."

"Want me to continue as planned?"

"Yes." His certainty was clear.

She didn't know a lot about computers, generally. Knew, intricately, the program she'd used for her work, and knew the number she dialed whenever something went wrong with the machine itself. Whether it froze, gave her an error report or a virus warning, she simply picked up the phone and dialed.

Or rather, the person she used to be had done that.

Thursday morning, it was just her and the machine, or rather, Scott's machine—which she'd never touched before, which she'd prefer not to touch, but she had little choice.

With Taylor and Dog sleeping soundly on Scott's bed behind her, Tricia clicked the help button on his Internet browser. First she had to learn how to clear history when she was finished, and then she'd search. There was no room for chance. No reason to implicate Scott in anything.

The violet-trimmed duffel that had been packed with periodically updated diapers, changes of clothes and emergency baby supplies, had been pulled out from beneath piles of fabric in the closet of her sewing room. As soon as Taylor awoke, ate, had his bath, they were heading to Coronado, to Patsy's to drop off the next three finished outfits she'd promised her friend—another pair of drawstring slacks, a flowing calf-length skirt and peasant top, and a pair of shorts with a button-up white blouse. After that, she had no idea where she'd go.

She had to leave. It might be illogical, rash, stupid, but she couldn't stay. She'd been followed the day before. A saner person might not think so, might think her imagination out of control, but she knew. There was no doubt. She knew.

The screen was too bright for her eyes in the early-morning dimness. But there was a little history button right on the toolbar where she'd found the help button. A click and another click, and any record of the sites she visited on the Internet would be erased from Scott's computer.

Turning, she watched her son breathe. There was such comfort in that. The simple in and out of air from his lungs, the rise and fall of his chest, had become precious proof that she hadn't lost yet. The baby, dressed in thin cotton footed bottoms that snapped into the short-sleeved matching shirt, lay sprawled crossways on the bed. He'd been like that most of the night.

Tricia knew because she'd been up watching him through every minute of it. She wasn't taking any chances.

Typing her request into the search bar, Tricia clicked *go* and waited.

She would've left the day before except that she thought she'd be making a mistake to leave prematurely. She was due to meet Miller later that morning and if she could find out who was having her followed—and why—she'd have more of a chance to throw him off. Show Thomas, or whoever it was, something that was the opposite of what he was looking for. Become something she was not.

Again.

She'd done it once. Could do it again. And again. And again. As many times as it took to get her son to his eighteenth birthday.

Besides, this way Dog only had to be alone in the backyard with the blanket and kennel and bowls of water and food she'd set up for two days instead of three.

The hourglass on the computer turned upside down one more time as the machine did her bidding. And then the screen flashed. There were pages of listings for Thomas Whitehead. She looked at the latest one.

Autopsy Reveals Conclusive Evidence
Thursday, May 5, 2005, 6:00 a.m.

San Francisco, AP. The autopsy of Leah Montgomery showed conclusively that the heiress sustained a blow to her back before she landed on the tree that held her suspended for three weeks, according to the Medical Examiner's office. Doctors say that the muscle and tissue just beneath Montgomery's shoulder blades bear evidence of severe bruising in the shape of handprints. Based on other injuries sustained during the fall, the area hit and the angle at which the body was found, police have concluded that Montgomery was pushed off the cliff. There was no other evidence of struggle or foul play, no signs of Montgomery having been restrained. According to a police source, whoever is guilty of this crime is someone Ms. Montgomery trusted enough to stand with at the edge of a cliff.

Though early reports show no indication of a previously announced pregnancy, and Senator Whitehead has an alibi for the time of the murder, prosecutors have not yet withdrawn charges against him. Further autopsy reports will be released. Prosecutor Amy Black was unavailable for comment.

* * *

"Hello."

On edge more often than not these days, Scott leaned against the station's backyard wall early Thursday morning and pulled his cell phone away from his ear as Tricia answered. He took a deep breath, then moved it back. The other guys were still asleep. He hadn't been so lucky.

"What's wrong?" Tension made the words stronger than he'd intended.

"Nothing! Scott, hi!" As curt as her voice had been seconds before, Tricia now sounded too joyful. Something was wrong. Very wrong. "I was reading—distracted. I'm sorry."

Reading at seven-thirty in the morning? "I figured you'd just be finished dressing, having your last peaceful cup of coffee before the troops awoke." He hated playing games. Most particularly with this woman. It was dangerous. Stupid. Too much was at risk.

His freedom. Hers. His heart. Hers. Taylor. The present.

"I am having my coffee. And reading."

She was lying. Or hiding something. Or someone?

He shook his head. Tricia just wasn't the type to have a lover on the side. Or if she was, he couldn't make himself believe she had one now.

"Reading what?"

"The paper." Which she rarely read at home when he was there.

"You already went out for it?"

"No. It's yesterday's. I never finished it."

Odd. But not unheard of. She'd told him she some-times picked up a paper on her morning walk with her son. But she usually didn't bring it home.

So what had she done yesterday instead?

And when had he started analyzing every word she said, looking for hidden meanings?

The woman was driving him nuts. Keeping him off balance. He couldn't afford to be off balance.

Nor could he seem to walk away.

"Anything earth-shattering?" They'd been too busy at the station for leisure reading.

"Nope."

Rubbing a hand across eyes that felt the pressure of too many nights of too little sleep, Scott studied the grass at his feet. "You sure everything's okay?" If he asked her any more than that, she'd run. He'd pushed her as far as he could.

"Yes, fine."

He asked about her plans for the day. She described a day like many others that had gone before. And he wanted to believe her. To accept the momentary peace her words brought him.

But he reminded himself that her words meant little. She was using a lot of effort to hide something from him. She wasn't about to disclose it during a casual run-down of the day's events.

"I love you." Her voice was soft. Completely Tricia. And Scott sighed, his shoulders, his stomach, relaxing in spite of everything that remained unknown.

"I love you, too." The admission was one of the few recent changes in their relationship for which he was thankful.

Beyond thankful.

"I mean it, Scott. I really do love you. A lot."

He believed her.

"I know. Me, too," he said quietly. And then, when the tension immediately returned to his stomach, he added, "Take care of yourself."

"I will."

Scott hung up, telling himself he was a lucky man to have the love of such a woman. And his freedom, too.

But the sound of those last two words—"I will"—echoed over and over in his mind. They'd been infused with intensity, too much intensity, almost as though she was saying goodbye.

While he sat helpless—like a man by the side of the road—watching a love die before his eyes.

He'd done what he could, short of marrying her, to keep her next to him. And that he couldn't do.

With a weary shake of the head, he pocketed his phone and went back inside.

"They're cops."

Walking from the door toward the chair in the back of Island Cleaners where Miller sat, unshaven and disreputable-looking as usual, Tricia stumbled.

"Cops?" He thought she was being followed by cops.

Patsy was wrong. This man wasn't any good at all. And if he'd ever been good, liquor had soaked up his skills.

He nodded, eyes half-closed. "Off-duty."

She stared at him, Taylor on her hip. "I'm being followed by off-duty cops."

His chin fell to his chest in confirmation.

"Taylor, don't, honey." She pulled the baby's fingers out of her mouth, kissed them, all the while watching the older man. Logic told her he was a farce, laughable, a waste of her time and money. Despite logic, she believed him. She preferred not to, but she did.

Frowning, Tricia dropped onto a wooden stool at the end of a long revolving rack holding plastic bags filled with clean clothes. Positioning Taylor on her lap, she pulled a package of crackers out of her bag and held it open for the boy, who happily crammed a pudgy little fist inside.

"San Diego cops?"

"Yep."

She wanted to yell at the drunk. Tell him he stank. That he wasn't earning his keep. And she felt strangely fond of him at the same time.

Swallowing, she peered over at him, not sure whether or not to like him, whether to continue this conversation or just run.

"And there are two of them?"

When all he did was nod, she wanted to scream. And cry.

"One of them is a woman?"

"They both are, although my source in San Francisco tells me the best people-finder in Northern California just returned from a high-paying San Diego stint last month."

"Oh." She blinked, her nerves jumping beneath her skin. The man on the beach? Had he been looking for her? Recognized her, after all? Reported back? Or not recognized her and given up?

But that didn't explain...

"You're sure both of these women are following me?"

"Positive." It was strange how a man could be such a complete, unwashed, disgusting bum and yet instill such confidence. "I saw them together in a bar," he was saying, "found the best-looking guy I could and paid him to hit on them, get them talking."

"One of those women was trailing me yesterday morning."

His only response was the protrusion of his lower lip, which Tricia couldn't translate at all.

Taylor dropped a cracker and she bent to pick it up, kissing the baby on the neck as she straightened. He threw himself forward again, obviously wanting to have another go at this entertaining game. She took a spill-proof cup of juice out of her bag and handed it to him.

And then there was nothing left to do.

"So who hired them?"

She knew, just didn't want to hear the truth, to face

the truth, to know that money had tentacles she couldn't escape. Not that she would ever stop trying.

"Fire chief named Scott McCall."

Taylor slid slowly off her lap onto his feet, the waiting dirty hands of the ex-detective steadying him. Tricia watched in slow motion, her gaze locked with that of the disheveled man holding her son upright. He was watching her intently, his watery eyes oddly compassionate.

She opened her mouth, but didn't know what to say. The room was spinning so completely she had no real comprehension. Scott McCall was having her followed, and her drunken detective was offering support. Meanwhile, in San Francisco, her husband had been charged with the murder of her best friend.

With one hand clutching the leg of her jeans, Taylor stared up at the smelly man with both hands around his waist, and even he was acting out of character. There was no recoiling as usually happened with strangers. The baby didn't hide his face against her, didn't cry. He just stared.

So did Tricia, desperately trying to hold on to any sense of reality. Sounds came from a distance, as though her head was buried in cotton. And she was hot. Too hot.

"What's wrong?"

She heard Patsy's voice. Hadn't seen her friend come in. Didn't see her now. But she felt Patsy's hand take hers, felt the other woman's arm around her. "Come on, honey, let's get you upstairs. Doris! Come get the baby!"

"No!" Tricia couldn't see much, her peripheral vision almost as dark as her heart, but she could see Taylor. With a fumbling hand she grabbed for him, catching his arm on the third try. "I can't leave him!" She could hardly believe that shaky, terror-filled voice was hers. She might not have believed it if she hadn't felt the scrape of those words passing through her dry throat.

"I know. Doris will bring him up," Patsy said, her voice uncharacteristically upbeat and as carefree as if they were discussing whether to put mustard and pickle on the hamburgers. Tricia wondered if her smelly drunken detective preferred hamburgers to hot dogs.

And like an electrical switch inside her, that thought took her outside the engulfing fear to experience a second's relief. It gave her a tenuous grasp on awareness, a brief liaison with the strength she was going to have to find deep within.

She stared at the two people hovering over her, at the baby who was reaching happily toward his friend Doris, toddling forward as she came in from the front of the store.

"I'll be okay," Tricia said, trying out her voice, reassured by her ability to make it sound more normal. "I just need to sit for a second."

"You need to come upstairs, have something to drink and maybe eat and spend the afternoon with nothing to do but relax. Sleep if you can, watch old sitcoms on TV or listen to music." Patsy pulled Tricia off the stool, holding one strong arm around her for support as she walked her toward the stairs. "I'll call Shauna in to watch the store so Doris can keep Taylor upstairs, close to you, but for these next few hours, madam, you will have no responsibility except not to think. Got that? *No thinking.* No worrying."

Tricia, walking slowly as she tested her shaky legs, nodded. It sounded like heaven.

"At least until dinnertime tonight, you are absolutely forbidden to make any decisions other than whether to chew or sleep. Got it?"

Still too weak to prevent the tears that sprang to her eyes, Tricia glanced over at her friend. "Thank you."

Patsy, her tough and capable companion, just nodded, brown eyes glimmering. There was a story there that Tricia wanted to hear.

She hoped, one day, she'd have the opportunity.

Miller faded silently into the distance, but Tricia knew she wasn't finished with him yet.

15

Amazingly, Tricia slept. Opening her eyes to the setting sun that shone in on her through the sheer white curtains on the bedroom window, she lay on the pillow-soft mattress, completely relaxed, trying to figure out where she was and why. The safe, peaceful feeling dissipated almost instantly.

Taylor! Where was Taylor? Flying off the bed, Tricia stumbled as her bare feet hit the wood floor. When she'd gone out the door and down the hall, she grew calmer, realizing she was at Patsy's—remembering that she had a friend, someone who'd taken care of her while she'd been incapable of doing it herself.

Slowing to a more normal pace, she pulled her T-shirt down over the waistband of her jeans, yanked the rubber band out of her hair, releasing a ponytail that had become scraggly at best. And, looking in every door she passed, found the bathroom, ignored it for now, and then found Taylor. The baby was asleep on a double bed in what was obviously Patsy's guest room. Her friend had insisted Tricia take her own room, saying the mattress was divine.

She'd been right about that.

Doris, ever-present playmate to her son, dozed in a large, overstuffed dark-brown armchair in the corner, reading glasses perched on the end of her nose and an open book in her lap.

The room was a lot like Patsy. Nothing fancy or colorful, but solid—solid wood, thick comforter on the bed, large and comfortable-looking armchair. Everything was serviceable, usable. Nothing extravagant or unnecessary.

How had she spent the first thirty years of her life thinking she needed more than this? Her baby, healthy, safe, sleeping peacefully—and friends to watch over them both.

"You're awake."

Startled, she jerked back from the door to see Patsy standing a couple of feet away in the hall. She was wearing the light-blue cotton drawstring pants and lace-trimmed tank top Tricia had made for her.

"Yeah." She ran a hand self-consciously through her hair. "Sorry I slept so long."

"I was hoping you'd make it through the night."

She couldn't stay. This was Patsy's place. But she felt her skin cool as she realized it had to be close to seven with the sun almost set, and she had no idea where she'd be putting her child to bed for the night.

"You're staying here," Patsy said, watching her.

Tricia shook her head, Patsy's white walls and wooden floor her only tangible reality. "I can't."

"Of course you can," Patsy said. "Furthermore, there's absolutely no reason you shouldn't. And at least one damn good reason not to go back to McCall's house. At least not tonight."

Scott. The pang in her chest returned, duller, but still too intense. "He's at the station, anyway."

Patsy's brown eyes narrowed. "You *want* to go back to his house? Sleep in his bed tonight?"

"No."

"I didn't think so." She grabbed a bag Tricia hadn't noticed on the floor outside Patsy's room. The overnight bag she'd packed with the few essentials she was taking from this life into the next, knowing when she left South Park this morning that she wouldn't be returning.

"You came prepared."

Patsy didn't mention the fact that Tricia had brought that bag along before she'd known about her lover's duplicity.

"I can stay in a hotel…."

"Not here on Coronado, and that little boy's tired," Patsy said, nodding toward her guest room. "He played until almost four. I suspect we'll be able to get him up for dinner and that will be that."

Especially since seven was his normal bedtime. With another pang, one of complete guilt this time, she wondered how life had become so impossible that even the simplest things no longer made sense. It was almost her son's bedtime and he wasn't even up from his afternoon nap.

Dinner was a surreal affair and yet, looking at it from the outside, Tricia supposed everything seemed normal enough. A woman cooking dinner for friends, setting the table with forest-green earthenware dishes and plain shiny silverware. Serving pork chops, rolls and asparagus straight from the stove, pouring sun-brewed iced tea into tall glasses. And the final touch, the plastic bowl of mashed pork and asparagus she'd prepared in a blender that until then, as she'd pointed out with her slightly acerbic grin, had only been used to make daiquiris.

Yeah, on the surface things could have seemed normal. If you didn't realize that the baby was sitting in a hastily borrowed high chair, or the guests were homeless.

Just as they were about to sit down, Tricia heard a shuffling gait on the stairs leading up to Patsy's apartment door, followed by a hesitant knock—almost as though the person knocking wasn't quite sure that was the right thing to do…or that an answer to the summons was desired.

Patsy dropped the napkins she'd grabbed from a cupboard. Bending to scoop them up, she mumbled, "I didn't think he'd actually come."

"Who?" One hand on Taylor's shoulder, Tricia was

ready to run. There was a back door through the kitchen, and a fire escape. She could—

"Miller."

"Miller?" She stared at her friend, wondering if that new textured bob had somehow short-circuited the woman's brain.

Glancing at the door, Patsy put the napkins on the table. "I had a feeling you might want to talk more once you got some rest. So I told him that if he found somewhere to clean up, he could come for dinner."

Mostly numb, Tricia nodded, watching from beside Taylor's tray where she was supervising the baby's attempts to feed himself with his fingers. Patsy wiped her hands on her pants and ran a hand through her newly styled blond hair on her way to the door, almost as though she was trying to impress the drunk.

Only good manners—and years of living in the public eye—kept Tricia's mouth from falling open as Miller stepped into the room. In a button-down blue shirt with the sleeves rolled up his forearms and a pair of clean jeans he'd probably stolen, with clean hair and a shaved face, the man had probably attracted the attention of every woman he'd passed on the street.

"You should do that more often," she said, when Patsy just stood there.

He shrugged, shoulders still bent with the weight of life. "I'll be drunk again by midnight," he said. "And it doesn't pay to shave drunk. Too many cuts."

"You ever think about sobering up?" she asked, and

then could have slapped herself. Like she had any kind of life to show for the great decisions *she'd* made.

"Every time I'm sober."

"And?" Patsy, moving toward the table, turned back to him.

He took one look at her, his eyes traveling blatantly up and down her body, and said, "Drunk's easier."

With dinner finished, Tricia expected Arnold Miller to leave. She really didn't have anything to talk to him—or anyone—about. His work for her was done. He'd found out what she needed to know. Or part of it, anyway…

"Did you see today's paper?" Patsy asked, glancing at Miller. She was holding Taylor, giving him the bottle of warm milk Tricia hoped would calm him enough to sleep. Her son's only fussy times were when he was off his schedule.

"Caught glimpses of it on my way over," Miller said.

"You saw the headline, then?"

"About the senator?"

Tricia sank down in her hard-backed wooden chair, suddenly cold. What now? Nervous tension burned through her. How soon could she be alone with a paper?

"What about him?" she asked.

Both sets of eyes turned in her direction. It was the first time either of them had looked at her since they'd begun this discussion. And her tension intensified under the scrutiny of those glances.

She sat up. Found a social smile she'd thought long gone. "You're talking about the guy from San Francisco, right? The senator? The one who supposedly killed his girlfriend?"

"Right," Patsy said, pulling the plastic nipple from the sleeping toddler's mouth, setting the bottle on the table slowly, almost deliberately. And then she looked back at Tricia.

"What about him?" Tricia asked again, keeping her voice casual. She was a middle-class stiff like all the rest, curious about how the other half lived—and got away with murder.

"The autopsy showed that Leah Montgomery had been pregnant. They're saying she miscarried when she went off the cliff."

Oh. God. Leah. I'll deal with this soon, my dear friend. As soon as I'm alone and can cry with you. For you. For us. Leah, I miss you so much.

So goddamned much.

Somehow, she kept her smile, but felt her lip twitching. She hoped it didn't show. She'd wait a minute or so, then excuse herself to the bathroom, taking Taylor when she left. She'd put him to bed, maybe lie down with him...

"And," Patsy added, "they've found an old hermit who lives halfway up Miner's Mountain. Apparently he knows Senator Whitehead. The man's bills, which have been in arrears since the government cut back on his welfare, have been paid in full every month since six months before the senator's wife disappeared."

Walter was on Thomas's payroll? He was one of them? Only her instinct for survival kept the food in her stomach.

"Someone must've leaked that little piece of information," Miller said, his too-clear gaze making her un-comfortable. "It's not the kind of thing the prosecution would normally let loose."

Say something, Tricia commanded herself. Act like any other middle-class working stiff having dinner with friends, discussing the soap opera-esque dramas played out by larger-than-life players—celebrities and political figures and movie stars. Everyone talked about that, right?

"Didn't the woman's sister appear on TV not too long ago claiming some kind of cover-up?" Hoping her voice didn't sound as shaky as it felt, she forced herself to continue, trying to convey just the right amounts of curiosity, compassion, horror and disgust. "Maybe they're letting things out to assure the public that they're actually working on the case."

"Maybe," Miller said. His hand lay on the table, thumb rapping a constant beat. Still, his gaze on her didn't let up.

What? Tricia screamed silently. She felt trapped. Caged. Needed to get out. To breathe.

"I read that the evidence established enough of a pat-tern and therefore probable cause to get an added grand jury indictment against Senator Whitehead in the death of his wife and unborn son. He's currently being held on a million-dollar bail." Patsy's words dropped quietly into the room, slamming into her like lead bullets.

What would a normal person say to that? Tricia tore a piece off her napkin. And another.

"Any half-competent prosecutor would've done the same," Miller replied to Patsy, but when Tricia glanced up, he was still watching her. "The two women were life-long friends. You have a pregnant wife who disappears without a trace and then, less than two years later, the friend—also claiming him as the father of her unborn baby—mysteriously disappears as well. Only this time they have a body. A dead body."

Was this what people were doing all over the state? Discussing her private hell over the dinner table?

"But why would he do such a thing?" Patsy's questions would logically have been directed at the man who sounded like he knew what he was talking about. Instead she was watching Tricia, too.

Tricia felt far too hot. Needed to take off her T-shirt, her bra. *Breathe.*

"If the guy's sterile like he claims," Arnold Miller was saying, "it wasn't something either of the women would have known, but it would certainly prove to him that both had been unfaithful."

"You think he did it out of jealousy?"

"It's common enough. He can't live without them, but can't live with their bastard children, either."

"Kind of odd, both women being unfaithful to him, though, isn't it?" Patsy asked thoughtfully.

Stop! Both of you, just stop!

Miller didn't answer.

"They're going for the death penalty," Patsy said.

Miller's presence scared Tricia into responding. "I hope they get it." And then, without looking at the ex-P.I., she murmured, "Well, I guess I should get this little guy into bed." She stood so abruptly her chair tipped over behind her.

"Tricia." Patsy's words came at her as she righted the chair.

"Yeah?" She didn't turn around.

"There was a picture of Kate Whitehead in the paper tonight."

She froze. Then turned, compelled by something deep inside her to play this one out. "I feel sorry for her." No one knew how true those words were, but she didn't say them because they were true. She said them because they were what she would've said if she'd been talking about someone else.

Miller's scrutiny detained her as surely as if he'd grabbed her wrist, and Tricia finally understood just how good the man had been at his job. And why. She had a feeling that if he wanted something from her he was going to get it. She just hoped to God he didn't want anything— and wished she had an open bottle of booze to hand him.

"It was the same grainy photo they splashed all over the papers when she disappeared," Patsy went on. "You know the one, with that beautifully wavy shoulder-length hair, eyebrows that were too perfect to be natural, those long lashes and curvy lips."

What the hell was going on here? Tricia looked from one to the other, wishing she had the energy to be angry with both of them rather than just frightened like a rat in a trap. She shook her head. "I don't know if I ever saw it." Thank God her upbringing had taught her how to lie—and how to do it artfully.

If only she could remember the lesson on detachment. It was the first key to survival.

"Yeah, well," Patsy said, "I don't know how anyone would recognize an actual person from that picture...."

Tricia's shoulders relaxed and she almost cried out in relief. They didn't know a thing. She was far too paranoid. Like that day she'd thought the guy on the beach was following her.

"...it was that bit about her being a fashion designer that got me." Patsy's gaze was compassionate and suddenly demanding, all at the same time. "The paper said the woman could make any body shape look good." Patsy's glance was pointed. "Even mine."

While Miller continued to tap his thumb and pin her with his unblinking stare, Tricia grasped the back of the chair she'd righted. Four hours' rest wasn't enough to sustain her through the beginning of her worst nightmare coming true. The light above the table was too bright. She was seeing spots.

"And then I remembered when you offered to make

me a new wardrobe. It was the day you saw that Kate Whitehead design and turned white. The day you asked me about finding Miller."

"Who got his ass sober long enough to call in some favors from San Francisco to find out about that pregnancy test strip they found in Leah Montgomery's apartment." Miller spoke—nailing her with her own words.

"Hi, it's me." The call came before dawn, Friday morning.

"Is something wrong?" Scott got up from his bunk, instantly awake as he spoke quietly into his cell phone.

"I'm not sure…."

Dammit, he should've listened to his instincts last night, run home to check on her rather than allowing his mind to convince him he was overreacting— That he was getting in too deep, caring too much. That he'd better learn to let go a little bit or he'd be sorry.

"What?" he said more harshly than off-duty Officer Deb Ball deserved. In T-shirt and hastily donned blue pants, he stepped outside the back door of the station.

"Have you talked to her?"

"Not since yesterday before lunch." They'd had a hellish day—three fires, a fatality on the freeway, a suicide and a heart attack victim. "I didn't get back to the station until after midnight."

"She didn't go home last night."

His shoulders fell so quickly he almost lost the phone

at his ear. Scott's stomach burned, his heart stalled, and then started to beat far too hard.

"Where is she?"

"I don't know."

He didn't say a word. He couldn't.

"I'm sorry, Scott. You save my kid from drowning and I can't even keep track of yours. I feel just sick about it…."

"Where'd you lose her?"

"At Island Dry Cleaners."

"On Coronado."

"Yeah. She went in yesterday a little after one. The place closed at seven and she never came out. She must've slipped out the back. I didn't pay attention. She always goes in the front and comes out the front."

Something was happening on that island. He'd known it since that Sunday the previous month, when she'd gone all the way to the Hotel Del to use the bathroom.

He tried to think. "It's too early to report her missing…."

"I have some favors to call in, too," Deb said. "You want me to ask the guys to keep an eye out?"

"Yes." If the city's police were helping him, he still might be able to save her. If it wasn't already too late.

Sick with panic, Scott forced himself through the calming exercises he'd learned during his paramedic training. He would be no good to anyone, not Tricia or Taylor, not himself, if he didn't stay focused.

She could've been abducted, could be tied up somewhere, or worse. If he'd known her secrets, he might know where to look…

"I have no idea what you thought I'd find, trailing her. Nor do I know why she didn't return home. But Betty and I haven't seen one thing these past three weeks that would indicate to us that she's in trouble."

The words were a relief and painful at the same time. More than anything, he wanted her safe. But if she was safe, why hadn't she come home? Or at least called?

16

San Diego Union-Tribune
Friday, May 6, 2005
Page 1

Police Look for Body of
Senator's Missing Wife

Searchers are combing the fifty-mile radius surrounding Miner's Mountain today, looking for the body of Kate Whitehead. Her husband, who yesterday was indicted for her murder and that of their unborn son, could be facing the death penalty. He is currently in jail, awaiting arrangements for the payment of his million-dollar bail. The senator, in a brief but emotional statement to reporters this morning, adamantly clung to his not-guilty plea, claiming that he loves his wife and prays daily for her safe return. When asked about the death of his wife's best friend, Leah Montgomery, the woman he's been seen with socially over the past year, he said only that he was grieved by her death.

Montgomery's sister, Carley Winchester, who appeared recently on Good Afternoon, San Francisco, told reporters that she's spoken to the old hermit, whom investigators discovered living on Miner's Mountain. She said the hermit corroborated her belief that Thomas Whitehead beat his wife. According to Winchester, Walter Mavis, who was born on the mountain, told her he saw Kate Whitehead with big sunglasses and bruises on more than one occasion. Winchester said that Mavis also told her that Whitehead visited the cliff top frequently with her drawing pad and pencils.

Whitehead, a gifted fashion designer, had been scheduled to have her first big show in San Francisco, with invitations allegedly accepted by most of the world's biggest buyers, less than a week after her disappearance almost two years ago.

Leah Montgomery, also pregnant and claiming Whitehead as the father, disappeared on the eve of a charity fund-raiser she'd arranged and was hosting.

Sitting at the table in the station's kitchen, surrounded by the aroma of coffee and pancakes, and the listless, intermittent conversation of the three men under his command Friday morning, Scott studied the small grainy photo that appeared next to the article. Told himself he was crazy.

And started to sweat.

He'd seen a couple of headlines in the last week or two about the Northern California senator's troubles, but hadn't paid a lot of attention. Living in California had a way of desensitizing a guy to celebrities and their riffraff. Especially a guy who'd once moved in those circles, who not only knew how much of their news was sensationalized, but who'd also sworn he was never going back to that society.

Glancing at the front page again, he calmed himself with empty assurances. He was tired. Sensitive to drama at the moment. The morning's early phone call was interfering with his ability to discern fact from fear.

"You want a refill?" Cliff was standing over him with the pot.

Shaking his head, Scott pulled the paper in front of his face. He'd heard the story back when Whitehead's wife had gone missing, but didn't remember much about it. Whitehead hadn't been a senator then. There'd been no charges. And very little press. He didn't think he'd ever seen a picture.

The photo bore little, if any, resemblance to her. It was ludicrous to link the feeling in his gut to the mention of that mountain cliff and its resident hermit. But for the first time since he'd become a firefighter more than eleven years before, Scott arranged for a replacement for the last twenty-four hours of his shift and went home.

Tricia knew two things. She had to go back to San Francisco.

And there was no need to rush.

If a dry cleaner and a drunken bum—okay, so he'd been the state's most sought-after P.I. in his previous life—could figure out who she was, so would others. The story wasn't going to stay out of the press this time. As the cliché had it, she could run, but she couldn't hide.

Neither could she stand by and see a man sentenced to death for two murders he didn't commit.

Climbing off the bus at her South Park stop late Friday morning, Tricia settled her purse and overnight bag on her shoulder, her son on her hip, and started the short walk to Scott's house. She had twenty-four hours before he got home. She hadn't meant to ever come back here. But that was when she'd thought she was living a life on the run.

As things now stood, she could take the time to pack. To plan.

Take the time to talk to Scott. If she could find the courage. She was done with running. From life. From fear. From herself. Leah had told her so many times that if she listened to her heart and made the choices it told her to make, life would do the rest....

She didn't know about that, but she'd been listening to her head and her fears for a long time now. It wasn't working very well. She was sick of avoiding her image in the mirror—avoiding the truth about who and what she was. She was sick of the lies.

Jabbering away, Taylor stuck a wet finger in her ear. Tricia left it there.

And what about him? What about the baby she'd do anything to protect? How could she be sure this latest choice wasn't going to be the worst yet? What if she went back and somehow Thomas got to them?

Fear shot through her stomach and up to her chest. Her step faltered. But only for a moment. Going back was the right thing to do. She believed that.

Thomas was being tried for her death, with the death penalty attached, and she wasn't dead. Yes, she was convinced he'd killed Leah, and she could do her part to see that he was punished for that, but he hadn't killed *her*.

Besides, she'd rather go back on her own terms than wait until she was discovered and exposed.

With a firm gait she turned onto Ivy, rounded the corner of Scott's drive, concentrating on the vivid reds and yellow and purples of the spring flowers covering his front yard. The miracle of new beginnings.

She had to believe there was a new beginning for her, too.

And then, as she made her way up the incline of the drive, she saw Scott's truck in the back of the carport. Saw her lover, dressed in tight jeans, a black T-shirt and sandals, his hair still wet from the shower, standing at the door watching her.

"Hi, Kate. Welcome home."

* * *

"You had me followed." She hadn't had the time she needed to rehearse, think, prepare, but knew defensiveness wasn't the approach she would have chosen.

Sitting out back in one of the two white plastic lawn chairs, upholstered pads making them relatively comfortable, Scott crossed an ankle over his knee, glanced at her and then away.

He'd been patient. She had to give him that. Patient and so much more. Other than the acerbic greeting he'd delivered when she arrived home an hour before, he'd been kind, playing with Taylor, waiting to talk to her until the baby went down for his morning nap.

But then, Scott *was* kind. His kindness was one of the first things that had attracted her in that bar those long months ago. One of the many things she loved about him.

"I was worried about you," he finally said, an elbow resting on the arm of his chair, his hand hovering near his chin. For all his relaxed posture, there was nothing calm about him. "I was afraid you might be in trouble."

She'd figured that out sometime in the middle of the night, lying awake in the dark at Patsy's home. Scott would have no other motive than to protect her. His life was about protecting people, saving them from harm.

"It scared me."

"I had no idea that you knew."

He didn't apologize for his duplicity. But if apologies for duplicity were the issue...

"I'm sorry," she said.

He peered over at her. The painful emotion shimmering in his green eyes broke a heart that was already completely shattered. Or so she thought...

"I don't even know where to begin...."

He hadn't asked any questions. Might not even want to know the answers anymore. She owed them to him, anyway.

"You're married." His voice wasn't accusatory. Wasn't angry. And yet it cut her more deeply than any of the horrible insinuations Thomas had made during the last six months of their life together. In part, perhaps, because Scott spoke the truth.

"Yes."

"To a state senator."

"Yes."

Dog, who'd been so overjoyed to see them when they got home that he'd tripped over his feet and done a full flip in the air, was lying in the middle of the small grassy backyard, chewing on a rawhide stick.

"I met him at one of Leah's charity functions, for an orphan relief effort in Afghanistan. He was being auctioned off."

"And you bought him."

"No." She'd been too dignified back then to do anything so overtly outgoing. "Leah did. And she gave him to me for my birthday."

It had been love at first sight. Or at least, the closest thing to it she'd ever known. But then, what *had* she known?

"Like you—and as you've already guessed—I grew up with money," she said, staring out at the wall several yards away. If it was painted something besides that boring gray, it wouldn't feel so…constrictive.

"Unlike your childhood, mine wasn't all that great." There was a long jagged crack in the wall, running almost from top to bottom. Even cement had its weaknesses.

"My father owned more car dealerships than God. He was everything derogatory you've ever heard about car salespeople. He could charm the peanuts away from an elephant—coaxed my finishing-school mother away from her old-money family—but in the long run, most of what he said had to be taken with the proverbial grain of salt. There'd usually be just enough truth for him to sail by, but if you lived with him, you could never count on any of it."

Scott said nothing. But he was still sitting there, so she kept talking.

"And when my mother or I said or did something that didn't please him, he'd think nothing of whacking us across the face."

"You were an only child?"

"Yes."

He nodded, his expression pained, but she couldn't tell if his pain was for her and the sordid story she was telling, or for himself. Or for them. Wasn't sure it mattered. She'd hurt him. That was enough.

"They divorced when I was twelve, but by then the damage had been done as far as my mother was concerned. She'd lost all self-respect. There were another six years of various men coming in and out of her life, using her, taking from her, hurting her."

"Then what happened?"

"I left for college."

"And your mother?"

Her stomach heaved with tension. "As of about two years ago…she was living in the mansion she inherited from her parents after their deaths, volunteering all over the city. She was on the board at the country club, too. About eight years before that, after Leah and I graduated from college and Leah became the charity organizer of the world, she drafted my mother's help and pretty much changed her life. Mom felt useful again, you know? It gave her back her self-respect."

"Sounds like she was finally happy."

"Until her only daughter turned up missing without a trace, you mean?" Tricia asked. There was so much guilt. She was responsible for so much pain. Yet what other choice had there been? To stay and be killed as Leah had? Have her unborn baby murdered as Leah's had been?

But if no other good came of going back, it would be wonderful to see her mother again.

Dog trotted over and Scott bent to scratch him behind the ears before scooping up the puppy and settling him on his lap.

"It's a classic story," she said, watching the puppy, wishing for that second that she could be as joyful, as carefree, as unfettered by life's choices. "Abused girl grows up to marry abusive man."

"Whitehead hit you."

Had he read about it in the papers, too? She hadn't been following the San Diego versions too closely.

"Yep."

He nodded, his gaze on the puppy he was fondling. "From the beginning?"

"We'd been married less than a month the first time."

"Jesus!" Scott looked over at her, his eyes hard yet brimming with compassion. "You're a strong capable woman, Trish—Kate, whatever your name is…" He glanced away and said, half under his breath, "You've been sleeping in my bed for almost two years, I love your son as my own, and I don't even know what to call you."

"Might as well call me Kate," she said softly. "It's my name."

He nodded. Stroked the puppy.

"Why'd you stay with him for so many years?" he asked after a time. She'd assumed they were finished with the conversation, figuring he could put the rest together for himself.

The sky was so blue, and the sun warm. Tricia slid down in her chair, closing her eyes, and turned her face up to the heat. "Thomas is a charmer. He can be tender and generous and funny. That was the man I married, the man I thought I loved. The other behavior was caused by stress, making him act out of character. It took me years to realize that the tenderness was the part that wasn't real."

She swallowed to rid herself of the dryness in her throat. It didn't work. But the sun on her face was warm. Nice.

"I threatened him after that first time. I said if he ever hit me again, I was leaving him and telling the world what he'd done. He was still under his daddy's thumb at that point and afraid of the fallout."

She and Leah used to lie out in the sun for hours, talking—until they were twelve and lectured about wrinkles and leathery skin.

They had much more effective sunblocks now.

She should start sunbathing again.

"As he got involved in politics and became more powerful, the violence slowly started up again. But not often. And he was always so…so apologetic. So sincere." She kept the bitterness out of her voice—and her heart—as best she could. She'd relived that time over and over in the past twenty-two months and she knew one thing for certain. She was never going to understand.

Not herself. Not Thomas. Not a love that would allow abusive behavior of any kind.

"It wasn't until I was pregnant with Taylor that things got really bad. The beatings, whether verbal, physical or both, were almost daily. I was terrified to wake up in the morning."

And terrified that she wouldn't.

"According to the paper, he claims Taylor isn't his."

The statement hung in the balmy late-morning air. On one level, she didn't blame him for raising it; she could see how she might have asked it herself had the situation been reversed. After all, what did he know about her except that she'd been living a lie—involving him in an adulterous relationship—for the entire time he'd known her?

"I've slept with two men in my life." She let him do the math.

"So he's lying."

"That's my guess." Though out-and-out lying hadn't ever been Thomas's style. Stretching the truth, dressing it up, withholding it, yes, but completely abandoning it? Never that she was aware of.

"Do you think he killed your friend?"

Tricia sat up. Opened her eyes. Scott was watching her, his gaze steady.

"I'm absolutely certain of it."

Chin jutting out, he nodded. His palm, still now, almost completely covered the puppy who'd fallen asleep in his lap.

"I had no choice, Scott," she whispered.

"You couldn't go to the police?"

"I threatened to once, but Thomas is one of the most powerful men in Northern California. His holdings touch just about every industry in San Francisco in one form or another. And his political ties put pressure everywhere else."

"Like the D.A.'s office?"

"That, and the sheriff, and the mayor and some cop's wife who works for an accounting firm that's housed in one of his office complexes. Or a city clerk with a kid who needs one of the many school programs he's funded."

"No one's invincible."

"No, but Thomas has another thing going for him that's probably as powerful as his money and status."

"What's that?"

"He comes across as a nice guy. Compassionate, generous. With an easy sense of humor. People *like* him."

She wanted Scott to touch her, take her hand—do anything other than leave her hanging out here all alone with her story.

"While I've always been more reticent than outgoing. And I'm the daughter of a shady businessman."

"Still, if you had proof…"

"That I was hit?" she asked, angry with herself, with him, when residual fear crept up her chest. "What he'd say is that I fell. And if they believed him, which they would, he'd make sure I paid for my indiscretion and disloyalty in a way I wouldn't quickly forget."

"Then you'd have proof of his abuse."

Trish scoffed. It was either that or lose control of the

sob lodged in her throat. "There are methods of intimidating someone that don't show at all."

"Like?"

Resting her head back against the seat, trying to pretend to herself that she was detached, unaffected, recovered, she turned to glance at him. "You don't really want to hear this, do you?"

"Yes."

And when he looked at her like that, as though he was driven by caring and not curiosity, she couldn't deny him.

Taylor would be awake soon. And then this would be over. She closed her eyes again. She couldn't talk about it with them open. It wasn't *her* she was talking about. It was that other woman—the one who'd died almost two years before, when she'd left everything she'd ever known, everyone she'd ever loved, to become someone she'd never dreamed of being.

"He'd treat me more like a prostitute than a lover in bed." Tricia swallowed. "Not in any way that would leave a mark, but there are many ways to hurt a woman that aren't discernible. Certain…movements. Words."

Hard to believe, but it had been the words that hurt the most. Always.

"And he said he'd make sure my mother was ostracized not only from the club, but from her place in our elite little society…."

Her poor mother who'd risen above her pain and humiliation far better than Tricia had. Her mother hadn't run.

"So why not just leave without accusing him of anything? People get divorced all the time."

"Thomas was in the running for big Republican backing for a State Senate seat. It's what he'd worked for his entire life. To him, that backing meant he'd become the man he'd set out to become. To him, image is everything…and he couldn't abide the image of a man with a black mark over his character…." Instinct told her to look around, check that they were alone, but Tricia couldn't open her eyes. Inside, she was all coward. "He said if I tried to sue him for divorce, he'd kill me." She'd whispered the words and was still trembling, almost awaiting the blow that would come for having uttered them at all.

Thomas was in jail. He couldn't have heard her.

But he was going to. And try as she might to be logical, to be brave, to remember everything she'd learned these past two years, what she knew in her heart was that, somehow, Thomas was going to get her.

"So why did you finally leave?" Scott's words dropped softly into the silence.

"I was six months pregnant, not feeling well, and he wanted to have sex. When I begged him to leave me alone, he became enraged. Started hitting me in the stomach."

"He could've killed the baby!"

Tricia kept her eyes closed, doing everything she could to blot out a memory she knew she would never escape. "He was going to kill our son," she said, her voice sounding faraway. "I knew the only way to stop him was to give him what he wanted."

"You had sex with him."

She'd lain there while he had sex. To her that was a very different thing, but didn't blame Scott for the disappointment she heard in his voice.

"The next morning, as soon as his car turned out of the drive, I got my purse and I left."

17

"I have to go back."

Scott stayed calmly in the chair, Dog in his lap, when every instinct compelled him to jump up, grab Tricia—Kate—and Taylor, and drive down to Mexico. She'd already run. Her whole life with him had been on the run. It hadn't been a bad life.

"You don't owe anyone anything." He had so much more to say, strong words to talk her out of this craziness. But his role was to sit and do nothing. He'd figured that out during the long hours of the morning, waiting to see if she showed up, wondering if he'd ever see her again.

His teenage vigil on the side of the road hadn't been wrong. It had been a manifestation of his character, a lesson he'd been meant to learn. A lesson he was still learning.

"I owe myself."

Part of her healing. He wanted that for her. Still…

"They're going to get him with or without you."

"Without me they might send him to death row."

"I would think you'd want that."

Tricia/Kate—maybe he'd just call her TK—chuckled, but there was no humor in the sound. "I want him dead more than you can imagine...."

The passion with which she said those words touched Scott. He glanced over at her, at the tremor in her hands as they lay on the arms of the chair, at the store-bought jeans and five-dollar T-shirt, the three-dollar flip-flops on her million-dollar feet, and at the moisture gleaming in her eyes. *This* was what he'd wanted—to see all of her. To have her come fully alive for him.

"...but I want him dead *honestly*," she finished, speaking slowly. "I've done enough damage with my cowardice. I already have enough on my conscience to give me dark nights for as long as I live because of the two deaths I already feel responsible for. I can't take the weight of another. At some point, I have to make reparation."

He frowned, studying the tortured conviction written in her slumped shoulders, weary posture and pain-filled eyes. "You didn't kill anyone."

Her lower lip between her teeth, Tricia said nothing at first. Tears dripped slowly down her cheeks, almost as though she was unaware of them. She didn't wipe them away.

"On the contrary," Scott continued, not understanding. "By all accounts you saved two lives—yours and Taylor's."

Not responding, she stared out at the yard.

"Tricia." Scott leaned forward, placing Dog gently on the ground as he reached for her hand. "Whitehead is in jail for your murder! The only reason you *aren't* dead is because you had the smarts to disappear before he could kill you."

Her face turning toward his, Scott saw what he suspected was only a hint of the anguish she was feeling. "Yes," she said, her voice tinged with a bitterness he didn't recognize. "And because I chose to save myself and Taylor, Leah and her baby are dead."

"You couldn't possibly have known—"

"Not about Leah," she said. "But I knew what he was. It stood to reason that if he'd do it to me, he'd do it to whoever came after me. If I'd stayed, I could've prevented that." She pulled her hand away, and Scott's stomach hardened. He was powerless here.

"By dying, maybe. And then only if someone could prove he killed you."

"I *have* to go back, Scott. For Leah if nothing else. A lot of the prosecution's case seems to rest on circumstantial evidence that connects his behavior with Leah with me. He's claiming he couldn't possibly be the father of Leah's child, which weakens their case. I can prove it *is* possible."

"With a DNA sample from Taylor."

"Yes."

He couldn't argue with that. He didn't like it. But he couldn't come up with one damned argument that was even remotely viable.

"I want him convicted for Leah's murder because he did it. And I want to clear my conscience of his death— which would be based on charges of killing me and my son—because he didn't."

Her face was so beautiful, her flawless skin and perfectly rounded eyes accented by the dark hair pulled back in its habitual ponytail. "But at what cost?" The question was torn out of someplace deep inside him.

She shrugged. "It's a price I have to pay." The tears had stopped falling, but her voice was still thick with them. "The price commanded of me. You realized who I was from one newspaper article, one picture in the paper. There are going to be a zillion articles before this is over, with many more photos. There's nowhere I'll be able to run to stay anonymous. It only worked before because there wasn't enough reasonable evidence for an indictment and Thomas had enough pull to keep things out of the papers."

"Then I'm coming with you." The answer was so obvious it should've occurred to him sooner. He had accumulated eleven years worth of vacation.

"No."

"Why?" Scott hadn't thought, after the phone call and the article that morning, that there was any hurt left to feel.

"I'm married, Scott."

And it wouldn't look good to have an adulterous lover in tow.

"Maybe you should've considered that before leaving the bar with me." The slap hit its mark. Her head drew back.

Scott wasn't proud.

"I'm sorry."

"No," she said, sitting as far away from him as the chair would allow. "You're absolutely right. I am what I am. But it's not going to help the prosecutors get a conviction if I give the defense evidence that I'm not faithful to my marriage vows."

"Tricia, I didn't mean that. I don't think any less of you for what you did. Nor do I regret one second of our time together."

Her face remained frozen. Driven by a desperation he didn't understand and wasn't willing to analyze, Scott moved closer, took her hand again and held it between his. Needing to connect with her even while he knew the effort was useless. She wasn't his to connect with. Never had been. She was a different woman who belonged to a different life.

Those blue eyes that he'd never forget, that were going to haunt his nights for a long time to come, softened as they turned on him. "I used you."

It was obvious to him that the regret she felt about that reached all the way to the core of her being.

"Yes," he acknowledged. He'd figured that out a couple of hours before. And wasn't ready to admit how badly the realization had hurt.

"They were looking for a single pregnant woman,"

she said. "I couldn't be that." She hadn't pulled her hand away, so Scott continued to hold it.

"I know."

Her eyes wide, she stared straight at him. "But I fell in love that first week, Scott. And that's why I stayed."

He wanted so badly to believe her. And yet he had to get through the next twenty years—the next twenty minutes—and knew he couldn't stand that close to the fire again. He released her hand, sat back and began preparations for a life without her.

"Where will you go?"

Now that there was no reason left to stay, Tricia had everything she'd brought into Scott's home packed before dinner.

"I'm going to call Carley from the bus station. She'll arrange something."

Lunch had been a horribly strained affair. Taylor had chattered away, smearing food in his ear, clapping when Dog grabbed the macaroni he'd dropped and generally being adorable and funny—and the two adults who'd spent his entire life adoring him were unable to crack a smile.

Her sewing room was packed up in boxes and waiting outside for the women's shelter to which she'd donated the stuff to pick it up. Patsy would be collecting the sewing machine the next day.

A bus was leaving for San Francisco before six. As soon as Taylor was up from his nap, they'd be on their way.

It meant another night of missing his bedtime, but considering everything else, that seemed insignificant.

Leaning one shoulder against the doorjamb, Scott watched as she folded the last of her panties and bras, placing them in one of the nylon knapsacks she'd bought earlier that afternoon.

"I don't know how long I'm going to need this stuff," she said, shaky and scared and falling apart inside. "I imagine Thomas got rid of all my things, and I don't know how long it'll take me to get new identification and bank cards and—"

"Tricia." He pushed slowly away from the door, came toward her. She could see him in her peripheral vision. Bracing herself, she continued to fold. Until one big hand covered the panties in her fingers, pulled them away, dropped them on the top of the bag.

"Come here."

She couldn't go where he was asking, couldn't afford to feel what she was feeling. That had to be over—as though it had never been. There was no other choice.

His arms were strong and comforting, offering a security and a warmth she'd never known in her life before him. A magic she feared she was never going to know again as long as she lived. Burying her face in her chest, Tricia promised herself she wouldn't cry.

"Ah, Trish, you feel so good." The words were little more than ragged whispers beside her ear and she shivered, with fear—and forbidden pleasure.

He felt good, too. So good it was more than she could bear. Just as she moved to push away from him, his hips pressed against hers, openly showing her just how much pleasure he was taking from the embrace.

"I have to go…." She clung to him. So much for her newfound strength. Her courage.

"Not yet," he said, holding both of her arms as his eyes beseeched her. "Just once more, let me lose myself in you." His words were no less intense for their softness. "Let me hear you cry out in pleasure one more time…."

Living a life of truth was a difficult thing. Looking up at him, Tricia knew that as honest as she was trying to be with the world, she owed him honesty even more. Reaching down to the hem of her shirt, she pulled it up, over her head and off, standing in front of him in a serviceable white bra.

"I have never loved a man the way I love you, Scott," she said, her fingers at the waist of his jeans. "I will never love anyone else like this…."

She might not know what was going to happen to her over the next days, she might not be able to predict even one month of her future, but this she knew.

Her body shivered again when his hands moved over her ribs, holding her at the sides of her breasts. With a quick flip behind her, she unfastened the bra and released them, then brought his hands to cover them, pressing her nipples into his palms.

If this was wrong, so be it. If she was a sinner, a

whore, sleeping with another man on the very day she was returning to acknowledge her marriage, then she was a sinner and whore. She was also a woman in love who had to speak her truth one last time. For that she would not feel shame.

"Will you call me?"

Standing at the end of the bed she'd shared with this man, dressed in the only pair of dress slacks she currently possessed, with a plain white cotton button-down shirt and cheap black sandals, Tricia shook her head. "I can't."

He nodded as though he understood—as though he'd expected nothing else.

"I'm just not strong enough…." No, that wasn't what she'd meant to say. "I have to give up this duplicitous life, Scott. Even though I knew it was saving my son's life, the guilt of living a lie was killing me, almost as surely as Thomas would have."

With his hands on her hips, he looked down at her, his eyes warm with support, and showing his pain as well. "I have no idea what happens next, or where I'll be living, but the one answer I do have, with a clarity that's probably so obvious because there's so little of it, is that I have to live the rest of my life honestly."

He swallowed, took a deep breath, but didn't look away. "If you ever get into trouble, need anything…"

"I have your number." But she wouldn't be using it. It wouldn't be fair to him. Nor did she trust herself not to need him so badly she'd forget herself, throw integrity to the winds and regret it all later, when people got hurt. As they would. They always did.

Her lips were trembling; she could feel them but was powerless to make them stop. Scott was the best man she'd ever met, the stuff of childish dreams she'd long forgotten, a good man in a world with too few of them. How could she possibly walk away?

How could she resume the life she'd lived of a wealthy fashion designer in San Francisco when she knew he was here?

"Can I ask you something, Scott?"

His smile was sad. "Of course."

"When are you going to quit punishing yourself— when is your sentence over?"

He blinked, loosening his grip on her.

"What sentence?"

"The life sentence you imposed on yourself when Alicia died in your arms that day."

Now wasn't the time for this, but there wasn't going to be any other time. And she loved him too much to leave without trying to help him.

"I don't know what you're talking about."

He did, though. She could tell not only by the way he evaded her eyes, but by the hands he'd suddenly put in his pockets. He was disconnecting. From her. And probably from himself.

"Why do you think you're still alone?" she asked him.

He didn't seem to have an answer, at least not one he was willing to share with her.

"It's because you think you're not entitled to that happiness after—as you see it—robbing Alicia of the chance."

"Were you a psychologist as well as a fashion designer in your other life?"

Tricia flinched, although she probably deserved the sarcasm.

"And how are you any different?" he asked, peering down at her with sharp eyes. "Aren't you throwing all of this away because you're responsible for Leah's death—as you see it—and have to make amends?"

In part. She thought about what he said, a glimmer of hope lighting within as she wondered if there might be a way to stay with him, yet still do the things she needed to do.

And then the light burned out.

"In the eyes of the law I'm a married woman," she told him. "And as long as that's true, I can't promise to share my life with anyone else. I intend to divorce Thomas, but with his connections and money, that could take years. But that's not all," she said. *Please understand, Scott. Please support me in this.*

"There's a man with a death sentence hanging over him, at least partially because of me. A state that needs to hear the truth about one of its leaders. Another woman who could end up married to him, being beaten at night while smiling for her friends all day. It isn't just about Leah."

Pulling her against him, Scott hid his face in her neck. There were no words of support, but it was enough.

At the risk of losing the warmth of his embrace, she had to finish this. She opened her mouth but no sound emerged.

"What?" he asked, straightening to see her face.

She'd promised herself no more tears. But they came anyway, blurring her vision. "It breaks my heart to think of you living like this for the rest of your life." Her voice cracked. "You're a great man, Scott McCall. Honest and loyal and reliable and kind and funny and sexy as hell…" The words broke on a sob and Tricia pulled away from him.

"I have to go…."

Without looking back—she couldn't look back—she went into Taylor's room, gently woke him from his nap and lifted him into her arms. All his things were outside waiting for the shelter pickup except the crib. Scott had said he'd move that outside later.

"Let me take you to the bus station." He was standing behind her.

With a nylon satchel on each shoulder and her son in her arms, Tricia shook her head. "It's not far. I can walk."

Just a few more steps and she'd be out the door. She heard the kitchen floor beneath her sandals, but didn't see the counters she'd wiped down every night. She didn't look at the refrigerator from which she'd taken the piece of typing paper with crayon squiggles that had been her son's first artistic effort. Didn't look at the puppy trying to tangle himself in her feet.

Out the door, down the steps. The evening air swooped over her, cool and bracing.

"Hey."

She stopped, but didn't turn. *God, if there's a heaven, if there's a way, give it to me now. This is it. The last chance.*

"Just remember one thing." Scott's voice came from several feet behind her. He wasn't following her. He was letting her go.

"When you're in front of the camera and they're asking you questions, smile big. I'll be watching you."

Tricia's eyes were red and swollen by the time she reached the bus station. Going first to the ladies' room, she set down her burdens within reach, blew her nose, rinsed her eyes with cold water…and avoided her reflection in the mirror.

She'd just said goodbye to Tricia Campbell.

Back out in the station, Kate Whitehead bought two tickets to San Francisco.

18

The silence in the house mocked him.

Attacking the emptiness with all the pent-up energy threatening to explode inside him, Scott dismantled the computer system in his bedroom, moving it—with Dog trotting at his heels, going after the cords—into the vacated spare bedroom. After a couple of trips out to the mall for a desk and fancy chair, office supplies and a new phone, he had an office of which his businessman father would be proud.

And another hour to kill before he dared lie down on the couch in the living room. Exhausted though he was, he didn't feel tired enough to sleep.

Cleaning up a little pile Dog had left in the kitchen, he glanced at the phone.

He'd thought maybe she'd call.

Or maybe, Scott acknowledged, wearily dropping into the plush new chair he didn't need, he'd known she wouldn't but had hoped anyway. She'd be in San Francisco by now. With Carley Winchester? Safely ensconced in her house?

Or alone?

Dog pulled at the hem of his jeans, growling.

With a haphazard punch of a finger, Scott flipped on the computer, just checking to make sure everything was reconnected and working, that he could still get online. Fixing a computer glitch could easily take up an hour or more. Or, if he was particularly lucky, it could take the entire night.

It booted up in record time. Or so it seemed. He'd been prepared to wait several minutes for the icons to pop up on the lower toolbar. Instead, he'd hardly blinked before the blue-wave wallpaper shone out at him. With one click, he was on the Internet.

And then off. It worked. He didn't much care at the moment what was going on in the rest of the world. He was too busy trying to make sense of his own.

When Dog started to whine, he picked up the puppy, held him in his lap, one hand haphazardly scratching his ears.

It breaks my heart to think of you living this way for the rest of your life.

He rearranged his desktop icons. Money management on the right. Internet on the left.

When are you going to quit punishing yourself? When is your sentence over?

Solitaire on the left. E-mail on the right.

Why do you think you're still alone?

Word processing on the...

Damn, he'd been too heavy on the forefinger, double clicked instead of highlighting and dragging. He waited for the program to finish opening so he could close it and wondered, a bit whimsically, if that was what his life was about: opening things just so he could close them again. Drawers, for instance. Doors. Relationships.

A white screen appeared with blinking cursor. And off to the left, in a side box, a list of recently open documents. *Taylor/Scott* was the first title on the list.

Slowly moving the mouse, he got closer to that highlighted listing. And eventually clicked on it. How could he be eavesdropping, trespassing, when he owned the computer and had authorized no one else to use it?

It took only seconds for the letter to come up.

But it changed something inside Scott forever.

To Whom It May Concern:

I, Kate Whitehead, being of sound mind and body, do hereby state my intent regarding my son, Taylor Campbell Whitehead in the event that I am no longer alive to care for him. I ask that the court appoint Scott McCall, of 624 Ivy Street, San Diego, California, as his legal guardian and caregiver and any monies belonging to me upon my death or accrued thereafter be kept in Mr. McCall's care for Taylor's use, the balance of which is to be conveyed upon him on his twenty-first birthday...

* * *

"Oh, my God! Kate?" Impeccably dressed as usual, Carley Winchester stumbled and almost fell as she climbed out of her Mercedes in the parking circle behind her San Francisco home. It was midmorning on Saturday.

She grabbed the doorjamb and hung on. "Is that *you?*"

Kate nodded, hugged Taylor close and tried not to cry. She'd meant to call. To warn Leah's sister that a ghost was about to appear in her life. But, in the end, not sure that Carley's phone wasn't tapped, she'd decided to wait out back at her friend's house instead. Carley had a habit of parking in the circle rather than pulling into the garage. Something her husband, concerned about her safety, had nagged her about for years. She'd always insisted that she couldn't live if she had to be afraid of her own backyard.

"I hoped you still had your Saturday-morning breakfast at the club."

Kate was referring to a standing engagement with a book discussion group, comprising mainly wealthy professional women.

"Oh, my God." Carley's knuckles, still clutching the doorjamb, were white. Her pale peach suit appeared vibrant against her washed-out skin as she stared at Kate.

"I'm sorry," Kate said, running a hand over the back of Taylor's head as the little boy laid it against her shoulder. He was still so shy with strangers. "I wanted to talk to you before anyone else discovers me. I've been following everything and knew I had to come back, but I have no idea what to do next."

"Kate?" Carley's voice squeaked again, her perfectly outlined lips trembling. One shoulder-length black curl had fallen onto her cheek.

Too weary to be self-conscious of the wrinkled jeans and shirt she'd spent the night in, Kate nodded again. Her shoulders and neck ached. She'd been lugging the two bags of belongings she'd hidden behind Carley's garage, as well as her son, for the hour it took her to walk to her friend's from the bus station. And then holding Taylor for the additional hour they'd had to wait for Carley's return.

"I can't believe it!" Falling away from the door, Carley launched herself at Kate, crying, hanging on to her neck, squeezing so hard Taylor started to kick. Kate didn't want Carley to let her go, the arms of friendship grounding her in a way she hadn't expected.

"I missed you," she whispered, drenching Carley's neck with her tears. "I missed everyone, so much."

"Mama!" Taylor squealed in a half cry, pushing against Carley—and against Kate. After a night of sleeping at the bus station he wasn't at his best.

With tears still streaming down her face, Carley backed up, stared at the baby. "He's yours?" she asked softly.

Kate gave a shaky nod. "His name's Taylor."

Dark eyes glancing from the baby to her, Carley smiled and sobbed at the same time. "He's beautiful…."

* * *

"I can't believe she's gone," Kate said softly, ignoring the cup of coffee in front of her on Carley's kitchen table. The Winchesters' housekeeper didn't work weekends and Carley's husband was out on the golf course for several more hours. Taylor, who'd finally dropped off into a restless sleep, was on a comforter spread on the floor in the next room.

Carley's dark eyes filled with tears again. "It's been over a month, but I can't believe it, either. She was so vibrant, you know?"

Kate did know. She, more than anyone, had known Leah Montgomery. "How am I going to live without her?" she whispered now, less sure of herself than she'd ever been.

One perfectly manicured hand, French-tipped natural nails fashionably long, covered Kate's. She'd forgotten how soft a woman's skin could be with regular care and lotions and spoiling. "We're going to be here for each other, that's how," Carley said.

And for the first time since she'd left home, Kate experienced a moment of complete peace.

"You're an amazing woman, Kate Whitehead," Carley said an hour later, having asked question after question about Kate's life in San Diego.

"Hardly," Kate said, grimacing. She lifted a hand to her ponytail, flipped it and let it go. "Look at me! My hair has no style and is full of dead ends, my hands are chapped and rough, my nails as short as a man's, from too much dishwater, too much stress and too many baby baths—and no manicures. I don't own a single outfit I'd feel comfortable being seen in…."

"You've lost weight." Carley got up from the table, peeked in on Taylor who, now that he was finally sound asleep hadn't budged, and moved over to the counter.

"I could afford to leave a few pounds behind."

"You could not," Carley said, returning to the table with fresh cups of coffee, to go with the coffee cake she'd cut and served half an hour before. Neither of them were touching either the coffee or the cake. "You always had the most perfect figure of any of us. Now you're just plain skinny. But we'll take care of that. Here—" she pushed a plate toward Kate "—have some cake."

Because she knew better than to argue with Carley when she got that tone, she helped herself to a forkful of cake. Took a bite. It was moist. Delicious. And it almost choked her.

She looked around the familiar kitchen, shaking her head. "I recognize all of this, and yet it's like I've never been here before. Like I saw it all on TV or in my imagination."

"I'm just glad you're back," Carley said, her voice catching again. "It's more than a dream come true. If only Leah…"

"I know," Kate said. And then there was nothing more to say.

* * *

"So now what?" Kate shifted on the soft suede couch, her knees to her chest as she watched her son playing with his plastic building blocks. She'd pulled them out of one of the bags she'd collected from behind the garage and now they were scattered across the Aubusson rug that covered the hickory-wood floor in Carley's family room. A state-of-the-art surround-sound entertainment center with a sixty-four-inch television set softly relayed the voices and pictures of Taylor's beloved Blue.

"After we get you into the shower, you mean?" Carley asked with a tender grin.

"I'll need to borrow some clothes until I can get hold of some money and buy some stuff."

She'd returned from the dead, had a mother to contact, a husband who'd threatened to kill her, a court system to answer to—and the thought of showering seemed overwhelming.

Carley nodded. "I've already thought of that," she said, kicking off peach pumps before stretching out on the couch, her toes barely touching Kate's calf.

Concentrating on that brief pressure, a tangible connection to reality, calmed the panic in Kate's stomach— even if only for a moment.

"You've easily lost a dress size," she continued, "but I've got a couple of suits that should fit you. Money won't be an issue. You'll stay here and I'll get you some cash...."

"I have a few hundred on me, but that wouldn't buy even one outfit Kate Whitehead might wear. And I have no idea how to access my own money here." The stomachache was back in full force.

Carley frowned. "I imagine they'll check dental records or something to establish your identity, and then it's probably just a matter of paperwork to get you a new driver's license, reissue credit cards, get you a way to access your joint accounts for cash."

She didn't want to access accounts with Thomas's name on them. But the money was half hers. Taylor toddled over, threw a yellow plastic square in her lap and moved back to his circle of toys, sitting down with a plop, his gaze focused on the huge Blue in front of him.

"Does it work that way?" Kate asked Carley, afraid for her son. And for herself. There was so much to think about. "I mean, is there a statute of limitations on someone's right to reclaim her life? Once I was declared dead, everything that was mine became Thomas's, didn't it? He could have remarried—"

Carley shook her head. "You were never declared dead."

"What?" Kate sat up so fast she saw stars. "How can Thomas be charged with my murder if I'm not declared dead?"

Carley's panty hose rasped as she rubbed her feet back and forth against each other. "I asked the same thing when I found out," Carley said, her eyes serious. "People might start to believe I'm as crazy as the press says I am if they found out how obsessed I've been with this whole thing," she admitted. "But I knew in my gut that Thomas killed my sister, and I haven't been able to think of anything but you and him and Leah ever since."

"You're not obsessed, Carl," Kate said smiling softly at her best friend's younger sister. "You're you, and thank God for that."

Carley nodded, her eyes softening.

"And you're certain Benny's behind you?" She asked the question she was almost afraid to ask. "He'll probably lose any further chance for political success in this state…."

"Benny's an honorable man, Kate." She smiled. "I know that's rare in our circle, but he really is. He'd go after Whitehead himself if he thought he had a leg to stand on."

In that next second, as she spoke of Thomas Whitehead, the detached veneer returned to Carley's demeanor—a trick Kate had watched Carley learn long before high school. She'd always considered it the result of a young Carley's desperate need to contain the natural intensity that was so unacceptable to her parents. Right now, she had a feeling it might be the only thing that would get either of them through this.

"In the case of a missing person, there has to be a motion made in civil court by a family member in order for that person to be declared dead."

Her face felt cool, as though a breeze were blowing in the white space surrounding her. "So how can they charge him with my murder?"

"That's a criminal court issue. Apparently a jury can listen to the evidence and decide you're dead, even if a civil court never finds you so."

"So I can be dead and alive at the same time."

"Yep."

"He can go to prison for my murder, but not spend my assets."

"Exactly."

Life was surreal. Twisting in so many directions she couldn't separate right from wrong. And then something else hit.

"Thomas didn't have me declared dead."

"Right."

"He never planned to marry Leah."

"It looks that way. He certainly couldn't have been planning to do it anytime soon, because until he files to have you declared dead, he's still a married man."

Shivering, Kate hugged her knees back to her chest. "So *why* didn't he have me declared dead?" she wondered half out-loud. "It's not like he needs my half of the estate, but it's not a small amount of money, either."

Carley tilted her head, eyes narrowed. "He claims— this is what I've been told by Amy Black, chief counsel for the prosecution—that he loved you so much he couldn't bear to give up hope that you'd be found…and able to take your rightful place as his wife. Just the way you'd want to."

Kate almost threw up. And then started to shake. All she could see was a red haze. She couldn't do it. Couldn't walk back into that insidious life of manipulation and control, his diabolical use of tenderness to soften his prey for the kill.

Because Thomas had the one thing that could tip the scales in his favor. The perception of honesty. In everything he said, there was *some* truth.

"Hey." Carley's hand was on her wrist, gently tugging. "It's okay. You can't—and won't—go back to him."

Kate could hear her words clearly, although they sounded as if they came from a great distance. It was the fervent support shining from Carley's dark eyes that reconnected her to the world. She listened to the cheerful and unnaturally high-pitched voices coming from the television set several yards away, watched her son happily trying to force a truck into a blue box half its size. And she thanked her best friend's sister for sending her strength where hers had failed.

"What *is* true?" she whispered.

"In the state of California, he could've been charged with your death even without a body if there'd been reasonable cause. His claims of undying love went a long way toward protecting him against that. He sure as hell wasn't going to rock the boat by having you declared dead," she said urgently. "It was all part of the act."

Yes, and that was what she had to remember every second of every day from now on. With Thomas, it was *always* part of the act.

"And…" Carley added, her glance sympathetic "…in

his own twisted way, Thomas does love you. As much as he can love anyone."

"Love to him is control," Kate said in a low voice.

"I know." Carley paused, squeezed Kate's hand. "But you broke away from all that, and you aren't going back." She said the words with such certainty Kate had to believe them. "In the meantime, the fact that he couldn't have you declared dead prevented him from stealing your life out from under you."

Yeah. Kate wanted to laugh at the irony of it all, but couldn't find any humor. Thomas had already stolen her life. Twice now.

A chord of fear chased through her again, leaving her weak. "What life is that?" she asked. Shook her head. "I can't get a grip on who might be living that life," she admitted, "or what it's going to look like."

Had she traveled so far, maintained her composure for so long, only to lose control now, when it was all finally coming to an end?

"Oh, sweetie, come here." Carley leaned over and pulled Kate close in a sisterly embrace. "It's all going to be okay," she half crooned, and while Kate knew her friend couldn't have any idea what she was talking about, she succumbed to the comfort she was offering. "You're worn out, and you're finally in a place you can relax your guard, and that's good. But don't worry, you're still you and you're going to be just fine."

"I don't know who that is," she mumbled against Carley's shoulder.

"You're a world-class fashion designer who'll be sought after just as zealously in a few months as you were two years ago. You'll buy yourself a beautiful new house—anyplace you want—and a new car, a few new pieces of plastic that'll get you in anywhere you want to go, enough clothes to tide you over until you have employees eagerly sewing up your newest collection…"

Kate slowly relaxed as Carley wove her fantasy. There was so much ground to traverse between where she was right then, destitute and unkempt on Carley's couch, and the woman her friend was describing. So many problems Carley casually forgot to mention. Still, this vision of herself was a diversion she couldn't quite turn away from.

"You're going to join the new mothers' group at the club, be inundated with suitors and invitations and…"

Scott. Her heart fell as a quick pain shot through her. She didn't want suitors. And Scott would never fit into this fantasy.

"But first," Carley said, sitting up, as though she knew she'd just lost Kate's attention, "we have some business to take care of."

Kate nodded. She moved through life one day at a time. The past two years had taught her that very valuable lesson. She couldn't forget it. Couldn't ignore the value gained from these lost years.

Or was it that she couldn't let go of two years that might've been the best she'd ever live?

* * *

"I'm going to suggest we keep your reappearance quiet for as long as we can," Carley said several minutes later. The women were once again on the couch. A new video of *Blue's Clues* episodes played in front of them, already entertaining the freshly diapered toddler who was half gumming, half chewing a cookie.

"I agree," Kate smiled sadly at her son as he swayed back and forth to the Blue theme song, his little bottom thick with diaper and overalls. "For his sake if nothing else. I don't want anyone near him."

Especially not his father.

"We won't be able to avoid the press forever," Carley warned. "Nor do I think we want to. We're fighting a very powerful man, here, as you well know. It's only because I went public that I've been heard at all."

"I understand." She'd known what she was getting into. She glanced at her son. "I just want to keep him out of things as much as possible. I'd also like the prosecutor's office to know about my reappearance before the defense does."

"Which is why I suggested we keep things quiet for now." Carley shot her an ironic grin. "It just means we're going to have to do something about your hair and nails ourselves."

Kate was almost comforted by the thought of living, even in this small way, the ordinary life she'd just left behind. She flipped her ponytail. "I think I want to keep it long, anyway."

"It'll be beautiful." Carley's smile touched the coldest places inside her. "With some wave and curls, you'll be rivaling Miss America again."

As if she ever had.

"I'll bet you never thought all those hours of begging you guys to let me do your hair would pay off, huh?" Carley's grin grew.

Kate meant to smile back. But her tears got in the way.

19

"I'm done." Kate set the pen down on the table with an aching hand, pushing the legal pad across the long Formica-topped wooden table. Along with several chairs, that table was the only furniture in the second-floor examination room at the San Francisco downtown precinct.

"It's all here?" Amy Black's gray hair was falling out of the neat twist she'd worn several hours before.

Kate nodded, still not used to the feel of curls around the sides of her face and neck. She wasn't quite used to the sensation of silk against her skin, either, though she'd designed the navy suit and cream blouse Carley had pulled from the back of her closet. "From the time I abandoned the car outside my home and walked to the bus station nearly two years ago, until Mrs. Winchester drove me to your door this afternoon," she confirmed.

They were alone at the moment, but Kate still couldn't relax. Detectives Gregory and Stanton had left to follow up on the results of the dental exam they'd ordered a couple of hours before, intending to hold her there until they'd confirmed she was the woman she claimed to be.

David Holm, Ms. Black's younger and more cynical partner, was out getting dinner for them. She hoped it wasn't Chinese. She didn't think she could handle the spices. Or the chopsticks. Or those cookies that told fortunes.

"Where did you say your son was?" Amy asked, her eyes kind behind the large lenses.

"I don't know." And even though that had been her choice, the fact was eating away at her. But she trusted Carley a whole lot more than she trusted the San Francisco police. "Somewhere safe." Carley had taken him to a cabin that belonged to a friend of a friend of a friend someplace outside San Francisco. She had a cell number to reach her, but that was all.

Amy nodded. "Probably not a bad idea."

Kate had no idea whether Thomas knew that she was back—she hadn't been out of that dirty gray-walled room in hours. But she knew for sure that he wasn't going to take the news gently.

"I'm prepared to bring my son in for DNA testing," she said now, keeping her wits about her through sheer force of will—and almost constant thoughts of Taylor and Carley out there waiting for her.

She'd had to break down and think of Scott more than once, as well, but no one need ever know that.

"I don't think that'll be necessary," Amy said now, frowning. "Once your identity has been confirmed, the state will be dropping the charges against your husband. There'll be no reason for us to confirm whether or not he's your son's father."

She stared at the older woman. "He is."

Ms. Black shrugged. "It's irrelevant."

Kate stared. "No, it's not! I'm not dead, but Leah is. Thomas is claiming he couldn't possibly have fathered her child. Taylor's DNA can prove that he's lying. He *is* capable of fathering children."

Amy Black didn't respond, other than through her sympathetic expression.

Something wasn't right. Kate's heart stopped and then jumped inside her chest, beating so hard, so fast, she could feel its pressure when she dragged in air.

"What?" Kate asked.

Amy shook her head. Raised her hands and let them fall to the table.

"Tell me."

"There's nothing to tell."

She'd spent the better part of a day with this woman, some of the most painful and difficult moments she'd ever endured. That had to count for something. "Please, Amy, what is it that you aren't telling me?"

The woman leaned forward. "The state's case against your husband in the murder of Leah Montgomery was based largely on the patterns set by the dual disappearances. Two women, best friends, both disappearing while claiming pregnancy by the same man…"

She was burning, sweating, from the inside out. "Thomas killed Leah."

Amy's smile, while filled with empathy, was no comfort as she shook her head. "His alibi checked out."

"So someone's lying. We know she was pushed off that cliff!"

"Yes, but—"

"No one knew about that cliff except Thomas and Carley."

Carley! Oh, my God. Taylor was with Carley! Lurching up, hardly able to see the door through the red fog in front of her eyes, Kate bumped her knee, catching her ankle on the chair Detective Gregory had vacated half an hour before, and still tore for the only way out.

"Mrs. Whitehead!" Amy Black was there, a firm hand on her arm. Kate flung her arm frantically, trying to get free.

"Mrs. Whitehead…Kate…"

Ms. Black held both her arms. Kate heard a scream, an animalistic cry. Felt the raw burn in her throat. And pulled for all she was worth.

"Hey…" Amy Black's arm was around her—at least she thought the arm belonged to Amy. "It's okay." The woman's voice had taken on the tone of an elder speaking with a very small child. Ordinarily such a tone would have sent Kate farther away. This time it called her back.

"It's not okay!" She shook her head, focusing for all she was worth on the other woman's gaze. "If Carley killed Leah..."

"She didn't!" Ms. Black said emphatically, then stopped and seemed to make some kind of decision. "Sit," she said more firmly, indicating the chair Kate had abandoned.

"You're sure?" Kate stood, still poised for flight.

"Positive."

Her breathing slowed. The frantic tensing of muscle and nerve began to lessen. And she saw herself from afar, saw that she was so completely distraught and at her emotional limit that she'd actually, for one moment, doubted Carley. Of all people.

"How can you be so sure?" It was no longer a question about Carley, but about the detective's confidence.

"Because—although this isn't information we're ready to divulge yet—we just found out who did."

Kate fell to the chair. Stunned. What had she just done? How could she possibly have thought Carley was capable of murder? Had her faith in humanity dwindled so far?

"Who did it?" she asked now, watching the prosecutor from a place of quiet detachment. Emotions still simmered inside her; she could sense them, feel them there. And was thankful for the rational stillness that had settled over her, due mostly to the older woman's calm certainty.

After watching her for several more seconds, Amy

Black took the chair next to Kate, between Kate and the door. "You aren't going to like what I have to say," she said, eyes narrowed as she studied Kate. She sat sideways in the chair, her knees almost touching Kate's thigh, her body a solid wall beside her.

"Thomas did it," Kate said.

Amy neither confirmed nor denied the statement.

"Walter Mavis came to us late yesterday," she said, instead, seemingly out of the blue. "He'd seen the article about the results of Ms. Montgomery's autopsy."

Feeling as though a shield of see-through cotton had fallen around her Kate sat quietly, nodded. She had no thoughts, no judgments. Or even suppositions. She just listened.

"He said he might be able to tell us something that could help us. He agreed to testify if we'd cut a deal with him."

Things like that happened. On television. In the news.

"His testimony in exchange for the state's agreement not to prosecute," Black continued.

Walter was a sweet old guy. She could see the value of that deal. But why would anyone want to prosecute him? Even if the hermit *had* spied on her and on Leah. He was the most harmless creature she'd ever met, carefully picking up the spiders that entered his home and taking them outside.

"He must've seen who went up there," she said. And it made sense that he'd tell the police.

"He did it."

* * *

Kate wondered how many times a person could be hit and remain conscious. Too many. Walter had pushed Leah? It wasn't possible. Didn't make sense.

"No," she said over and over. She just couldn't accept that. It was too much. "He was our friend…."

"He was an alcoholic who had to have his alcohol. Thomas paid his liquor store tabs."

"He killed her for a bottle of whiskey?"

She had to lie down. Sleep until she had the energy to go on. Escape. But then the nightmares would start. She wasn't sure which would be worse.

"He admitted to pushing her over the cliff. He said he'd done it because Thomas threatened to expose him if he didn't."

"Expose him for what?"

"Obstructing justice in the investigation of your disappearance. He had the old man convinced he'd go to jail for keeping quiet about the fact that you visited Miner's Mountain the day you disappeared."

"And Mavis bought that?"

"You said yourself how secluded the old man is. He's never seen a television show in his life, which is unfortunately how most people gain their legal knowledge. And he panicked at the thought of being locked up."

It was typical Thomas, preying on a person's weaknesses as a means of control.

"Apparently, after pushing Ms. Montgomery, he

couldn't live with himself," Amy continued. "Luckily for him, Mavis talked to a guy where he gets his liquor who told him to call an attorney before he came here. The guy gave him Dan Hillier's name. Hillier showed him the article about the autopsy results."

"His attorney cut the deal," Kate said, almost thankful for the diversion of this little side story, as though its impact wasn't changing her life.

"Dan Hillier knew we'd want Thomas Whitehead badly enough to give Mavis a buy." The disgust tingeing Ms. Black's voice brought Kate closer to the life she was trying to avoid.

"So you've got Thomas," she said, remembering how the woman had implied earlier that the state had nothing on him. When, in fact, she'd merely been telling her why the state didn't need a sample of Taylor's DNA….

"No, unfortunately, we don't," she said.

"Sure you do." Kate nodded, even that slight movement making her dizzy. "Hiring someone to kill another person is the same as killing that person yourself…."

Amy sighed heavily. "We made the deal last night and spent the morning investigating Mavis, trying to build our case. Now that we know what we've got, we also know the defense has enough evidence to discredit Mavis's testimony from here to New York."

Kate felt the blood drain from her face.

"He's an alcoholic. He eats weeds, thinks crickets are

members of his family. At one point he called you his daughter."

He'd told her if he'd ever had a daughter, he'd have wanted her to be like Kate. She'd said she'd much rather have had him for a father…

"The onus is on us to prove beyond reasonable doubt that Thomas Whitehead hired the hermit to kill Leah, and with Mavis's testimony as our only real evidence, we don't have a hope in hell of convincing a jury."

The prosecution had been planning to use Kate's death, the pattern of her and Leah's disappearances, as evidence, thinking that, with Mavis's testimony, even discredited, that would be enough.

"You believe Mavis murdered Leah, though," Kate said.

Amy nodded. "The handprints on Leah's back measured the same size as Mavis's. He said she scratched him, grasping for his arm to save herself as she went off the cliff, showed us the scar. And forensics found his DNA under her fingernails. Thomas withheld liquor money and Mavis was in bad shape, mentally and physically. He wasn't himself. So when Thomas threatened to expose him, he became convinced he'd go to jail for keeping quiet after you disappeared. And he believed it when Thomas said no one would ever find out about Leah. No one knew about him or the cliff, and he'd seen how easily doubts about Thomas were dismissed in connection with your disappearance."

The lump in her chest constricted her breathing. She

could imagine Leah, knowing she was going to die, grabbing for the old man who'd been like a father to them....

"And now, because the state made a deal, he just walks," she said when she could think clearly enough to speak.

She sensed more than saw Amy Black's nod. "In this case, the deal was made pursuant to the witness's *agreement* to testify in court, not on his actually having done so. I've wanted Whitehead for a long time," the woman went on. "Giving up Mavis seemed like a small thing. The man lives on a mountain. He's no danger to society."

"What about Leah's blood on Thomas's car seat? It's clear now he was lying about that, since she obviously wasn't having her period."

Amy Black's face was impassive. "Maybe she scratched herself."

"Maybe he hit her."

"I'm inclined to agree with you but since there's no evidence, my opinion is worth nothing. She had a massage that afternoon, and apparently no one noticed anything out of the ordinary."

Kate welcomed the numbness that spread through her. If only it could last until she'd taken her last breath on this earth.

"It would've been better if I'd stayed away," she said, almost to herself, leaning on the table with both forearms. "Without me, you could have convicted Thomas...."

Amy Black's gaze was open, sincere. "We might've sent him to his death for murders he didn't commit."

A burst of anger shot through Kate, fierce, bitter. She sat back sharply. "So instead he walks—despite the murders he hired someone to commit?"

Black shrugged.

"Wait a minute!" Kate suddenly said. "We can still get him," she said. "If I get on the stand, testify to his abuse." The very idea of finally having her say, coming clean, getting the shameful secret out into the light gave her momentum. "The jury will see his violent nature, the DNA test will prove he's a liar, and then, with Mavis's testimony added to the fact that only a handful of people even knew about that cliff…"

Amy Black shook her head and Kate wanted to hit her. Hit something. She'd seen a prosecution similar to what she was describing on television once. It could work….

"What you're describing is called character evidence, and that's not an element of the offense with which Mr. Whitehead's been charged. Even if we tried, the defense would bring forth a motion to disallow it after pretrial, where we have to disclose our evidence." She spoke slowly, like a teacher to a child. Kate hated her more with every word.

Hated how powerless Amy Black's words were making her feel. How helpless.

And hopeless.

"Any judge would rule that evidence inadmissible," the prosecutor continued anyway. And in the city of San Francisco, hell, the whole state of California, they wouldn't be dealing with *any* judge. They'd be dealing with someone Thomas most likely knew, someone Thomas had served in some capacity.

Arms back on the table, Kate leaned forward, unable to hold herself upright any longer, but turned her head sideways to look at the older woman. "So what you're telling me is that we all know Thomas is guilty of a Murder One felony for conspiracy to murder and because we don't have enough irrefutable proof, he's going to walk. Just as he has with every other wrong he's committed in his life."

"We have a fiduciary duty to the people of California," Black said, her words mere background for the darkness that was overcoming Kate. "It costs hundreds of thousands of dollars to go to trial. We can't spend that money unless we have reason to believe we can win…."

She couldn't think of a thing to say. Yet she couldn't just sit there and take it, either. "But…"

"After Mavis's testimony and now with your reappearance, which destroys our ability to show there's a pattern, we have *nothing*," Amy Black said, more strongly now. "No motive, no pattern, no previously questionable behavior. And the defense has plenty—including a so-called accomplice who's got no credibility at all. An alibi. They have a defendant whose charitable heart is known far and wide. The fact that the state was ready to put the man to death for a murder we have living proof he did not commit..."

It was as she'd said. Her return had bought Thomas his freedom.

She spent another hour there before she was free to go. Dinner had come and gone. The sun had come and gone. All that was left was darkness.

Her dental records had proven her identity. First thing Monday morning, when banks and the drivers' license bureau opened, she'd have her life back. Such as it would be. For as long as it would be.

"Do you have a place to stay tonight?" Amy Black asked quietly as everyone packed up pens and pads preparing to leave.

She nodded. Somehow or other, she was going to get out to the cabin where her son would undoubtedly be asleep. She'd never spent the night apart from him and now wasn't a good time to start. For either of them.

The rest of the world might underestimate Thomas Whitehead, but she did not. Once it was known she was back, that she was alive, she would never be free of him. She'd either play by his rules or end up rooming with Leah.

If she didn't have Taylor to consider, the latter would be her choice. She'd already wasted too many years in Thomas's power. It was a no-win situation.

"Mrs. Whitehead." She turned as David Holm, prosecuting attorney and partner to Amy Black, called her name by the door. His worn leather satchel was tucked beneath his arm.

Kate's feet hurt in Carley's pumps. Her legs ached from too much sitting and too little rest. And her head felt as though it was on the verge of exploding. Still, she tried to find a polite smile. "Yes?"

"There's someone here who's very anxious to see you," he said. Exhausted as she was, she couldn't tell whether his smile was genuine or completely put on, but she experienced a moment's relief.

Her mother. They'd called her mother for her. She'd been waiting to find out what would be required of her before contacting her mother, so she'd have some answers with which to reassure the vulnerable older woman.

With the first real smile she'd managed in many hours, Kate glanced behind the attorney to the hallway beyond.

The room went cold. Her smile faded away.

It couldn't be. They wouldn't do this. Not here. Not like this. Not yet.

Kate leaned one fist on the table beside her as her knees began to shake.

"Hello, my love. Thank God it's really you."

Thomas's voice cracked, his eyes filled with tears as, moving past Holm, he came into the room and took her into his arms, lifting her off the ground with the strength of his embrace.

20

"You have no idea how glad I am to see you." Thomas's fervent words, whispered just above her ear, sent chills through Kate's body. Trapped in his grip, she struggled to breathe, wondering if she was suffocating because he was holding her too tightly. Or if, perhaps, his suffocation of her was less a physical thing, and she was only now starting to manifest the effects of inner death.

Either way, she gasped for air.

"It's okay, baby, don't cry," Thomas crooned softly, molding her body against his. There was no other sound in the room but Thomas's voice, his breath in her ear. Had everyone else left? Was she alone with him?

She couldn't open her eyes to find out. Was too light-headed.

"Shhh, I know you've been through a lot, but I'm here now. Right here."

I'm not crying. She tried to say the words. *I'm too dead inside to cry. Numb.* The muscles in her chest ached as she forced them to work, to get in even a small bit of air.

Something dripped down her neck. And then again. "We'll get through this." He shuddered against her. "I know we will."

Yes. They would get through this. Didn't he always? She got in another small gulp of air.

"Oh, my love, you feel so good." While he still held her close, one hand ran up and down her back, between her shoulder blades, the small of her back, over her buttocks. "So damn good."

There was something laughable about that—saying this when she was slowly dying. She'd never felt worse in her life.

He sniffled, and only then did Kate realize that the wetness on her skin was his tears. She sucked in another breath.

A vision of Leah, her usually smiling face stern, floated behind her closed lids. She'd looked that way when Kate had come to her, beaten and bruised by her father, but refusing to tell anyone what had happened. Leah had begged her to turn him in. Kate had known her mother would pay the price if she did.

Thomas lifted his head. She felt the movement, but wouldn't look. He could stare at her if he liked, but she wouldn't let him in. She needed to sleep.

"They've left us alone," he said. "I don't know what you did with the kid, gave him up for adoption, whatever, but I want you to know I forgive you for all that."

Her head was thick and it felt as though someone had filled it with cotton. But the cotton, while soft and white, was heavy, too.

"Let's get out of here, honey," he said.

Had she finally escaped reality, only to end up living in a hell in her own mind? She couldn't be in Thomas's arms, listening to him speak as though nothing had happened between them but a cruel twist of fate, an accident, a mistake beyond his control and hers. Listening to him so blithely dismiss his son, *her* son. The best part of her.

"Ah, baby, you haven't said a word." His voice was so soft, so loving, she shivered. "What have they done to you?"

Leah's face swam back and forth before her eyes. Leah's expression remained stern, but it was filled with the light of knowing. They were twenty-one. Kate had just been offered her first chance to have her designs shown. She'd lacked confidence, hadn't thought she was ready. Somehow Leah had found the spark of strength and drive inside Kate and ignited it.

Leah believed in her.

Thomas's grip changed. The arm around her waist moved lower, behind her knees, lifting her until she was cradled like a baby in his arms. Her eyes flew open as he started to walk with her. Outside the door, lining the hall, was a row of faces. Some she recognized, most she didn't. With one quick frantic spin, she sought Amy Black. Couldn't find her.

These were all Thomas's friends. Kate quickly shut

her eyes and let the man who'd raped and beaten her carry her gently out into the night.

He was glad he'd driven himself. Glancing at the woman passed out beside him, Thomas Whitehead drove slowly through the relatively quiet San Francisco streets. He'd found a trial pack of a nighttime pain reliever in Kate's expensive leather purse and had, with the help of a rookie female officer at the door of the precinct, gotten one down her. From the little he'd heard, she'd been up for more than forty-eight hours. She'd sleep a while now.

And he had her all to himself, didn't have to keep up appearances with anyone, not even Sammie, his driver— the son of his father's driver. The boy he'd grown up with, played with like a brother, before he'd recognized the great gulf between him and the kid his age who played on the property of his home, but would never be like him.

Sammie had been with him since he'd graduated from college. Drove him anywhere, everywhere, without question. Thomas trusted him more than he trusted most people. But tonight he was tired. Tonight he was thankful.

Tonight he wanted to be completely alone with his wife.

She sighed and he looked over, pleased to see that she was still out. There'd be time enough for conversation later. Tonight she needed him.

He liked that. Always had.

Squinting against approaching headlights, he remembered back through the years of his marriage to

Kate. The good times. Choosing to ignore the bad. They were over. Behind them. She'd come home to help him. That was all that mattered. No matter what had gone before, in the end she'd saved him.

Blinking lights, yellow and red and blue, drew his attention to a marquee. Lonnie's Bar had dancing until two. Maybe another night when Kate felt better.

She wouldn't have come back during his darkest hour if she didn't love him. At least a little bit. She might not realize that yet, but he'd show her. She was an intelligent woman. She'd understand it eventually.

And in the meantime, he wasn't going to let her out of his sight.

San Francisco Gazette
Sunday, May 8, 2005
Page 1

Senator Exonerated.
Welcomes Home Wife Returned from the Dead

All criminal charges against Senator Thomas Whitehead were dropped yesterday when his missing wife appeared at a downtown precinct of the San Francisco Police department, proving that her husband could not possibly have killed her. Her return invalidates most of the circumstantial evidence showing the alleged pattern between Leah Montgomery's pregnancy and death and that of his wife. The state had planned to use this pattern to convict the senator for last month's murder of Montgomery. According to an unnamed source, there was a claim yesterday that Whitehead blackmailed Walter Mavis into pushing Montgomery off the cliff, but there was insufficient evidence to substantiate that. Mavis drinks heavily and apparently suffers from hallucinations.

The senator was joyful as he arrived at the police station just after 9:00 p.m. last evening to collect his wife. Little is known at this point about Mrs. Whitehead's whereabouts over the past two years, who she was with or how she was treated, nor is anything known about the child she'd been carrying when she disappeared. She was unconscious, sources say, from exhaustion and distress, as the senator lovingly carried her out to his waiting car shortly before ten o'clock. No doctors were called to the scene.

Senator Whitehead was not available for comment, but a spokesman who is close to the senator stated that the senator cried when he first heard the news about his wife's return and dropped everything to hurry to her side. When asked about the senator's thoughts on the Leah Montgomery issue, the source said that while Senator Whitehead was unaware of her pregnancy, he knew Ms. Montgomery to be a highly moral woman who would have been devastated at the public humiliation of an illegitimate child. According to this spokesman, who asked to remain unnamed, the senator also believes the bruised tissue on Ms. Montgomery's back resulted from her fall and that Ms. Montgomery might have taken her own life to protect the father of her baby from exposure, guessing that the man is both prominent and married. He didn't come forward with any suggestions as to who the father might be.

"Carley? Thomas Whitehead." Holding the phone to his ear, he stood in his office at the mansion that had been a wedding present to him and Kate from his parents. Looking out over the lush green grounds, interspersed with trees and colorful flower beds, he waited for the sun to rise. Sunday mornings had always been his favorite time of the week. This morning was particularly nice.

"Where is she? What have you done with her?"

He paused, bit back the instantaneous reply that rose to his lips. Counted flower beds. There were fifteen of them on this side of the house. Leah's sister was one of the few women he truly despised.

"I've done nothing with her," he said when he was calm again. "I love my wife. I've spent the night thanking God that she's back home with me, safe and sound."

"She's there? At your house?"

"It's her home," he reminded her. "She's upstairs sleeping."

Where he'd been until half an hour before. He'd come down to make coffee. And take care of this one pressing matter. He couldn't have a troubled bitch like Carley Winchester running amok with stories of Kate gone missing again.

"You're telling me Kate just showed up there last night and announced that she was staying?"

"No." There it was. The first streak of blinding light sparkling through the trees. Day had begun, and it was going to be a good one. "I went down to the station and we left together."

"She went with you willingly." It wasn't so much a question as a statement of disbelief.

"I certainly didn't carry her kicking and screaming out of the police station while a dozen police officers stood by and watched," he said with a hint of humor. "As a matter of fact, one of the female officers downstairs got her a cup of water as we were leaving so she could take an aspirin that was in her purse."

"That was a nighttime pain reliever!" Carley said. "It had a sleeping aid."

So Carley was closely enough involved with his wife to know about the contents of her handbag. He pinched the bridge of his nose.

"It was the only pain reliever in her purse," he said again. That was the point here. And hardly worth mentioning. "She had a headache."

"I don't know what you're up to, Whitehead, but if you hurt one hair on her head—"

"I've said it before, and I'll say it again, Mrs. Winchester. I love my wife. I'm thankful beyond comprehension that she's home and—"

"I'll just bet you are." The vituperative woman just wouldn't let up. "I just heard the radio news. You walked again, you bastard."

"Lovely conversation, Carley, and I'd be delighted to continue, but I have a wife who'll be waking up soon, and as you can imagine, I'm anxious to get back to her. I placed this call on her behalf so you wouldn't worry about her. I understand she was planning to stay at your place last night." He chose his words carefully, as always, speaking only truths. Selective truths. He hadn't been told where Kate planned to spend the night. But he knew her well enough to know that was where she'd run. He knew her well enough to know she wouldn't want to worry Carley.

"She asked you to call me?"

"How do you think I got your cell phone number?"

He couldn't lie. But that didn't mean he had to answer every question he was asked. The number had been scribbled on a scrap of paper in Kate's purse. There'd been very little else. Although he'd looked diligently, he hadn't found one piece of identifying information among his wife's things. Nothing to give him a clue about the missing two years of her life.

"Something stinks here, Whitehead. You just tell Kate I'm keeping Taylor safe until I hear from her personally."

The day darkened perceptibly.

"Taylor?"

"Just give her the message."

He wasn't going to be threatened. "I—"

Thomas stopped, anger surging through his chest when Carley Winchester hung up on him.

Taylor had to be the kid, goddammit. Thomas threw the phone, watching as it bounced off the leather couch and landed on the plush carpet of his office with barely a sound. Why hadn't someone at the station mentioned that she'd brought the kid back with her? He'd assumed she'd left the bastard behind. Another son of a bitch's kid. He'd assumed that since she'd come back, she'd seen the light—known how unfair it would be to ask him to raise her lover's son.

He'd assumed. Whitehead, Sr., had delighted in pointing out to him on numerous occasions that *assume* made an *ass* out of him. He'd heard that throughout his childhood, but apparently he hadn't learned it as well as he'd thought.

Half an hour later, Thomas sat still behind his desk, staring out at the morning.

The Winchester bitch had said she was keeping the kid—Taylor—safe. Which led to a fairly logical guess that Kate had left him in her care.

He ran through the months in his head. Adding, subtracting. He'd be nineteen months old now—this child of his wife's. Pain shot up into his shoulder. Loosening his death grip on the arms of his chair, Thomas slowly opened his aching hands, flexing them. Anger was good. It instilled enough strength to prompt action. But it had to be used properly, in the right measures at the right time.

He stood, stretching, letting his anger fuel a resurgence of passion as he thought of the beautiful woman sleeping upstairs. Now *wasn't* the time for anger. He was too close to the perfect life he'd scripted, worked for, deserved. He couldn't act out of turn. Besides, he reminded himself with a grin as he sprinted up the stairs. His wife was home.

The sheets were cool, smooth and soft against her bare legs. Kate stretched, wondering why she'd forgotten how good four-hundred-count cotton felt against naked skin. Turning over, she slid a hand under her pillow, wallowing in that state between sleep and wakefulness, enjoying a few minutes of utter relaxation. She'd slept well. Better than she'd slept in a long time.

The bed sagged behind her and a gentle male hand slipped under the covers, finding her thigh, drawing slowly up to her hip and then down again to her knee. Mmm. Scott. Delicious shivers followed that tender touch and she moaned softly, encouraging the hand to continue. It did. Rounding her bottom, sliding up her back, over to the side of her breast and then across to her other side.

She'd roll over in a minute, revealing her breasts to

his touch, but first she just wanted to lie there, enjoying the perfect moment. The hand seemed agreeable to her silent choices, moving over her back, down her bottom, around to the back of her leg.

And then the quality of its motion changed. A couple of fingers darted between her legs from behind, entering her quickly, and Kate recognized the touch instantly. Fully awake, she shot up so abruptly that her movement jerked the fingers painfully from her body.

"Don't you *dare* ever touch me like that again," she choked out, her long hair falling in her face as she clutched her husband's expensive sheets to her naked body.

"Kate, love…" he started, reaching gently to brush the hair from her face with the same hand that had just been inside her.

"Don't say the word 'love' to me." That tone of voice would have garnered her a slap in years gone by. At the moment, she didn't care if he beat her to death, she wasn't going to let him touch her that way again.

She'd learned what it was like to have her body loved since she'd last seen this man. It was something she'd never forget. A memory she didn't want diminished by settling for less. For *accepting* less.

Watching her with those all-seeing gray eyes, he nodded, propping himself up on a couple of pillows on the other side of the bed. The unusual retreat confused her.

"It's okay, honey, I understand. Men tend to believe

that physical love leads to the development of emotional bonds, while women need the emotional connection first."

What? Kate stared at him. She wanted to get out of the bed, had to use the bathroom, but didn't dare move for fear he'd grab hold of the sheet that was her only covering, leaving her completely exposed.

"How did I get here?"

How did I get naked? was the real question. It was one she couldn't ask. Because the answer was going to be more than she could bear.

Please, God, tell me he only undressed me. Only fondled me. She knew Thomas would absolutely have done that much, played with her breasts once he had them naked, teased the nipples to life, getting off on the proof that he could arouse her even during unconsciousness. She didn't want to know—ever—if he'd done more than that. The thought of Thomas mounting her unconscious body made her heart so sick she refused to consider it.

She was on the pill, thanks to the free program at the women's shelter where she'd first found a bed after abruptly leaving her life in San Francisco behind. There would be no consequences, no matter what he'd done. Assuming she got to Carley's today, where her pills were.

The thoughts took only seconds to chase across her mind. She stared at the devil who starred in so many of her nightmares. She had to remember the hard-won lessons of the past two years. She was strong. Capable. Intelligent and worthy of love.

"How did I get here?" she asked again, her voice more controlled.

"I brought you, of course. When they called me from the station, I went immediately to get you. You were overwrought, passing out from exhaustion. I carried you to the car, brought you home…and…put you to bed."

His eyes took on that seductively slumberous look she'd once loved and had grown to fear even more than she feared his anger. He'd touched her, the bastard.

"Where are my clothes?"

He pointed. "Over there."

All she saw "over there" was an empty love seat, where the chaise longue used to be. Okay, so she had to keep her wits about her. At least she'd slept. Her head was throbbing, but it wasn't pounding, wasn't obliterating every coherent thought. On the surface, he had the upper hand. She couldn't very well escape without clothes.

Not unless he made it a matter of life and death.

She glanced back at him, determined now to read him as he'd always read her, to engage in his mental battle and, for perhaps the first time, be a credible opponent. He was physically attractive, this demon she'd married. His hair, still naturally blond at forty, was thick and cut so that it looked sexy and windblown, even first thing in the morning. His shoulders were broad, the sandy hair on his chest adding to the youthful appearance he retained.

Her eyes moved lower and she wasn't surprised to see that he was as naked as she—and not the least bit concerned with modesty. His penis lay against the bed of hair spreading across his pelvis, hard and ready for the sex he'd tried to initiate.

She'd never been so repulsed in her life.

21

"I have to call Carley." Kate sat up straighter in Thomas's bed, clutching the sheet more tightly around her, thinking of her ally. She wasn't all alone this time around. Someone else knew that Thomas was deranged—evil. Somehow she had to get out of this house.

"Done."

"You called Carley." Why didn't that surprise her?

He nodded, a small grin softening his mouth. She'd once melted at that look, had pressed her lips eagerly against that mouth, as anxious as he for their tongues to meet, mingle, start the foreplay that would inevitably lead to his invasion of her body.

She'd given up expecting to enjoy the event years before. He'd always told her that her lack of pleasure had been her own fault. And what had she known? She'd been a virgin when she entered Thomas Whitehead's bed. He was the one who'd had all the experience.

"What did you tell her?"

Arms folded across his chest, he shrugged easily.

"That you were sleeping. That I was calling so she wouldn't worry. She'll expect you to phone her soon. We need to make arrangements to collect Taylor."

Her heart started to pound. Who'd told him her son's name? Or that Carley had him? Her son had not been mentioned, other than with Amy Black, when they'd discussed possible DNA samples. At Carley's insistence, she'd given her story only to Amy, who'd agreed to let Kate keep her son out of the fray for as long as she could.

What had Carley thought of her being here, sleeping in Thomas's bed? Did her friend know they were dropping all charges against him?

Thomas sat there with that smile on his face, looking like every girl's dream of a charming, kind, rich husband who wanted only to please the woman of his heart. And anyone who could see him now would fall for the act. He could commit murder and sit naked in his bed with his murdered lover's best friend and smile as if he didn't have a care in the world.

Collect Taylor? He'd said they were going to collect Taylor?

She couldn't do that. Even if it meant she never saw her beloved son again. She had to protect him from this maniac.

"Come on, baby, it's been two long years. What do you say we…uh…reunite, and then we'll handle everything else together…." He leaned over as he spoke, ran the back of his fingers over her nipple in a way he knew would get him the response he wanted. It hardened instantly.

Kate hated herself for that.

She let him play with the same breast that had fed their son all those months, wondering which would be worse—lying there, spreading her legs for Thomas; or risking his immediate wrath if she tried to reject him.

History pretty much told her she wouldn't succeed. She could take it gently, like she was doing now, not fighting him as his hand slid across to her other breast, teasing that nipple into a tautness that matched the one he'd started with. Or she could resist and take it hard, fighting him while he jerked her legs apart, pushed himself into her with one harsh thrust and cursed at her until she was raw and praying for his orgasm so it would all be over. But one way or another, she was going to have to take it if she hoped to get dressed.

With a soft tug of the sheet she was still holding, he silently demanded complete access to her breasts and Kate released it, watching as if from afar as his finger stroked the tip of one breast. He pressed his tongue against her, nipped tenderly while his hand played with her other breast.

She couldn't think. Couldn't remember. Falling back against the headboard, she lay there, propped up, an object for him to conquer. His mouth moved to her second breast and his hand slid lower, caressing her stomach, continuing down.

He was going to be dipping his fingers between her

legs momentarily, pushing against her inner thigh, demanding she spread her legs. And then it could be another hour before he spasmed inside her with his final orgasm. Thomas had an armory of creative ways to touch a woman, kiss her, enter her body.

"No, please." The whimper came from someplace deep inside her. He wouldn't care. Sometimes she'd wondered if Thomas got more personal pleasure out of her resistance than he did her compliance—even in the early days, when she'd been a willing participant in anything he'd suggest, pretending orgasm after orgasm in her attempt to be even half the woman her adored husband thought she was.

"What?"

Blinking, Kate came back to the present to see the fiend's soft blue gaze on her. Her nipple puckered anew as the room's cool air touched the wetness left by Thomas's mouth and tongue. His hand stilled on her crotch.

"What?" he asked again.

He knew damn well she didn't want what he was doing to her. She'd told him so many times in the past she'd been like a broken record.

"I asked you to stop."

He didn't say anything, just continued to peer up at her, his breath on her breast, his hand a pressure between her legs.

"I…we…have so much to discuss," she stammered. *We haven't even seen each other in two years, you bas-*

tard. I don't know you. I certainly don't love you. You don't own me. And I don't want your fucking body anywhere near mine. "I'm confused. A-a-and tired. I… can't…concentrate on…this…right now."

Bending to her breast, he licked her nipple once. Looked up at her. Licked it again. "Your body begs to differ with you."

"Thomas, cold air of any kind makes that happen. Whether I'm getting out of the shower, walking outside in the wintertime—" breastfeeding "—or having sex, it does that. It doesn't mean I want you to do this right now. I don't."

"You didn't object last night…."

Oh, God. Don't tell me I already have his sperm swarming around inside me. Normally she could tell and this morning she still felt—dry.

"I was asleep!"

"I mean before that, at the station." His eyes were wide, clear, as he stared at her. "When I walked into that interrogation room, you practically fell into my arms. And once you knew I was there, knew you were safe, you gave in to the exhaustion overwhelming you and left it up to me to get you home and into bed."

"Last night I was out of my mind with exhaustion, yes, but with confusion, disorientation and grief, as well. I'd just been through more than eight hours of questioning, hearing too many things I couldn't cope with. I—" She stopped. She'd told him more than she'd ever intended.

He knew the truth of their relationship. He *knew* why she'd run away. And Leah's death was proof that she'd had just cause. How could he possibly believe she'd fallen willingly into his arms the night before? He'd grabbed her in a way she couldn't have resisted without a lot of physical and mental effort. She'd been fresh out of both.

She'd never planned to leave that station with him. Still wasn't sure how that had happened.

"So what are you saying?" His eyes had narrowed.

Kate stiffened, prepared for the onslaught. But she was glad she'd spoken. She might not be able to prevent his invasion of her body—she could scream and no one would hear, try to get away and he'd catch her. But she didn't have to lay down her spirit for him to rape, too. She'd rather take his abuse fighting than lie there submissively. The physical pain would ease eventually. It always did. It was the mental and emotional anguish of submission that never seemed to heal. She'd learned that in the past two years.

"I'm not prepared to do this." *I don't love you! I despise your touch! I wish you were in hell which is where you take me every time you get near me!*

The pressure at her crotch deepened—and then vanished. Thomas pulled the sheet over her breasts, sat up. "Then we don't do it," he said, his tone as congenial as it had been the time his mother had tried to force a living-room couch on her that she'd abhorred and Thomas had supported her desire to refuse the gift.

Of course, he'd abhorred his mother, so it hadn't been any great sacrifice on his part.

Lifting the seat of the new bench at the bottom of the bed, he pulled out Carley's beautiful silk suit, wrinkled from the previous day's wear. "You can put this on until we have a chance to get your things out of storage."

Staring, mouth open, Kate said, "You stored my clothes?"

He stopped on his way to the bathroom. Turned to look at her. "I always hoped you'd come back."

When the door shut behind him, Kate quickly stood, pulling on the clothes so fast they tangled. She should feel relieved. Satisfied, if perhaps confused.

She should.

But gazing at that closed bathroom door, wondering what diabolical new tactic the man behind it had concocted, all Kate felt was sick.

As soon as she heard the shower, Kate went downstairs in the home she'd lived in for years, looked briefly for the purse she'd borrowed from Carley and, not finding it, walked out the front door empty-handed.

"Welcome home, Mrs. Winchester, ma'am." Sammie, her husband's chauffeur, appeared from the side of the house, almost as though the front door had somehow been rigged.

Don't let your imagination run away with you, Kate reminded herself. She had enough problems without seeing things that weren't there.

"Thank you, Sammie. It's good to see you." She'd always liked him, although she was under no illusions. Sammie was Thomas's man, through and through.

Not that she'd ever thought the chauffeur actually liked or even respected Thomas. He was one of the few who saw her husband for the cold calculating man he was. But Sammie received a large paycheck for his loyalty.

With a quick nod, she started down the walk.

Kate had often suspected the other man often laughed all the way to the bank.

"Can I drop you someplace?" He was her husband's age and, though his hair was mostly gray, he was in good physical shape. He stood on the cement directly in front of her.

"No, thanks," she said, squinting up at him as she stepped around him.

He was in front of her again. "Mr. Whitehead told me to make sure I took you wherever you wanted to go," he said. "You wouldn't want me to get into trouble with him, would you?"

Two years ago the plea would have worked. That was back when Kate took responsibility for her husband's abuse and had done whatever she could to protect others from it.

"I'd guess your orders were more like 'don't let her out of your sight,'" she said, walking on. "And no, I don't particularly care if he gets angry with you or anyone else. I'm a free woman and I choose to leave, now and on foot."

He was in front of her again, his hands out as though he needed to intercept her, but wasn't sure how. "Please, ma'am, you can go wherever you like, just let me take you. It's a mile walk into town from here."

"A five-mile walk is not unusual for me these days, Sammie," she said, smiling at him. She picked up her pace as she reached the front gate. "I'm going now," she added, opening the wrought-iron door on the right side of the sliding gate. "Tell Mr. Whitehead I'll be in touch."

"But—"

"You come near me, Sammie and I'm pressing charges." Her tone stopped him. Probably because he was so shocked to hear it coming from her.

Kate didn't much care why the chauffeur finally gave up. She just thanked God he had. She'd gained a lot of strength in the past two years, but coming home had thrown her back into the feelings and fears of the woman she'd been when she left. Confusing her. Scaring her. Weakening her. For the next hour, skating in and out between trees in the surrounding neighborhoods, traveling by backyards, snagging Carley's skirt as she climbed over a rock wall, Kate willed the shaking in her muscles to stop.

You don't have to worry, she kept telling herself, although the mantra didn't seem to be doing much good. She *didn't* have to worry. She wasn't going to fall prey to his abuse again. She had an edge this time.

She knew how to run. And she had a job to do.

There was a little boy who'd woken up this morning

without his mother's smile to greet him. She had to get to Taylor. She'd worry about everything else once she'd held her baby close and let him know that his world was safe.

It was after noon by the time Kate arrived, barefoot and blistered, at Carley's back door. She'd had to circle around the neighborhood and come in from the opposite direction when she'd noticed Sammie in a car she didn't recognize, parked in a driveway down the street.

Trembling, hungry and tired, she knocked on the door. *Please, someone be here.*

The door flew open immediately, as though the occupant had been on the other side waiting for her.

"Kate! Thank God you're here! Come in."

Benny Winchester, a short balding man with glasses and the readiest smile she'd ever seen, stepped aside and then, after closing the door behind her, took her into his arms for a very welcome hug.

"Carley's been frantic to hear from you," he said a couple of seconds later as he stood back, looking her up and down. He was dressed just as she'd always seen him, in dark casual slacks, a button-down shirt with the sleeves rolled up his muscled forearms, and loafers.

"Thomas took the purse she gave me," Kate told him, able to find a wry smile in spite of the stress she'd been carrying alone. "And the money she also gave me was in it." With a tilt of her head, Kate met Benny's gaze, relaxing more than she had in a long, long while. "I can't thank you guys enough for everything you're doing, Benny. I'll pay you back, I prom—"

"Don't even say it." Benny cut her off with a shake of his head. "You've been a member of Carley's family a lot longer than I have," he said. "We're all in this together. For better or worse."

For the past two years, her memories of San Francisco had revolved around the debilitating life she'd lived at the hands of her wealthy father and then her equally wealthy husband. But there'd been so much more. She'd been beaten down and abused, but Kate was only beginning to realize how very rich she'd been, too.

Stopping in Sacramento for Kate to pick up enough things to get her by, Benny—once he was satisfied they weren't being followed—drove her to a beautiful, two-story cabin in the woods a good hour and a half from San Francisco. Carley was waiting outside with Taylor in her arms.

"Ma-ma-ma-ma-ma," the little boy called happily, stretching out his arms. Wearing the jeans and light-weight sweater she'd pulled from Carley's closet, Kate ran to him, tears falling down her face, holding him against her, feeling clean again although she still hadn't had a shower. She'd been too eager to get to her son.

Taylor didn't let her squeeze him for long, pushing away from her and wiggling his legs to get down. He toddled over to the plastic ball Carley had been rolling for him, picked it up, dropped it, followed where it rolled, picked it up and dropped it again.

Crying and laughing at the same time, Kate watched him. "He doesn't seem nearly as traumatized by our separation as I was," she commented to the other two adults.

"You've done a good job with him, Kate," Carley said wistfully. "He's happy and secure."

Kate frowned at her friend. "I thought you hated babies. That you never wanted one of your own."

Carley and Benny exchanged a telling glance and when Benny nodded, Carley said. "Yeah, well, you know how it is when you finally grow up and realize you were wrong about certain things?"

"So you two are trying?" Kate grinned.

"We've been trying for a couple of years," Carley said.

"We're due for another bout of artificial insemination next week," Benny added, standing beside his wife. "Hopefully, this time it'll take."

Taylor's gleeful scream rent the air. His ball had rolled down a slight incline. Kate kept her eyes glued on his tiny body as he made a stumbling run to retrieve the toy.

"How many times have you tried?" she asked her friends. She'd missed so much while she was away. Not only the support she'd desperately needed, but the opportunity to support the people she loved, as well.

"Three," Benny said.

"Two didn't take." Carley took up where he left off. "And three months ago I miscarried."

Kate's heart twisted. "Not long before Leah disappeared."

"Yeah," Carley said, tears in her voice. "Right when I needed her most." And then, that signature Carley veneer coming over her face, she looked at Kate. "That's why Leah told me about the baby, about the father who swore it wasn't his," she said. "She'd asked Benny and me to adopt it…."

And that was why Benny Winchester would fight Thomas Whitehead to the end. In killing his sister-in-law, the senator had also killed the other man's adopted child.

22

"We can't hide out here forever," Carley murmured.

"He's going to find us sooner or later, anyway," Kate agreed in a worried voice.

"We aren't hiding, my dears, we're taking a time-out to plan." This was from Benny.

Cup of hot chocolate in hand as she lounged in a corner of the long tweed couch, Kate smiled at him. At his suggestion, Carley and Kate had embarked on nothing more taxing than lying around, reading, watching television or napping the rest of that afternoon. He'd grilled steaks for the three of them for dinner and, with Kate's help, had ground up steak and carrots in the daiquiri blender—just enough to make them easier to chew— for Taylor. Only now, with the baby safely ensconced upstairs, pillows and blankets tucked around him on the bed he'd be sharing with Kate, had they broached the future.

"I thought time-outs were for bad kids," she said. Her life was a shambles. She was a woman without an identity, married to a man she both hated and feared, in love with a man she'd never see again, trying to protect her son from the father who denied him and yet, she felt… loved. Protected. Even if the feeling was an illusion, she was grateful for it. It gave her a little more confidence in her ability to cope with whatever lay ahead.

"Haven't you heard?" Carley asked, sending her husband a wry smile. "It's the bad kids who have all the fun."

The conversation wasn't funny. They laughed anyway. And then, as if on cue, all three sobered.

She'd talked to her mother that afternoon. Vera Peters was in Europe but was getting the first flight home she could.

"I didn't come back to hide," Kate said. Although the weather outside was a cool forty degrees, the cabin was warm, cozy, with a fire burning in the fireplace on the opposite wall. Benny had turned off all but two of the lights when he'd come down from checking on Taylor one last time, before joining Carley and Kate in the living room.

"No, but you came back thinking Thomas was going to prison," Carley said.

"I knew he was out on bail." Kate took a sip of her hot chocolate, hoping to regain even a fraction of the peace she'd felt most of that afternoon. "But yes, I did think that with my testimony, with the proof of Taylor's paternity, he'd be back in jail immediately…and then in prison."

Instead the man was free—and expecting her to simply resume her previous existence. She shook her head. "I've known Thomas all my adult life," she told the other two, glancing from one to the other. "I've seen what he's capable of, and I still can't believe he really thinks we can pretend the past two years didn't happen. I ran away from him, changed my identity, went to extreme lengths to ensure that he couldn't find me, that I'd be free of him forever—and he thinks I'm just going to forget all that and go back to being his wife?"

She'd been avoiding the thought all day. It was too bizarre to understand—and how did one cope with what one didn't understand?

"It scares me, you know?" Her words were almost a whisper.

"Scares you how?" Benny asked. He'd poured himself a scotch and soda and returned to his lounge chair.

"I don't know…" She paused, tried to put into words something that she could recognize, but never completely quite grasp. "Thomas has this ability to say something with such authority, and repeat it often enough, that somehow the absurd becomes reality, fantasy becomes fact. It's as if…as if he's this powerful being who has a control panel, and when he pushes the right buttons, people eventually do exactly what he wants them to. It's like they've been programmed."

There was a horrified but knowing look on Carley's face. "Leah said something similar to me once, shortly before she was killed…."

Benny put his glass down and sat forward, clapping his hands together. "Okay," he said. "I don't think you're going to be safe here for long. If Thomas doesn't already know where you are, with his connections, he will soon. If nothing else, he's bound to find someone who knows someone who knows that Zack Wilson and I went to college together...." He included both of them in a concerned gaze. "I think you'll be safer in the open, in the city. I'd feel a lot better if you'd come back to our house in the morning Kate."

She was fine with that. Carley nodded, too. "Then what?" she asked.

"Thomas Whitehead is a charmer and a manipulator," Benny said. "He thrives on control and has a shit-load of money. He's also smart enough never to tell an out-and-out lie, which gives added credibility to what he does and says...."

"I'd agree with you completely," Kate interrupted. "But how does my son fit in there? He's Taylor's father, Benny. I was a virgin when I met Thomas and I never even looked at another man while I lived with him. I didn't dare."

"And you know he was the father of Leah's baby," Carley reminded him.

"I know." Benny nodded. "But consider this." His eyebrows rose as he looked back and forth between them. "What if he *didn't* falsify those medical records from twenty years ago? The scar his doctor described could be so minimal no one but a medical professional would notice it. Which means he actually might've had that vasectomy and he really believes he's incapable of fathering children."

"You think it reversed itself?" Carley asked. "I've heard of that, but it's kind of rare."

"Either that, or that quack he used didn't do it properly."

Implausible as it seemed, Kate wondered if he was right. "Amy Black told me they hadn't done a sperm-count, yet. The doctor's records were sufficient at this point. And he does pride himself on the fact that he doesn't speak untruths," she said, and then couldn't help adding, "he thinks his way of choosing to tell only half the story, or not to speak at all, means he has integrity."

"So we have Taylor tested," Carley said, sitting forward, too. She'd showered and changed into a pink silk lounging suit that was a striking complement to black hair.

"They do buccal testing now," Carley continued. "It's a swab taken from the mouth. Not painful at all."

Kate nodded. She'd researched it on the Internet the other day. "But with Thomas free, do I want him to know that Taylor's his son? Look how adamant he is about getting me back. He's called, what, no less than ten times today?" Benny had fielded several calls that morning before Kate arrived, and there'd been another half dozen on Carley's cell phone that afternoon and evening. Eventually they'd shut the thing off.

"If he knows for sure the boy's his, he's going to demand rights to him," Benny agreed.

"Forget that." Kate sat up, put her cup down on the wood-planked coffee table in front of her. "I'll die before I let that man anywhere near my son. He's not going to have even a remote chance to hurt that baby the way he's hurt everyone else he gets close to."

"You aren't going to die," Carley said abruptly. "Don't talk like that. It's not funny."

"I wasn't being funny," she said, then gave her friend a sheepish look. "Sorry, Carl, I'll be more careful."

"Thank you." The other woman's face didn't soften noticeably. "I will fight this man for the rest of his life, but I will not lose another person I love at his sick and greedy hands. I don't think I can live through it again."

"I know." Leaning sideways, Kate reached over to the other end of the couch, grabbing Carley's hand and giving it a squeeze.

"I understand your reluctance to hand Thomas his son," Benny said, his serious expression sending a shard of fear straight through Kate's heart. "But have you considered the alternative?"

She had, but wanted to hear about the one Benny had in mind.

"Let's say you refuse to go back to him—" he paused, glancing at both of them "—which is your plan, right?"

"Of course," Kate told him. "That's a given."

Benny nodded. "So you refuse to see him. Thomas,

being Thomas, is never going to blame himself for that. He's the victim. His type of person always is. So, who's he going to blame?"

"Me?"

"Yes, but not completely. Because he wants you back, he's going to make excuses for you."

Kate felt the blood drain from her face. Her hands and feet grew instantly cold. "He's going to blame Taylor."

Terror unlike any she'd known before took possession of her body, her mind, holding her captive in the worst kind of hell.

"You think I should get Taylor's DNA test done to protect his life."

"You should consider it." He nodded again. "A man like Thomas Whitehead is not going to murder his own son."

"He'd beat him, kill his spirit, but not his body, you mean," Carley scoffed.

"That's the second part of this," Benny said, his look grave. "He needs you, Kate. His image, which is everything to him, has taken a hit over the past month and your sudden reappearance could eradicate most, if not all, of the bad press. The whole reason the prosecution dropped the charges against him is because they knew what the jury would conclude. The allegations against him couldn't possibly be true with his miraculously returned wife come back to protect him, standing lovingly at his side." Benny walked over to the fire, facing it for a time, then slowly turned, his shoulder against the stone edging. "With very little effort on his part, the whole situation gets tied up very nicely. He once again comes out the victim, because of the false charges against him, and gets a resurgence of public sympathy, to boot. Then he continues on his merry way."

"And if I don't go back to him?"

No one said a word for long minutes. Kate didn't look at either of her friends as she searched desperately for alternatives.

Carley grabbed the pillow she'd been holding on her lap, threw it across the room, and watched as it slid to a halt in a corner of the dining area. "I will not have another Leah," she said through gritted teeth. "That man has to be stopped."

"If I go back to him, that would mean he'd be raising Taylor, pulling out his belt whenever the little guy spilled his milk on Thomas's wooden floors, putting him down constantly...."

Benny lifted one brow. Said nothing.

"You aren't suggesting I adopt out my son are you?"

"I'm wondering if your mother might be persuaded to raise him."

Or Scott. Scott would. Taylor would be safe there.

Or...Carley and Benny.

And she'd die a slow and painful death without him.

"The man has to be stopped," Carley said again, her voice rising. "We *cannot* let him do this, not to Kate and not to an innocent little baby who deserves a shot at happiness."

Pacing the far side of the living area, Benny scratched his head. "People like Thomas Whitehead succeed, but only for a while."

Kate's gaze flew to him. If he had even a hint of an idea...

"You have to know what drives him, beat him at his own game...."

"Get him to reveal himself for the bastard he is," Carley muttered.

"Okay, how do I do that?"

Benny sat back down. "That's what we have to figure out and I'm guessing we don't have a lot of time."

Thomas Whitehead paced the plush carpet in his downtown office, his tense body jerking to attention every time he heard a sound in the room. The window-sill cracked, settled, as it adjusted to the warmer temperatures of a mid-May Monday in San Francisco. It had been twenty-four hours since Kate had walked out the front door of his home, past the chauffeur he'd fired, and gone...where?

He wasn't going to let her disappear again. Now that he knew she was alive, he wouldn't give her up. The damn fool he'd hired had come back from San Diego with nothing except a dead end on Coronado Island. That was one private investigator who was going to have a hard time finding work in this town.

The distant honking of a horn came from the street far below. Thomas glanced down at the stopped traffic, trying to determine which vehicle had made the noise—

which one contained the idiot who thought that blaring his horn would suddenly clear up the accident that was the cause of the jam.

Why couldn't the guy get on his cell phone, do some business to occupy his time, and be thankful he wasn't trapped in the smashed car a few yards ahead of him? Be glad it wasn't his family that would be receiving a tragic call.

Speaking of which, Thomas checked his watch. The doctor was fifteen minutes late in getting back to him.

Impatient, Thomas forced himself to put his hands in the pockets of his pants and wait. He'd get Kate back one way or the other, but if the doctor phoned with positive news, he was home free.

Of course, that was the only thing that concerned him, he thought as he moved slowly toward the wet bar in his office, poured himself a whiskey straight up. He didn't want children. Had never wanted them. If, by some fluke, the two women who'd accused him of fathering their children were actually correct, if the child—this boy, Taylor—was his son, it wouldn't change his life, other than to solidify the image he'd spent a lifetime creating.

Still…to have a son, to bring forth another generation to carry on the Whitehead tradition of public service he'd begun in this state. To eradicate the memory of his tightfisted and heartless father…

"I have to tell you something," Kate said. She and Carley sat at one corner of the dining table in the cabin on Monday morning, sipping cups of coffee they didn't really need. They were waiting for Benny to get back to town, talk to some people, see what he could do to help Kate cut through the necessary red tape to reestablish her identity. He wasn't Senator Thomas Whitehead, but he knew a lot of people and had his own clout. Kate had shown Carley how to mix homemade play dough out of flour and water, and Taylor was happily chattering on the sheet spread out a few feet away from them, plastering himself and every toy within reach with the stuff. He'd asked for Daddy when he'd first awakened that morning, but had been easily distracted. He was used to Scott's long absences.

"What?" Carley asked, frowning.

"The other day, at the police station, Amy Black said you and Thomas and I were the only ones who knew about the cliff...."

She couldn't look her friend in the eye. But she couldn't continue to accept Carley's help without confessing, either.

Carley's brow was still creased in confusion.

"She'd just told me they knew it wasn't Thomas who'd killed Leah, and I went crazy. I thought of you and Taylor together, and I panicked! I doubted you, Carley." The words came out in a rush.

"Oh, hon, don't worry about it!" Carley said, her expression clearing into a warm smile as she lifted a fallen strand of hair away from Kate's face.

"For a second there, I actually thought you'd killed Leah!"

Carley chuckled. "No, you didn't. You were on emotional overload. You'd been given more than you could handle, especially without sleep."

Kate couldn't absolve herself so easily. "I didn't trust you."

"You came to me, Kate," Carley said. "You left your son with me. And you're here with me now. You're also human. We've got some real issues to deal with here, okay? Let's not make another one up to add to the bunch."

Kate tried to smile, didn't quite succeed, but knew that she would never again doubt Carley—about anything.

"Now can I ask you something?"

"Of course," Kate said, wondering as she watched her son if she'd ever again experience an entire morning without a knot in her stomach. She was going back to San Diego tomorrow—but only long enough to beg Scott to take her son, to keep Taylor safe until she could return to him.

It was too much to ask, she knew that, but she also knew she was going to do it anyway. Scott loved Taylor as much as any father had ever loved a child. He'd do as Kate asked.

And she would ask. She'd do whatever it took to keep her son safe.

Even if that meant leaving him.

Because as soon as she had Scott's agreement to

take care of Taylor, she was coming back to San Francisco, to move in with Thomas, resume her role as his wife for as long as it took to gather enough evidence to hang him.

She and Carley and Benny had talked far into the night and all three believed this was the only way. They'd all lost so much that could never be returned to them—a sister, a best friend, a child. And they couldn't escape the fact that if Kate didn't do something to stop Thomas, he'd kill her eventually. None of them doubted that....

"This person you know in San Diego, the one you won't name but whom you trust with your son's life, he wouldn't happen to be a man, would he?"

Over the past couple of days, Kate had exposed every intimate detail of the horrors of her life to Carley, but she couldn't find it in her to disclose her relationship with Scott. Nor did she really want to consider the reasons for that.

"Why do you ask?" God, she sounded just like her husband, avoiding the truth with diversions.

"Last night, when you were talking, you said you hadn't looked at another man the entire time you lived with Thomas. You didn't say the entire time you were married."

"Which I still am."

"That doesn't answer my question."

"I thought we'd decided that the less anyone knew about where Taylor's going, the better."

"Yes..."

She couldn't stand the hurt in Carley's eyes. Couldn't stand to keep secrets from her friend. They were in this together. Were going to work together to lure Thomas into believing his own fantasies. And all the while, Kate was going to be searching his home, his records, watching every move he made in an attempt to find the chink in his armor, to identify the one mistake that would allow them to stop him.

"I can't ask someone to wait for me while I move back in with my husband," she said, cringing inside as she thought about the weeks ahead. At least tomorrow evening, when she returned from San Diego, she'd get to see her mother. She was very much looking forward to that.

"Kate, we have to find another way," Carley said for about the thousandth time since they'd gone upstairs late the night before. "I can't bear the thought of you going back there, sleeping in that man's bed...."

"I know." And it was Carley's abhorrence, in part, that was giving her the strength to do just that. "But I did it for years, Carl, without any hope of salvation. This time I'm doing it for Leah, and for justice. And for Taylor. We can't live our whole lives in fear and on the run. We didn't do anything wrong!"

The baby squealed, threw a wad of dough and fell down laughing.

23

Benny was a miracle-worker. With a judge's affidavit in hand, Kate was met at the door of the DMV office closest to the Winchester home mid-afternoon on Monday. She was escorted directly to the X in front of the camera, where she had to stand for a new identification photo, then shown to a small private office while the paperwork was done, signed her name and within ten minutes had a brand-new California driver's license.

"How's it feel?" Carley asked, leaning over to get a look as the two women headed back out to Carley's car. They were going to the bank next, and then home to Benny and Taylor for dinner.

How did it feel? Like she was going to cry. She was legitimate again. She was paying a high price but still, being someone was better than being no one. She glanced around automatically as they burst out into the bright San Francisco sunlight—not that she'd be able to tell if someone was spying on her in any one of the hundreds of cars nearby.

"Like I'm glad I let you talk me into curling my hair and leaving it loose for the photo."

She'd worn one of her new outfits, too, a pair of black linen slacks and a tailored white blouse with double cuffs rimmed with black and silver thread.

"I almost don't recognize you with all that makeup on again," Carley said lightly, but the smile she gave Kate was filled with warm understanding.

"Yeah, well…" Kate slid into Carley's sleek new Mountaineer. "I figured if I'm coming back, I might as well come back."

Carley started the SUV, put her hand on the gearshift and studied Kate. "I kind of miss the wholesome look," she said.

Kate kind of did, too. But right now it was more important that she keep up appearances. Her life—and her son's life—was very likely going to depend on that.

Kate stared out the window as they drove the streets of San Francisco, taking in the familiar sights with a dreamlike nostalgia. She'd always loved the city—the narrow streets with hills as high as mountains, the busy wharf, people hurrying to and fro. There was always something going on—a feeling of opportunity. And a curious sort of benevolence. A sense that if you needed help, or acceptance, San Francisco was a place you could probably find it.

"Are you planning to call your friend and let him know you're coming?"

After a quick glance at Carley, who was concentrating intently on her driving, Kate looked out her window again. "I never said it was a he."

"I know." They passed through an intersection. And another. "So are you going to call him?"

She shook her head and then, remembering that Carley wasn't looking at her, said, "No."

Carley tapped one perfectly polished fingernail against the leather steering wheel.

Kate sighed. "One reason is that I don't want to give Thomas a chance to trace phone records."

"Oh." Carley turned briefly in her direction. Grinned. "That makes sense."

And the other reason? The mere thought of seeing Scott again, even for an hour, sent the blood dancing through her veins. She didn't trust herself to actually hear his voice until she had to. Her love for him was the one weak link in her resolve. She had to do this. She was never going to be a free woman and Leah's death would not be avenged, until she had the courage to stand up to Thomas.

There was no one to meet her at the door of the bank. That was Kate's first clue that things weren't going to be so easy this time.

"Can we see Marissa?" Carley asked the receptionist while Kate hung back. So far she'd gone unnoticed by the press and cameras that were sure to descend on her soon.

The gray-haired receptionist frowned, looked at a sheet on her desk. "She signed out at lunch, said she was taking the rest of the day off. Is there someone else who can help you?"

Kate stepped up. "The manager? Is Doug Cloud here?"

The woman shook her head. "He's off this afternoon, too." She said in a confiding tone, "He went golfing with Senator Whitehead!"

"He did!" Kate was impressed by how naturally Carley played along. "Does he do that often?"

"Nope," the older woman said. "First time."

"How about an assistant manager?" Kate asked. "Is there one on duty today?"

"Yes, that would be Roger Whittal," the woman said with a smile, apparently relieved to finally give them an affirmative answer. "I'll call him for you if you'd like to wait over there."

"Guess Benny's connections weren't as loyal as he thought," Carley said, and if she was upset she was hiding it well as they stood beside the chairs the receptionist had indicated.

"Thomas has that kind of power over people." She wasn't doing as well at masking the tension racing through her as Carley was. Her stomach hurt so badly she had to fight the urge to bend over. She settled for hugging her arms across her midsection instead.

What the hell did she think she was doing? She'd done the impossible once—escaped Thomas Whitehead. The man had friends everywhere. From fast-food managers to city managers, he'd spread his tentacles too deep to be avoided.

"Sure is taking a long time," Carley muttered, shifting her weight from foot to foot as she frowned, scanning the room. "Someone's head's going to roll for this."

"Not if Thomas is involved."

It was revealing that Carley said nothing at all to that. Some things just were.

Kate wanted this over and done with. The pain in the side of her head was back, radiating from her neck. And she was cold again.

Taylor would be waking from his nap. Asking for her.

"Mrs. Kate Whitehead?" The man who approached her hadn't come from the bank offices as she'd expected. He'd come through a side door, from the outside. And he wasn't alone.

"Yes?"

"I'm Detective Rodriguez, ma'am." The plastic wallet he pulled from his pocket and flashed in her face identified him as a detective with the San Francisco police. Oh, God, if something had happened to Taylor…

"This is Detective Martinson." The older blond man, nodding silently, flashed his ID, as well.

If Thomas's thugs got to her little boy, she'd hunt him down and—

"We'd like you to come down to the station for questioning, ma'am…."

There was a small crowd gathering. Kate could sense them more than see them. The detectives blocked most of her view. She was thankful when Carley moved closer and took her hand.

"She answered all the questions she had to answer on Saturday."

Detective Rodriguez's gaze never left Kate's. "We'd appreciate it if you'd come with us, ma'am."

"Does she have to?"

"No." The detective slowly shook his dark head. "However, if you don't come now and answer some questions, you'll leave us no choice but to press charges against you and issue a warrant for your arrest."

"Charges…against…me?" Kate couldn't react to what she was hearing because it simply made no sense. "For what?"

"Custodial interference."

She would've fallen onto the chair beside her if Carley hadn't been there, holding her up. "What?" She could barely get the word past the dryness in her throat as, with a backward glance at Carley, she was led away. She was shaking, trying desperately to keep her thoughts in some kind of coherent order.

Thomas was behind this. It had to do with Taylor.

And she'd thought she'd known all sides and depths of fear.

She'd known nothing.

* * *

"You can't take my son from me!" She'd been sitting in the cold gray room for more than an hour. It wasn't the same room she'd been in two days before, wasn't even the same precinct. But it looked exactly the same. Except for the two detectives facing her, who lacked even a hint of Amy Black's understanding and compassion.

She'd considered asking to see the other woman. But had soon dismissed the idea. If Amy Black could help her, Thomas wouldn't allow Kate to see the other woman; if she couldn't, Kate would only get Amy into trouble for asking her to try.

She'd considered asking for a lawyer, too, except she didn't know how she'd be able to tell whether or not a particular attorney was in some way tied to Thomas. So far there'd been nothing but threats, and the minute she could get Benny on the phone he'd find out who to call, who could be trusted. She'd already tried calling him twice.

She knew how this game was played.

But she had no idea how to win it.

She couldn't lose. She just couldn't. The stakes were too high this time.

"As we've explained, no charges have been laid yet," the blond guy—what was his name, Martinson?—said.

"I've told you all I have to say," she repeated. "What more do you want from me?"

As far as she could tell, they were going nowhere.

Either they were planning to press charges against her—for taking Taylor away from his father almost two years before—or they weren't.

"You admit the boy is Senator Whitehead's son," Rodriguez said.

"I've never denied it."

"But you didn't put his name on Taylor's birth certificate."

"My husband was abusive, Detective." She was out of patience. She'd told them, repeatedly, why she'd run. They didn't want to believe her. But keeping her there, haranguing her with questions, wasn't going to change the facts.

"You never pressed charges," Martinson said. "As a matter of fact, you never even called the police. Or reported anything to a doctor."

She glared up at him from her seat at the scarred table, hating him for standing over her like that. "My husband's a powerful man."

Taylor was safe with Benny at the zoo. She had to believe that. Still, she was frantic at the thought that these men were holding her long enough for Thomas to kidnap her son.

They fell silent again, staring at her, as they'd done twice now. And the desperate energy that had been sustaining Kate sifted away. She could go to jail. That hadn't even occurred to her.

She'd risked everything to come home to save a man from the risk of being put to death erroneously, to testify so he'd be sent to prison for the crimes he'd actually committed—and *she* might end up in jail? Her stomach roiled with nausea. She couldn't go to jail. She couldn't protect Taylor from there.

Couldn't see him.

Couldn't keep him from his father…

The door flew open. "Kate! Sorry, dear, I got here as quickly as I could."

She should've been surprised to see Thomas standing there in his green golf slacks and white polo shirt, but somehow she wasn't.

She'd known they were waiting for him to do something.

Just as she'd known that her nightmare was only beginning.

"Your husband would like to hear you admit, here in front of us, that Taylor is his son," Rodriguez said as soon as Thomas entered the room. The man was enjoying this. Kate hated him.

"Yes, he is."

"Yes!"

She jumped, hit her knee on the table when Thomas whooped.

"Congratulations, sir!" Martinson said as the detectives took turns shaking Thomas's hand.

Kate wanted to stand, to walk out that door, but she was, for all intents and purpose, a prisoner. She couldn't afford to show any vulnerability.

"Thank you both!" Thomas was saying, his handshake effusive. He even wiped a tear from his eye. This crying thing was new to her.

If she didn't know him better, she'd think her husband was honestly moved to learn that he'd fathered a child.

"I told you this two years ago," she said dryly.

Thomas turned to her, his grin fading as though he'd just remembered she was there. "And this morning's test results confirmed that you might have been telling the truth."

Nothing felt real to her.

"You mean you really thought you couldn't?" she asked, mostly with derision, but some curiosity, too. Had Benny been right? Had Thomas honestly believed he couldn't possibly be Taylor's father?

Or the father of Leah's baby, either.

Had he killed her friend because of that? Because she'd dared to sleep with another man—or so he believed? Just as he'd almost killed Kate?

"I had a vasectomy when I was twenty-one."

"You never told me." Not that it mattered.

"I never told anyone."

Kate wondered whether, over time, his body had healed itself, or the procedure had been performed incorrectly to begin with.

"I want a DNA test done immediately," he was saying.

She glanced up to find him giving the order to Detective Rodriguez.

"I've told you he's yours."

"But my name is not on his birth certificate." His voice softened as he spoke, as though he'd been so beside himself he'd forgotten the role he had to play. "I intend to petition the court to have that changed, and I need the proof to do so."

"Or you could get a signed affidavit from me."

He already knew that. Kate used every ounce of determination she had to stay focused.

Rodriguez looked from one to the other. "What do you want us to do now, sir?" he asked.

And suddenly Kate saw it all with lethal clarity. She wasn't going to jail. Thomas would have to press charges against her for that to happen and he didn't want his public to see him as a man who would do such a thing—even to a woman who'd wronged him as horribly as he wanted them to believe she had.

"That depends," Thomas said, pulling out a chair to sit beside her. She had to refrain from yanking her arm—hard—when he sandwiched her right hand between both of his. At least until she knew her next move.

Benny's suggestion would work. They had to play him at his own game, find his weakness. While Thomas had held her hostage for ten years, he was held hostage, too. By his own belief that he had to appear in a good light to his public at all times.

She wasn't sure how she could use that information yet, but it was the way to get this man. Of that she was sure.

"I know you've been through more than any one

woman could bear," he said now, his blue eyes sympathetic.

If he was speaking of her years with him, then yes, he was right.

"I understand you aren't yourself right now."

Another truth. She was a woman without a self. She waited to hear what he was going to do with that.

"So I can forgive the way you ran yesterday, making me relive my horrendous experience of two years ago, when I couldn't find my wife anywhere, not knowing if she was dead or alive."

She could tell he'd repeated that story many times over. He had a hard time maintaining the level of emotion it required.

How come I can see through him so easily now? Kate wondered. *And why couldn't I see this years ago?*

He stared at her, his gaze deep. If he was waiting for an apology from her, they'd be there for a very long time.

"But now that my son is involved, I can't afford to let my love for you cloud my judgment."

He wasn't going to throw her in jail. It wouldn't look good. Kate played that thought over and over in her mind. And still, she felt her blood run cold.

Now that Thomas knew he could father a child, he was apparently quite taken with the idea of having one. Of course, that made sense. People had a soft spot for men with children, tended to trust them more.

"That said, I love you and just want my family home with me."

The detectives, white-shirted arms crossed over their ties, stood by the wall, an avid audience. They'd shed their jackets an hour ago.

It made Kate sick to her stomach to see the hero-worship on their faces as they watched Thomas.

Bottom line, Thomas, I can't take much more. Nor could she make herself speak up. Right now, sitting in that room with two cops under her deranged husband's influence, she was virtually powerless. And experience had taught her a little too well. Whatever he had in mind, Thomas would go easier on her if she submitted with docility.

"So, if you'll agree to come with me now, introduce me to my son, let us resume our lives, I'll refrain from pressing charges of custodial interference against you for robbing me of the first two years of my son's life."

The son he'd almost killed.

"You're going to hold me hostage," she whispered. She had no doubt that once she went with him, she'd be chaperoned twenty-four hours a day.

"I'm sorry you see it like that," Thomas said now. "In reality, all I'm doing is trying to protect you, baby." He gently shook the hand he still held, laid it on his knee, holding it there, covered by his own. "You're obviously having severe emotional problems. We knew that before you left two years ago. The pregnancy messed with your hormones. It happens that way sometimes."

Kate was furious at those words, the condescending tone. And she slowly wilted inside. He was winning. Again.

Maybe he was one of the few who always did.

"I want you home. But I also want to know that my son is safe."

If she'd been stronger, she would've laughed out loud. As if Taylor would ever be safe around his violent-tempered father!

"Tell me what you want, Kate. Do we go get our son, or not?"

She couldn't make this decision. He was offering her hell…or hell.

Except that in one hell, she'd also have a piece of heaven. And a chance to see justice done. Their plan could still work. She'd still be in Thomas's home, with the determination and opportunity to find whatever evidence she could. Money disappearing without explanation, as must have happened with Walter Mavis. Conversations or messages that resulted in some benefit to Thomas. Threats… The last thing in the world she wanted was to expose Taylor to the man, even for a minute, but Thomas had managed to take that choice out of her hands. The best she could do now was to make sure she was there, too, protecting her child.

"I'll call Carley and tell her we're on our way."

24

Sitting with his back against a hard cement wall, long legs cramped from being pulled in beneath the shrubbery providing his cover, he watched as the shiny black limousine came slowly up the drive just before dinnertime. He'd been crammed into so many tight spaces in the past couple of days, he wasn't sure his body would ever unfold completely again.

He kept his gaze on the car as it stopped before the massive front door of one of San Francisco's more elaborate mansions. Whitehead would get out, run up the steps, disappear inside. A light would come on in what had to be his study. The shadow of a man would cross the room, probably toward a bar, because shortly after that, still shadowy and indistinct against the light, he would move to the window, raise a glass to his lips.

Eventually the light would go out. The man was boring. At least if the night before was anything to go by. The night before that, Scott had been up in the mountains outside Sacramento.

She hadn't been there.

And last night she hadn't been here, either.

He was running out of options. But was determined to watch out for her anyway. Somehow.

The chauffeur, a man who lived in a smaller house on the premises, got out—a different chauffeur from the previous night. He opened the back passenger door. The man Whitehead had fired, the one Scott had gone for first, had been only slightly reluctant to give Scott security codes and all the information he needed to get around the Whitehead estate undetected—after he'd been offered a large enough sum of money.

A leg appeared. A leg that wasn't wearing dress slacks. Or any kind of slacks. It was long but slim, a familiar smooth ankle beneath a pair of Capri pants. And then the rest of her body slid out—showing him a woman he hardly recognized. Her hair was glossy and curling around her face like that of some beauty queen. Her face looked different, too. Her mouth larger, more seductive. Her eyes more pronounced.

Still, it was her.

He wasn't sure if the heavy breath that escaped him held relief or disappointment.

She was here.

He had to restrain himself from rushing out to greet her, grab her, run with her. That wasn't why he was here.

He sat on his hands when she reached inside the car, held the position for several long seconds, and then backed out carrying her son.

The breath that time was just painful. They were together. Here. He didn't belong. Should have stayed home.

As diligently as part of him said to leave, another part made him stay, straightening first one leg, then another, as darkness fell, giving him more freedom to move about. An hour passed. Two hours. Lights had gone on—then off. Other lights had come on.

And now, three hours after they'd arrived home, the couple was upstairs in what he'd determined the night before to be the master bedroom.

Like a passerby held mesmerized by the horror of a car accident, he sat and watched as the man approached the woman. The curtains were wide open, as they'd been the night before. Lights were on, revealing the occupants of the room in almost vivid clarity to anyone roaming the estate grounds.

Which, as far as he could tell, was only him.

Move, he urged himself when the man reached out a hand to the collar of the woman's white tailored blouse. It was easy enough to tell what the man in that room was doing. Slipping buttons through their holes. Slowly. Seductively.

Taking his time.

Tell him no, Tricia. Scream. Run.

She wasn't listening. On the contrary, she didn't even raise a hand to stop the exploration. The blouse fell open. He tried to close his eyes when the man's hand reached behind her back, but he just couldn't. Something masochistic held him captive to the agonizing scene playing out before him.

He saw her breast the second it was exposed. First the curve of the underside, and then, horrifically, all of it as the man's thumb ran across the nipple before he bent and licked the tip.

He'd thought he'd lived through the worst day of his life at eighteen.

Scott McCall couldn't have been more wrong.

"This is nice, don't you think?" Thomas's voice wasn't quite even as he bent to her breast, touching her in ways that made her want to take a shower.

"No, Thomas, it's not nice. I told you yesterday morning that I don't want this."

He continued to toy with her nipple, sliding his free hand up to start on her other breast, as well. "Our situation's changed since then," he said, catching the tip of her breast between his teeth as he spoke.

She did her best not to flinch. Not to show any vulnerability that would turn him on hotter, faster. And tried to think of her baby safely asleep down the hall. He'd refused to go to his father, but had spent much of the evening staring at him, and Thomas had been satisfied with that.

He'd thought it a sign of respect.

"How has our situation changed?" she asked, more as a delaying tactic than anything else. She couldn't think of Taylor right now. Didn't want to remember the number of times he'd asked for Daddy or Dog when she was putting him to bed. Didn't ever want her son to know this about his mother, the degrading things she'd submitted to because she was too stupid or too weak to free herself.

Because she was such a bad judge of character she'd married a maniac.

That's not true. You're not a bad judge of character— he fooled everyone. Leah's voice floated into her mind. And from a distance Kate recognized the truth of the words her friend had never uttered to her. Because Thomas's abuse was the one thing she'd never shared with Leah.

To Leah's detriment.

"We're officially back together," Thomas said. "And tonight I plan to enjoy the best part of having a wife."

"Even if I don't want it?"

Thomas had always insisted their sevants not live in the house with them, and she knew this was why.

"Of course." He glanced up at her, smiled. "Especially then. I can always *make* you want it. You know that. You're a whore at heart, Kate, always have been."

He was going to hurt her. She knew that. But she couldn't just stand there and let him browbeat her into believing lies about herself.

"No, Thomas, I'm not."

"You going to tell me that in the time you were gone you never slept with another man?"

Yes, she was going to tell him that. She was going

to renounce Scott as if he'd never been. Because she had to.

She stared up at the only person she'd ever truly hated. Opened her mouth.

"You did!"

"No, Thomas, I—" Kate heard the fear in her voice and knew she'd lost. She hadn't even made it through one night.

"You little bitch!" The slap across her mouth was familiar, even after a two-year respite. "You fucking whore!" The name-calling seemed to excite him. His eyes were glazed, his hands shaking as he ripped her shirt off her shoulders, bruising her shoulders as he yanked off her bra.

She raised her hands to protect herself. He slapped her again, then grabbed both breasts, squeezing them. "Did he touch you here, baby?" he sneered. "Like this?"

"Thomas, no!" With a strength she'd had no idea she possessed, Kate pulled away from him, ran for the door, was halfway down the hall before he caught up with her.

"Not with Taylor here," she said, appealing the new-found fatherhood he apparently prized.

His eyes didn't clear as she'd expected. Instead, they took on a gleam she didn't recognize. There was no calculation there, no awareness of the pleasure he took in violence, just the look of a crazy man bent on retribution for all the sins against him.

"He's not mine, is he?" he screamed, clutching her by the shoulders, shaking her so hard she almost lost consciousness. "I knew it! I knew it was too good to be true. A whore like you? You wouldn't do anything so right as to give me a son."

As if completely repulsed, he pushed her away from him so hard, the force of her fall knocked the wind out of her. And bruised the back of her head.

Through stars, Kate saw him head into Taylor's room, saw the light come on.

"No!" Her screams scraped her throat. "No! You will not hurt him!"

Taylor's angry wail drew her up from the floor and into his room. The baby hung suspended between his insane father's hands.

Thomas's head turned, his glare aimed straight at her. "Whose is he?" His roar scared the baby.

"Mama! Mama!" The shrieks tore through her, but it was the frantic look in her baby's eyes that broke her heart.

"He's yours!" She had to convince him. It might be the only way to save Taylor's life. She hung on to Thomas, barely noticing her state of undress, the tears pouring down her face, the pain throbbing so fiercely in her head she could hardly focus.

"Please!" The word was a cry and a scream. "We did the test today! Do you think I would've done that if he belonged to anyone but you? What would've been the point?" She was rambling, her words only half decipherable even to herself. "You'll know tomorrow, Thomas! He's your son!"

"You whore!" he shouted again, shoving at her face with his elbow. The crack made her dizzy. She tasted blood in her mouth. "You have no friends!" he continued. The diatribe was familiar. She'd heard it innumerable times and, knowing what would come next, almost gave up, gave in, almost slid to the floor and let oblivion take over.

"Mama! Mama!" The dark-haired little boy was terrified. But so far he wasn't hurt.

"Thomas!" She stumbled but straightened in front of him. "Do whatever you want with me. I'm your wife. All yours." She coughed as a trickle of blood ran down her throat. "But don't hurt him! You don't want to! I promise, he's yours."

He stared at her. At the overwrought baby flinging himself wildly in her direction. "Stop it, son," he commanded with a hard shake.

Oh God. His neck. "His neck!" The words burst from her as he shook the child a second time.

She didn't see the foot coming until Thomas had landed a blow between her legs. "You fucking bitch! When you die I'll be glad, you hear me? Glad!" Spittle sprayed her forehead. "No one's ever liked you. No one! The world'll be a better place without you!"

Maybe.

"Mama!" Taylor's voice moved farther away.

"Give him to me!" She tried to yell, but the sound was weak, her throat hoarse.

"Look at him!" Thomas hollered, seeming to take

some kind of powerful pleasure from shaking the baby. "He's *not* mine! If he were, he'd obey me! Whiteheads always obey their fathers. Who does he obey, bitch?"

"Mamamamama!!!"

"Give him to me!" She was seeing stars. And shadows. And Thomas over by the window. Opening it.

"You want him so badly, don't you?" Thomas said, his voice dangerously low and laced with a sickening glee. "Tell me how badly!"

"Thomas, please."

Kate was out of her mind. Her heart was going to stop soon. No heart could beat that hard for that long, endure that much pain and still keep pumping.

"Mamamama! Down!"

"He wants down, love," Thomas said, his voice sounding almost curious. "What do you say we put him down?"

With one thrust he had the window open and, before she'd even realized his intent, had Taylor hanging, suspended by his armpits out the second-story window.

"Dadadada!"

Kate might have laughed at fate's final, bitter irony, but then everything happened at once. As hopeless as she knew the act would be, she lunged for her son, but was held back by a strong male arm that wrapped around her middle, pulling her kicking and screaming away.

"No, honey, you'll force him to let go…"

The words whispered in her ear were an illusion, as

was the arm around her waist. She must have already lost consciousness.

But that didn't explain why she saw Thomas let go of one of the baby's arms. Heard him taunt her.

"You want him, baby, come and get him. And watch him fall…"

The last she remembered was an image of Scott lunging for her son as Thomas let him go.

"Hi."

Kate blinked at the light that was blinding her. Heaven's light. The one dying people always saw at the end of the tunnel. And Scott's voice.

"Hi," she said, figuring it made some kind of sense to hear Scott's voice now that she was dead. She could feel herself smiling, although it hurt to smile.

"How are you?"

There was movement beside her. The touch of a hand against hers. Just a touch. She hadn't expected to feel anything after death.

"Fine."

"You are, huh?" More movement. Another soft touch—this one against her forehead. Just there and gone. "You don't look fine."

"Oh. I'm sorry." It hurt to talk. In her mouth. And her throat. And probably her head, too.

"Don't say that." Scott's voice was stern and she felt like crying. "Don't ever say that," he went on. "You have nothing to be sorry for." His words just kept coming so she listened, starting to make out shapes through the light. "You are an incredibly intelligent, courageous, loving woman who has more inner strength than I can ever hope to have."

"I hurt."

"I know, honey."

He sounded sorry. Sorrow and pain. In life—and death.

"Taylor?" She wanted to turn her head, to see if her son was there. Couldn't see him.

"He's here."

Oh. "Thank you," she whispered.

Kate closed her eyes.

It was dark. She hated darkness. "Excuse me?" Kate called out, scared when she felt the movement of her tongue in her mouth, when she heard the garbled sound that came out.

"Kate? Thank God you're awake!"

"Mom?"

"I've been here for three days, sweetie. So have Scott and Carley. I've been so frightened, so scared you wouldn't ever wake up."

"Mom? Can you turn on a light?"

Someone had put marbles in her mouth. They hurt.

"Of course, sweetie."

She heard the click, and shut her eyes. "Okay, I guess not," she mumbled around the marbles. "It hurts."

"She's awake! Excellent." Kate didn't recognize the

male voice in her room but didn't care enough to risk the pain of opening her eyes again.

"Yes, and she's talking and coherent." That was her mother.

"Why are you guys talking as if I'm not here?" she asked, slightly irritated. "I'm in a lot of pain, is there something you can do about that?"

"Yes, as a matter of fact, there is…."

That voice again. And then blessed relief.

Kate only knew that two weeks had passed because Carley had told her. Or had it been Scott? Or maybe Benny? She couldn't be sure. They were all hanging out together, and she was kind of jealous she'd missed so much of the party. Mostly she was aware of the male voice that had been new to her at first but had quickly become familiar. He was her doctor.

About a week before, when she'd finally been able to see clearly, she'd been surprised to find him so young. And a redhead.

Though it still hurt like hell to move, she turned her head to see if she was alone. Scott was sleeping in the chair a few feet away from her, his head at an awkward angle, as if he'd been fighting to stay awake. Then, almost as though he could feel her watching him, he opened his eyes.

"Hi." She smiled. It hurt, but she managed.

"Hi."

"What time is it?" A recessed light burned dimly in the wall.

"One in the morning." He grinned, nodded his head as though proud that she'd asked.

"You don't have to humor me," she told him. "It's really me this time. I think I'm back."

He approached the bed with careful, quiet steps. "How do you feel?" he asked, half sitting on the mattress beside her.

"Like I laid down in front of a train."

He grinned again. "You don't look quite *that* bad." His eyes perused her slowly. She knew she had to be repulsive, but it didn't seem to matter to him.

Which mattered to her.

"Am I going to need plastic surgery?" she asked.

He shook his head. "They were able to set the bones in your cheek and jaw. That was the worst of it. Once the swelling and bruising is gone, you'll be back to normal."

Kate shuddered. "I'm never going to be normal again."

"Sure you are, honey. It'll just take on new form. A better form."

She wanted him to hold her. "I love you."

His gaze warmed, his feelings unmistakable even in the dim light. "I love you, too, Kate, more than I ever knew."

She was glad. Because that was how much she loved him.

25

"Can I touch you?" he asked, his voice a hoarse whisper.

"Of course."

"I don't want to hurt you."

"Scott, it seems like I've been in a haze of pain forever. Another ache or two isn't going to faze me."

He laughed softly. "You *are* better."

"Yeah," she said, and then felt tears trickle down her cheek. "For better or for worse."

"What does that mean?" he asked, his dear, unshaven face close as he bent to wipe the tears gently away.

In spite of what she'd said about touching her, she winced.

"I'm sorry, honey. He broke your cheekbone."

She nodded. "He almost killed me this time."

"Yes."

The tears came again and pretty soon they were dripping down both sides of her bruised face.

"It's going to be okay, now, Kate…" She liked hearing that name from him. "He's going to jail for a long, long time."

She didn't believe that. Thomas was facing more of a challenge this time, since there was a credible eyewitness, but he'd find a way. A prosecuting attorney who'd make a mistake, which would result in the suppression of key evidence. A judge who'd make a mistake, which would allow for the calling of a mistrial. There were a number of ways it could happen.

At the most he'd get a light sentence in a minimum-security rich-boy country-club prison—and freedom within a year or two.

Her tears continued to fall. She knew she had to stop them or soon she'd be sobbing and her ribs weren't going to tolerate that.

"Hey, what's this about?" Scott crooned. His expression was clearly worried as he glanced around the dark-ened room, obviously looking for help.

She could tell him the tears were for herself. For the fact that she'd never be free of Thomas Whitehead or his abuse. But... She took a breath. Tried to calm herself. And couldn't.

"Taylor's dead. Isn't he?" The sob she'd been dread-ing accompanied the words. And it hurt as badly as she'd known it would.

Hearing the words hurt far worse.

"No, he isn't!" Scott jumped up, strode through an adjoining door she assumed led to the bathroom—prob-ably to get her a box of tissues.

He needn't have bothered. There was one on the tray at the side of her bed.

Kate cried helplessly, wishing he wouldn't humor her now, not over this. Not ever. Maybe she wasn't strong enough to take the news a week or two ago, but she'd had a lot of unconscious time to process the truth.

He was back almost immediately, wheeling something toward her.

It was a little bed, not much bigger than a bassinet, with bars and blankets and something in the middle of it. A bundle, with only a face poking out. A precious little face, eyes closed, mouth open, cheeks slightly flushed.

"He was due to be released today, but everyone thought it would be better to keep him close to you for now."

"Taylor?" She couldn't even feel the excruciating pain in her ribs as she sat up, reached over and touched her baby's head. "Oh, my God! Taylor!" She cried out, laughed, sobbed all at once, her hand lightly against the sleeping child's head.

"He landed in a bush," Scott was saying, tears in his eyes as well. "A concussion, some stitches, a little whiplash and a bruise or two, but he's over it now. They removed the last of the stitches today."

Ten minutes later, her hand still on her baby's head, Kate asked, "Who's going to take care of him until I get out of here?" She couldn't stop staring at the beautiful sight of that little body, warm and secure and sleeping soundly.

"We are," Scott said, pulling a piece of paper out of his back pocket. "And until you're ready to chase him around the room, I'll be doing that."

She recognized the letter. It was the one she'd meant to have notarized that Monday at the bank. It seemed like years ago.

"He's staying here?"

Scott nodded. "Sometimes it pays to have a bit of extra money."

"When does he go to trial?" An hour had passed and Kate was tired.

"Next week. They expedited things. I guess he's not as popular a guy in jail as he was on the streets."

"Yeah, he was pretty tough when it came to sentencing legislation."

"Seems kind of fitting, though, doesn't it?" Scott asked, as he sat gingerly beside her. "After what he's done, he *should* spend some time with people who hate him."

"He'll get out."

"I don't think so, honey."

Kate wanted to shake her head, but it ached too much. She lay there, eyes half-closed, and watched Scott in the reclining chair he'd pulled next to the bed. He'd moved Taylor back into his room so the incoming nurses wouldn't disturb him during the night.

"I can't sugarcoat this one, Scott. Thomas Whitehead will always get away with anything he does. It's the way of the world. Sometimes evil does win. If I'm ever going to live a full life, become a whole and healthy woman, I have to accept that I'm always going to be watching over my shoulder. And I have to do it knowing that eventually he'll catch up with me again."

Thomas Whitehead was a fact of her life.

Two days later Carley was there, holding a sleeping Taylor, when Kate woke up from her nap. "Hey, woman, how are you?" her friend asked.

"Not ready to climb trees, but I walked around the entire wing twice this morning."

Carley's head tilted back, her eyes wide. "That's quite impressive. You whack anyone with that pole of yours?"

She glanced up at her IV drip. It was due to come out the next day, and although she was used to it, she wouldn't be sorry to see it go. She wanted to be able to hold her son without having to constantly watch the tubes.

"Nope. I was perfectly nice for once."

Carley grinned at her. "This little guy sure is a hit up here."

"Yeah, but that's because I have my own private suite with built-in nannies," she said. "I'm just so glad they broke every rule in the book and let him stay."

Eyes filling with uncharacteristic sensitivity, Carley said, "Yeah, well, I think everyone knew that the best healing balm for both of you was each other."

She nodded. And would have added a third name to that small list if Carley hadn't suddenly blurted out, "I've got news."

And suddenly she knew. "You're pregnant!"

Carley's happy smile was one of the best sights she'd seen in ages.

Life ebbed and flowed; seasons came and went. For the first time in years, Kate was ready to look ahead to the seasons in her future.

"So, I have this thought to share with you," Scott said a few days later. He was sitting on a blanket on the floor, opening the doors and sliding the windows of a brightly colored plastic activity box with Taylor.

"What's that?" she asked, smiling down at them. Dressed in a silk gown and robe, she was sitting up in bed. She'd spent most of the day in the chair she'd seen Scott sleeping in before. She was hoping to be set free when Dr. Grant came around tomorrow.

"I've been operating under a false assumption."

Her heart caught, her battered spirit still too tender not to protect itself against the onslaught of bad news. Too tender not to expect to be hurt and run for cover. "What false assumption?"

Scott didn't look up.

"I thought I'd guard myself from the chance that the worst day of my life might repeat itself by refusing to plan a future."

She didn't know what to say. If that assumption was

false, did it mean he was now ready to plan a future? And if so, were she and Taylor part of it? Or were they still just here and now? They'd talked about many things these past days, including their love for each other, but he'd never mentioned their relationship. And she'd been too unsure of her current ability to cope with the answer to ask.

"How'd I do?"

She frowned and glanced at the toy, which seemed exactly the same as it had moments before. "With what?"

He looked up then, his gaze open, serious, and completely, honestly, vulnerable. "Protecting myself from the worst day of my life repeating itself."

Her heart started to pound. "You tell me," she said without taking a breath.

Scott shook his head, held her eyes and said, "I hope never to have a day as bad as the day I saw you walk into that man's home. Or the one when I watched you walk down my driveway and out of my life, either."

Kate smiled, but felt her lips trembling. He was learning. And so was she.

"Dadada, see-ee!" Bending over until his head was almost in his diapered lap, Taylor put his face down to a plastic mirror in the middle of his toy.

Scott glanced at the boy, then back at her, something between panic and hope on his face.

"We can take things slowly," she suggested.

He nodded. "Good."

She couldn't look away. "I love you."

"I love you, too, Kate." The name still sounded odd coming from him.

"You can call me Trish if you'd like."

He shook his head. "No more hiding."

"But it could be our private name, couldn't it?" she asked. "I've grown fond of that woman. I think she saved my life."

Scott rose, hands on her bed, and leaned over, kissing her softly, just the lightest touch to a mouth and jaw that were still far too tender. "I know she saved mine."

"Mr. McCall, can you please tell the jury why you were on the grounds of the Whitehead residence on the night of May ninth?"

"I knew Kate was going there to confront Thomas Whitehead and that he'd been violent with her in the past. I just wanted to make sure she was okay." *She'd gone there to testify against him for murdering her best friend,* Scott wanted to say, but had already been warned that the fact was considered informational and therefore disallowed. They were having to tread extremely carefully through every aspect of the trial procedure to ensure that there'd be no cause for mistrial, that Thomas Whitehead would be convicted. And that afterward, there'd be no cause for reversal.

He kept his gaze on the prosecutor. If he looked at the blond man in his expensive but sedate blue suit and Italian leather shoes, he'd forget that he wasn't some Neanderthal and tear the bastard to shreds.

And if he looked at Kate, sitting gingerly on the hard wooden bench, her back still sore from the nearly healed hairline fracture she'd suffered when Whitehead had thrown her against the wall more than four weeks before, he'd never be able to get through the next few moments. This was only the third full day of trial and already she was fading. If it weren't for the fact that they had to put Whitehead away for her to be free, he'd say to hell with the trial and take her to some island in the Caribbean. Someplace where she could lie around in the sun all day, sip mai tais, play with her son, and learn not to glance over her shoulder every time she stepped outside.

"Describe for us what you saw."

Resisting the urge to yank at the red silk tie around his neck, Scott stared at the back wall of the courtroom, catching his father's nod. His mother, sitting in the next seat, had Taylor on her lap. She was going to take the child out the minute he got fussy. He wished that had already happened so she wouldn't hear what was coming next. He wanted to spare not only his mother but Kate, too.

Carley and Benny flanked Kate in the front row. When he'd taken the stand, they were each holding one of her hands. *Please God, let them be holding her now. Surround her with love...*

"I saw the defendant and his wife enter a room upstairs. The curtains were open and the light was on, so I could see them clearly." He, the prosecutor, Kate—

they all knew what he was going to say. They'd gone over his testimony early that morning—not exactly how he would've chosen to spend a lovely mid-June day.

"It was dark outside?" Prosecutor Black asked.

"Yes."

The older woman, dressed in another of her gray suits, stood just to the right of the witness stand.

"Go on." She faced the jury.

"He started to undress her. To fondle her." He swallowed. Stared at Black, who was now standing right in front of him. Her eyes held his, reminding him not to glance away, even for a second. She was going to guide him through this.

"How was he fondling her?"

"He…her blouse was undone…"

"And her bra?"

"Yes."

Black nodded. *Go on.* Her eyes said, *She needs you to do this.* Those eyes gave him no mercy.

"He was touching and kissing her breasts."

"And then?"

"She shook her head. Backed away. It was obvious they were arguing about something."

"What happened next?"

"He slapped her face. Twice…"

"And then?"

"She jerked away from him and ran for the door. He chased after her…."

He looked over at the jury, as he'd been instructed

to do. "That's when I broke the window in the back door, let myself in. By the time I got upstairs, they were in the baby's room. Mrs. Whitehead was bleeding from the mouth, barely conscious. Her body was at an awkward angle."

He'd never forget that sight. Ever. Not in a million lifetimes.

"And her son?"

"He was holding the baby by his armpits, dangling him out the window."

Every face on the jury flinched. And Scott knew a second's satisfaction. This was going to work.

"Go on."

He shook his head, glanced at the prosecutor—and at the back of the room. His mother's seat was empty. Thank God. His father sat upright, hands on his thighs, his gaze intent—and encouraging.

They adored Kate, had been a world of support. As he'd known they would be. They also adored Kate's mother, who was up front, sitting between Carley and her mother. This was hard on all of them, but the women were drawing an immeasurable amount of strength from each other. Patsy and Arnold Miller were there, too. They'd driven up the coast together to be with Kate during the trial.

"Kate lurched toward the defendant, begging him not to hurt her baby. I guessed that he was just waiting for her to get close to him to drop the boy, so I restrained her. I hoped to use the element of surprise—and my superior strength—to grab him around the waist and pull him back from the window before he had a chance to drop Taylor."

He swallowed again. Hated the moisture that swam in his eyes.

"I grabbed him, pulled him down, but he dropped the baby before I could—"

His voice broke. Amy Black shook her head. He'd said enough.

"Mr. McCall, you just implied that the intimacies you witnessed between Senator Whitehead and his wife were somehow enacted against her will."

"They were."

"You sound certain of that."

"I am."

"I'm a little confused here." The defense attorney leaned a forearm on the witness stand. "I must have missed something in your description of what you saw."

Scott waited. Angry. Ready to step down from the stand, take his lover in his arms and lead her home.

"What did Mrs. Whitehead do when her husband unbuttoned her blouse?"

"Nothing."

"He did it quickly, then? So quickly that she didn't have time to protest?"

His hands shook against the arms of the chair. "No."

"And when he—how did you describe it? Fondled her breasts. Did she raise her hands then, maybe push him away?"

"No."

"Did she even step away?"

"Not then, no, but—"

"Thank you, Mr. McCall. I have another question. Just how can you be so certain that the injuries you saw as you came into that nursery were inflicted by Mr. Whitehead?"

"I saw him slap her!" Acid, like fire, spread through his stomach.

"Yes, but a playful slap across the face is a far cry from attempted murder." The defense attorney leaned so close now that Scott could see the coffee stains on his teeth.

"He'd hit her before."

"Objection, Your Honor. There's no evidence to support that. It's hearsay only."

"Sustained."

"As a matter of fact, Mr. McCall, when the injuries actually took place, you weren't there to see anything at all, were you? You were breaking into the couple's home at the time…."

Scott's hands itched to punch something. He'd never known he was capable of feeling such rage. "Yes." The single word scalded his throat.

"I have no further questions, Your Honor."

"State your name for the record."

"Kate Whitehead."

"Thank you. Tell me, Mrs. Whitehead, what do you remember about the activities that took place on the night of May ninth?"

From his seat in the front row, Scott ran sweaty palms down the slacks of his black suit. The sixth day of the trial, and it wasn't getting any easier. The prosecution had not called Kate to the stand, but they'd known the defense was planning to do so. She'd thrown up twice during the night, and spent the rest of the hours lying awake in his arms in the room they were sharing in her mother's home.

Good news had come that morning. Her divorce from Thomas Whitehead would be final the next week.

But it hadn't been enough to dispel her unequivocal belief that they were going to lose. Thomas Whitehead had done his work well. His soon-to-be ex-wife believed, heart and soul, that he was, at all times, a winner.

"Mrs. Whitehead?"

The judge, an older man with a thick nose, reading glasses and a few tufts of gray hair growing over his ears and around the back of his head, stared down at Kate.

"Answer the question please." At least his command was gently issued.

"N-n…" Kate started. Her eyes filled with tears. "I remember nothing."

"State your name for the record please."

Scott took Kate's hand between both of his. Carley, on her other side, slid an arm around Kate's shoulders. Her mother and Scott's dad, immediately behind her, both placed hands on her shoulder.

His mother was at Kate's mother's house with Taylor. Scott hoped that was what Kate was thinking about. She'd promised she'd try.

"My name is Thomas Whitehead."

He was wearing brown today. Brown suit, beige shirt, brown tie, brown shoes. To go with his filthy character.

Concentrate on the color, man. If you get any more personal than that you're not going to be what Kate needs today.

His mother was probably feeding Taylor way too much sugar. And the toddler would be up half the night. He hoped so, anyway. Kate actually smiled some when her son was consuming her attention.

"Mr. Whitehead, would you please tell the court what actually happened at your home on the night of May ninth of this year? The night, I might add, that you and your wife and son were finally reunited as a family since your wife's tragic disappearance—"

"Objection, Your Honor, irrelevant." Amy Black's gray-suited back appeared in Scott's line of vision as her strident voice rang out in the packed courtroom. The trial had been blocked from the press, but there were supporters on both sides of the room.

"Objection sustained," the judge said. "Stick to the question, counselor."

"Tell us what really happened that night."

Really happened. As though every bit of evidence presented by the prosecution had been incorrect. Scott's knee started to bob.

"My wife and I were in our bedroom making love…."

Kate choked. And had four hands patting her back. Scott reached for the bottle of water he'd had with lunch, unscrewed the lid, held it to her mouth.

"She...occasionally...likes to—" Whitehead glanced down sheepishly "—enact fantasies..."

"And you play along with them?"

He shrugged, gave the jury a look that was a masterful mixture of innocence and knowingness. "She's my wife. I love her. It's all in fun."

"Tell us about this fantasy..."

"Objection, Your Honor, this has no relevance to—"

"Overruled, Ms. Black. Please sit down."

"She likes me to pretend to treat her like a...you know..."

"No, Senator, please tell us."

"Like a woman who's been very naughty."

Kate's whimper turned heads throughout the audience. Scott held on to her hand for dear life, willing all the energy, strength and love he had through his skin and into hers.

"Thank you, Senator. I apologize for having to do that."

Whitehead nodded graciously.

"Tell us, sir, what happened next."

"Our son started to cry. Kate was worried about him being frightened, as it was his first night in his new home and he'd already been tired by the time we arrived. When she heard him upset, she pulled away from me and ran from the room. I was particularly eager for him to adjust to his new home—and to me, his father—

and I ran after her. I made it to the hallway just in time to see her slip on the wood floor. I tried to catch her but her arms were flailing and she flew backward, slamming into the wall behind her.

"I reached for her then, but the knock on her head had been pretty severe. She didn't seem to recognize me, or our son, either. I've never personally witnessed anything like it. She went crazy, hitting at me. Lunging for him…"

"And that's how her face was hurt?"

"I'd put up a knee upon which to rest the baby while I got a better grip on him and she smacked right into it."

"Then what happened?"

"I tried to calm her down, but I knew that my first priority had to be protecting the boy. She kept coming at him, clutching at him, screaming horrible things. In a desperate and incredibly stupid move, I resorted to hanging him out the window because it was the quickest way to get him away from her…."

"Has the jury reached a conclusion?"

At the back of the courtroom, where Kate had chosen to sit so they could make a quick exit, Scott sent up fervent prayers for the first time since Alicia's death. If the verdict was in Whitehead's favor—as Kate, the press and even he feared it would be—Kate was never going to be the same. Their lives together would be forever marred by fear and mistrust. Expecting the worst.

"Yes, we have, Your Honor."

He and Kate knew the truth. Even the jury might

know the truth. But there'd been little proof shown that was beyond the shadow of a doubt. Kate couldn't remember anything about the night of the attack. He'd been thankful for that when he'd first found out.

Now he thought it was a cruel joke.

"Will the defendant please stand?"

Whitehead and his chief counsel rose together.

"On the charge of attempted murder of Kate Whitehead, count one, how do you find?"

"We find the defendant guilty as charged, Your Honor."

And just that quickly, it was over.

"On the charge of attempted murder of Taylor Whitehead, count one, how do you find?"

"We find the defendant guilty as charged, Your Honor."

Scott's arms were ready when Kate fell sobbing against him. Picking her up in his arms, kissing her all over her face, laughing and crying with her, he carried her out into the bright June sunshine to take her home to their son.

It might take a while for her to really believe it was over. But it would happen. Their time had come.

San Francisco Gazette
Sunday, August 21, 2005

Fashion Designer Weds Fireman

San Francisco-based fashion designer Kate Whitehead, now Kate Trica McCall, wed millionaire firefighter and paramedic Scott McCall yesterday at

San Francisco's Lady of Hope Church. Guests, including a fireman's honor guard in full dress and what appeared to be the entire world of San Francisco fashion design, flooded the three-story church, filling every crevice, spilling out to the sidewalk and street beyond, taking up more than a city block. The bride was elegant in one of her own designs, a long white satin-and-lace beaded gown. She was attended by Mrs. Carley Winchester, whose dress, also designed by the bride, had guests wondering if the matron of honor was pregnant. Sources told *The Gazette* that Mrs. Winchester was to have adopted the unborn murdered child of her deceased sister, Leah Montgomery. The only other attendant, the ring bearer, two-year-old Taylor Campbell Whitehead, walked in with the groom, who, next week in adoption court, will become the boy's legal father. The family plans to honeymoon in Paris over the next two weeks, where Mrs. McCall will be showing a brand-new line of casual wear that has already won her acclaim this summer, here in the States.

Scott McCall has just signed a contract on behalf of Angels of Mercy, his new paramedic service, to be one of the primary providers of San Francisco's paramedic and ambulance services. Angels of Mercy reportedly has more than thirty ambulances and over a hundred trained employees, who will be on call twenty-four hours a day, ranking San Francisco among the top five in the nation in ambulatory care services.

San Francisco Gazette
Sunday, August 21, 2005
Page 21. Section E

Former Senator Dies In Jail

Impeached Senator Thomas Whitehead died in jail early this morning after a late-night skirmish involving several inmates. Details of the event are not yet known, but the senator sustained the only reported injuries. Official cause of death was repeated blows to the head with a blunt object. The former senator was impeached earlier this summer after being convicted of attempted murder on two counts for the near-deaths of his wife and son, for which he was sentenced to eight years in a minimum-security prison. He was in the county jail awaiting a decision for reversal of the findings from the San Francisco Court of Appeals at the time of his death. That decision, which had been reached and communicated to the state and defense attorney on Friday but won't be written until sometime late next week, granted Whitehead's plea for reversal. This was based on evidence submitted that, while in an unsanctioned